DOES GOD FORGIVE SURFERS?

LOCALS ONLY

Kooks
Go
Home

HOPE MILLER

A NOVEL

© Copyright May 2018 by Hope Miller

Author: Hope Miller

Editor: Michel Miller

Cover Design: Kalynn Campbell

Graphics & Layout: GRIFFITI

ISBN-10: 0692123113

ACKNOWLEDGEMENTS

Dedicated to Butch Towers
1950-2015
If it wasn't for Butch there wouldn't have been an
Anacapa Surf Shop. And without that our Tribe may
never have been born.

To My Husband Skip
Thank you for letting me throw my hat in the ring, and
for being my barometer. You completely changed my life
into what I dreamed it could be. Thank you. XOXOXO

To My Daughter Arielle Love
I not only adore you, I admire you. My love for you is
unconditional and forever.

Acknowledging my friends
Thank you for your constant encouragement,
suggestions, and overall excitement for this fictional
story that happened like I was in a dream. Love you
guys. Thank you!

I would also like to acknowledge my wonderful Editor,
Michel, who is consistent, thorough, and very groovy.
And my beautiful Aunt Linda, thank you
for your Artist Eye and your tremendous help
with this project.

Table of Contents

Table of Contents

Introduction

When people refer to their childhood, they often say it was a simpler time. When I think of being a teenager raised on the shores of Southern California, I know that is untrue. Without cell phones or the Internet we had more time to get out into the real world with each other and tangle up our lives in alcohol, drugs and too much sun.

We made our own families from our group of friends. We had our own pecking order that was established on looks, popularity, surf skills, musical talent—and raw aggression toward anyone attempting to displace us from our thrones within our rightful territory. This was our home: the beach breaks, the bonfires we hid from cops, the dirty music venues and the spontaneous house parties. Our erupting hormones urged us into careless choices, unleashing both our angst and devotion.

We were a lost tribe defining ourselves by the other lost tribes up and down the coast, but we didn't know we were lost. Only looking back at what became of our "brothers" and "sisters" is it apparent that many of them never really did grow up. Some we lost to drugs and alcohol, others remained stuck in the rage of puberty long past an excusable age.

This was Oxnard in the 1980s. This was our heaven on earth. The following accounts will take you inside that circle of surfers, skaters and punk rockers at Silver Strand, Oxnard Shores, Hollywood Beach and Hueneme Beach. The places are real, but the characters stem from the Author's own delusions.

LOVE CANAL - OXNARD SHORES

It was discovered in 1985 that a 100-lot subdivision in Oxnard Shores was built on a toxic waste dump. Upon learning this, a teenager took spray paint to the outside of one of the more visible homes in that area and wrote "Love Canal" in huge letters to mark the neighborhood's protest. It was a *symbolic memory* for this first story. Teens at this time were surviving broken homes and recession; and no one was watching out for them. Just underneath the surface of what appeared to be an idyllic beach existence, toxic waste was waiting to engulf them.

CHAPTER ONE

Kia Wilson, 15

Summer of 1985 – Friday

"Do you think that when we die God looks at the way we lived our lives and overlooks the stupid stuff we do at this age?" Kia mumbled. She sat staring at the Pacific Ocean, watching the small 2- to 3-foot sets roll in. She pushed the long, blonde strand, whipped by the wind, away from her heart-shaped face, her light blue eyes trying to focus on the rapidly disappearing horizon as the sun kissed the world goodnight.

"Huh? What are you talking about, you kook?" Ami shot her a dismissive look, then turned back to the ocean taking a big gulp from the cheap Boone's Farm Strawberry Hill wine they had talked a man into buying for them at the Corner Market. She passed it to Kia, who took a strong sip and passed it to Brooke, on her right. The three 15-year-old girls sat with only the sound of the tide going in and out.

"I don't know. I guess I was thinking if Vienna gets an abortion I was wondering if, you know, will she be forgiven?" Kia uttered.

Ami looked over at Kia with disbelief. "Of course she'll be forgiven! God! Are you Catholic or something? Don't be ridiculous, are you drunk already? Brooke, pass that bottle over here," she demanded and bent forward to grasp the bottle's neck as it was passed to her.

Kia took her long blonde hair and twisted it on top of her head into a bun, emulating something she had seen the very-popular Kristen do at the beach earlier that day. It took a couple of tries with her being buzzed on the strawberry wine. She momentarily forgot what they were pondering and focused on her task. She stood up and bent at the waist to gather all her hair together, and almost flopped on her face.

"Whoa!" She righted herself, laughing. Her hair, refusing to be contained, flew around her face.

"So," Ami interrupted Kia's moment, "what the fuck are we going to do about Vienna? We can't have her shipped off to live with her grandparents to have that baby."

Kia turned to face her, remembering they were trying to figure out how to rescue Vienna from her horrible fate.

Kia didn't have any idea, and at the moment she was a little too drunk to think any further about it. She looked to Brooke who was putting on lipstick and staring at the ocean.

"Who knows?" Kia shrugged, "Let's figure it out tomorrow."

Ami stood up quickly and a little wobbly to loudly defend her mission to figure this out immediately, but all that came out of her mouth was a defeated, "Fuck, fuck, fuck!" and "This is bullshit!" before she landed on her behind and fell backward into the sand.

Brooke and Kia burst into giggles as Ami rolled onto her stomach flopping around like a beached whale trying to rise up again.

Brooke, elegantly as always, maneuvered her way up and over to Ami to assist her. She stood with her feet planted a foot apart into the sinking sand and reached down to Ami, but the girth of Ami's huge breasts pulled them both down into the sand by sheer gravity.

This time they all three burst out laughing.

"Shit! Ami! Come on, get up."

Brooke's sweet little voice was more like a purr than a roar, "Let's go over to Mickey's party, I gotta pee." The ocean breeze blew her long, brown hair back from her face. She looked like Bambi, except with perfect tits and ass.

Kia helped them both up. She was at least three inches taller than all of her friends. They were petite girls (despite Ami's breasts.)

"Yeah, OK," Ami resigned to the muddled state she was in, "But this conversation is not over! We can't let Vienna leave. She's our friend. No, she's our family!"

Kia looked at Brooke who nodded before attempting to wipe the sand off her denim miniskirt and oversized thrift store sweater. Ami finished off the bottle of wine and chucked it toward the ocean.

Brooke looked in the direction the bottle flew. "Oh my God, Ami, what if that breaks and someone steps on it?"

Ami looked her in the eye and then shrugged while smirking. Her face could get really ugly when she was acting like an asshole. She was already dealing with squinty eyes and wildly curly hair that looked like it could break a brush in half. What saved her was the tanned, voluptuous body that held up that unfortunate head. There was also her house that was almost always "parent-free."

While Brooke ran down to the shore to retrieve the bottle, Kia wiped the sand off her butt and legs and shook the sand from her half-cab Vans before putting them on. She straightened the old-school OP shorts that were an exceptional thrift store find even though they were a tad big for her. She patted down her tank -top and grabbed her Senor Lopez she used as a blanket to sit on.

As Brooke made her way back to them, Ami reached for Kia to get steady, grabbing her by the hair that was almost past her ass.

"Oww!" Kia yelped. She pulled her hair around so it was away from Ami. "That hurt."

"Yeah, sorry. You have so much it must have blown around my hand somehow," Ami replied without an ounce of sincerity.

12

Kia rubbed her scalp where the hair was tugged and headed toward the street wondering how much of an accident it really was. "Bitch," she whispered to herself.

She stepped over the curb on Ocean Avenue and waited for the other two. She felt chilled from the breeze that had kicked up after the sun set and pulled her Senor Lopez on. Once again she bent over to gather her hair securing it into a loose knot on top of her head.

Ami and Brooke joined her and they crossed the street to head down to Mickey's party.

There was laughter in their shuffle-walk together. Ami tripped on the curb and stubbed her toe. Brooke and Kia tried not to laugh but she made the ugliest face.

"What the fuck?! Oww!" She shrieked so loud that the people in an adjacent house peeked out from behind their curtains. Brooke and Kia couldn't help but laugh and steady her between them to amble forward. Kia smugly realized that instant karma had just been dealt.

They turned onto Mickey's street and Ami looked at her toe. The nail was all bloody and was dripping off her flip-flops. She thought, "Aww shit," and kept walking, not wanting Kia and Brooke to laugh at her again. Plus, she was drunk, and in a minute she forgot about it. They got to Mickey's and the open doorway was crowded with some of the local guys drinking beers and talking about the Lakers game that was on TV in the living room.

The girls brushed by them into a room packed with dudes sitting and standing, watching the game oblivious to their entrance. Kia didn't like being ignored. It made her feel awkward and uneasy. Brooke and Ami's boyfriends were seated on the couch where the girls joined them to make sure everyone knew they belonged. Since Kia didn't have a boyfriend, she hoped that just by being with them it was understood she was supposed to be there, too. It was an older guy's party. Since she wasn't "doing" any of the guys, she felt like a third wheel. She just hoped that one of the older hot guys had a secret crush on her and had been wishing she'd show up. But none of them turned away from the game.

A minute later Kristen and Erica arrived with two 12-packs, and every guy said hello to them. Kia studied them and how they looked—what they were wearing, how tan they were—and felt immediately like an immature girl who hasn't fully blossomed into those ripe, perfect breasts that give their owner confidence. She prayed a growth spurt would happen soon.

Brooke and Ami went to the kitchen for beers, and Kia shuffled behind. Erica was Brooke's older sister, so they were allowed.

Kristen and Erica were putting the beers in the fridge when Kia glanced out to the back patio where about six older girls were sitting in beach chairs drinking and smoking. She spotted Melissa and froze with fear. Melissa hated her and Kia didn't have a clue why. She'd heard rumors from Brooke, since Melissa and Erica were best friends. Supposedly, Kia reminded her of some chick Melissa saw on the dance show MV3. Of course, Kia watched that show, everyone did. MTV had recently been added to the cable TV lineup and music videos were the hot new thing. This show featured a bunch of cool kids dancing as videos played in the background. It was the best way to keep up on "in" clothing and dance trends. There was only one girl who Kia thought might look like her, but she was the really pretty and cool one who stood out on the show. Kia was simultaneously flattered and confused by Melissa's hatred of her. She wasn't that girl, and if it was that girl, shouldn't Melissa like her instead? Aren't the popular girls the ones you should be nice to?

Kia turned back to the kitchen before Melissa made eye contact with her and tried to stifle her fear. Be cool, she thought. But Kia felt trapped. She definitely didn't want to go outside, but was too shy to hang out in the living room. She got a beer and tucked herself into a corner of the kitchen where she could see anyone coming from either direction. She turned toward Kristen to listen in on what she was saying.

"So, Dave got Vienna pregnant," Kristen said to Ami in a tone that suggested skepticism, "Are you sure?"

"That's what she said," Ami nodded. "She told me her mom is sending her to live with her grandparents up in Chico."

"Hmmmm . . ." Kristen took a sip of beer before setting it down gingerly on the countertop.

"It's not that I don't believe she's pregnant, I guess, but I heard it may not be Dave's baby."

She then hopped onto the counter. As her impeccably suntanned legs dangled, she lifted the beer up to her lips, smirking before taking another sip.

Ami's mouth fell open and her eyes got wide, which was a good look for her. She rushed up to Kristen, fishing for information. "What did you hear?" she whispered almost in her face.

Kia was shocked. None of the girls ever said anything mean about Vienna or called her a slut. Vienna and Dave had been boyfriend and girlfriend for two years and that was considered a long time. Dave was the lead singer of Mohawk Disco, the local beach band, and he was hot. But he was obviously dedicated to her. Vienna was sort of "in charge" of their relationship, and Dave pretty much did whatever she said. They made an interesting couple. You could tell they loved each other, or something close.

In their group of friends, Vienna was definitely the leader. She was only a hair taller than 5 feet but she was loud and brash and didn't take shit from anybody. Girls tried to pick on her in junior high school and she never backed down. She got right up in their faces like a crazy person. For someone so small, she was scary. Vienna got her first tattoo at 13. It was a flower band that went around her right ankle. She told Kia her brother did it for her in their garage. It was badass.

Kia heard the screen door open to her right. She glanced over to see Melissa enter the kitchen.

"Hey, what's up Kristen? Erica?" Melissa glanced at Brooke and Ami, then saw Kia and gave her a dirty look before dismissing her.

Melissa got a beer from the fridge, opened a cupboard and

16

grabbed a bottle of tequila. She passed it to Kristen who took a pull and gave it to Erica who did likewise and passed it on. Everyone took a drink, but Melissa grabbed it from Brooke just before it got to Kia, and walked outside with it. The girls in the kitchen pretended not to notice the blatant snub.

Kia's face turned red from embarrassment. "Kristen," she squeaked, "What did you mean about Vienna?"

Ami's head swiveled to her then Kristen.

"Yeah, what did you hear? I'm her best friend! I'm sure I'd know something about that," she said accusingly.

Kristen's chin rose and her eyes looked down on Ami. "Well, maybe you don't know everything" She turned to Erica. "Tell these little she-grommets about seeing Little Miss Vienna in the backseat of a Trans Am, of all things, with three dudes at the Pierpont Chevron gas station a few weeks ago."

Ami, Kia and Brooke all looked at Erica who began to open her mouth just as Vienna ambled into the kitchen with a beer in one hand and a joint in the other. She was smiley and slightly buzzed.

Kia could hear Dave's voice from the living room and lots of "What's up, brotha?" and hand slapping.

Erica grabbed the joint from Vienna who kind of bumped into the counter. Erica took a drag and passed it to Kia with a nonchalant wink. She wasn't like Melissa though they were best friends. She was the nice one. Kia dragged on it twice before handing it back.

"Soooooo," Vienna slurred, "I'm knocked up." She laughed a little too loudly.

"Yeah," Kristen said, "We heard. Moving to your grandparents?" Kristen rolled her eyes as she took a hit off the joint.

"Fuck no," Vienna laughed, "Fuck that."

Ami maneuvered her way over to Vienna, still incognizant of her blood-caked big toe.

"What happened to you?" Vienna stepped back and bent down, peering at her toe.

Ami was momentarily stupefied, "I tripped. I forgot! Ha! Ha!"

"Ewwww," Vienna exclaimed, grabbing the joint.

"So," Ami pressed up to her, "what are you gonna to do about the baby?" Her eyes drunkenly fixed on Vienna's nonexistent belly bulge.

"I don't know." She lifted her shoulders in an inebriated shrug, then smiled, thinking it was funny.

CHAPTER 2

Kia watched the girls from the corner of the kitchen and it seemed like she was seeing what was transpiring through tunnel vision. She could feel her heart pounding out of her eyes. Strong weed. Her forehead began to sweat, but she didn't want to say anything.

Christian entered the kitchen just then. Kia's heart skipped a beat. He was the best looking person she'd ever laid eyes on. His blonde hair, bleached from the sun, cascaded in waves around his shoulders. When he smiled, huge dimples indented his cheeks and his blue eyes danced with laughter. His tanned and just-right muscular chest, arms, legs and butt were perfectly sculpted from years of surfing. She sighed and maybe drooled a little.

He walked over to Kristen, his eyes locked on her, taking it all in. She tilted her head and gave him a mischievous grin. He grabbed her beer, finished it, then took her hand and led her outside. Kia hoped they'd all gravitate outside so she could get some fresh air. She forgot about mean bitch Melissa.

A few more guys ventured into the kitchen roughhousing and whooping, grabbing beers and walking out back signaling the end of the basketball game. The Lakers must have kicked ass against the Denver Nuggets, but you would think from all the trash talking that these couch surfers did all the work themselves. The girls in the kitchen followed them outside.

Kia stepped onto the back patio, spied Melissa and moved as far away as possible. Luckily her girlfriends walked over to the skate ramp where their boyfriends were taking turns with all the other grommets. A couple of the older guys busted in and grabbed boards, but they were drunk and fell on their asses— except Tony Zane (everyone just called him Zane, sometimes Insane Zane). He was the lead guitarist of a straight-edge punk band from Hueneme Beach. He grabbed one of the boards as it flew up the opposite side and jumped to the top of the ramp pulling perfect 1080s.

Kia watched him, grateful to have something to focus on. Her friends had moved closer to the group of girls Melissa was hanging with. Stoned out of her mind, Kia watched Zane skate. She wished she could skate that well. She'd rather skate the ramp than be paranoid that Melissa might smash her face into it. She wished Melissa didn't hate her. It was rumored that she beat up her own boyfriend. He was a tough-looking punk and if Melissa could beat him up, Kia didn't stand a chance. She shivered just thinking about it. She wished she was ballsier like Vienna, or had the anger of Ami, or that people would leave her alone as they did with Brooke since she was so pretty and girly. Kia tried to emulate Brooke, but she just couldn't get it right; it wasn't who she was naturally. Kia wasn't even her given name. It was Lisa. But there were a million girls named Lisa out there in the world. Nothing grossed her out more than being ordinary or easily forgettable. She had changed her name to Kia when her family moved to Oxnard. It was a combination of two words: kicking and ass. This was supposed to make her unique. She was a left-handed, bow-legged, slightly tall, pigeon-toed girl who was surrounded by petite girls; and the guys all seemed to like the little girls' body types.

Kia watched Zane and the grommets skate some more, then had the realization that watching them by herself might seem weird, so she sauntered over to her friends. Vienna was sitting in Melissa's lap with her head thrown backwards over Melissa's shoulder laughing, looking like a baby herself, small as she was.

Melissa took a shot of tequila from the bottle and gently pushed Vienna up, calling out to Dave, "Come get your drunken ass wife off my lap!"

"I'm not his wife!" Vienna slurred. "He would be soooo lucky!"

Christian and Kristen were sitting next to each other flirting when Christian looked up and yelled, "Dave! Come get your wife!"

Dave stumbled out of the screen doorway looking confused when he saw Vienna sitting on the ground. He offered her his hand and lifted her up. She fell into his arms and everyone chuckled.

21

"Dude," Doug called out, "take her to Vegas and marry her."

Every guy there booed and hissed at the suggestion. Kristen chimed in, "You knocked her up, be a man." Everyone knew it was a joke. There was no way were they that serious.

"Yeah, right," Dave snorted as Vienna crumpled into his arms. He gently lowered her down into one of the beach chairs.

Erica looked up slyly from her chair where Mickey was trying to ply her with alcohol. "Come on, Dave. She's carrying your love child." Erica's voice was so cute and sweet that you almost had to take it as a serious proclamation of what a good person should do.

Dave blushed. "Come on, Erica." He put his hands out in a gesture of resignation. "Get married? I'm 19."

"I'm 15," Vienna burped.

Everyone laughed. Dave blushed again. The matter was dropped when Dave was called into the living room to do a sound check. Mohawk Disco was setting up to play the party.

"He's fucked," Kristen said into her beer, but loud enough for everyone to hear. Looking at Christian she shrugged and smiled, "Get me a shot?"

Kia was able to remain invisible for the next 30 minutes while Mohawk Disco set up. Everyone crammed into the living room and kitchen while more locals showed up for the party. Kia blended in, grabbing a warm beer off the counter ever wary of Melissa's gaze. The band played and Kia got pushed against the living room wall as everyone jumped, raised their fists and danced.

Kristen and Christian were directly in front of the band singing along and smiling at each other. God, they are beautiful. Kia thought, Two perfect human beings, tailor made for each other. Then she noticed Mickey had Erica cornered in the kitchen playing quarters at the dining room table with Melissa, her boyfriend and some punk chick she'd never seen before. Melissa was getting aggressive and loud and was whispering to the ugly punk girl next to her and laughing like a donkey,

Kia turned her attention back to the band. She looked to her right to see Zane standing next to her, eyes on the band, nodding his head in time to the music. The scent of his sweat was a bit suffocating with so many bodies in the living room but it had a good muskiness. She suddenly wanted to lick his neck. She turned back to the band keeping Zane in her peripheral view, nodding her head in time with him.

The night roared on and when the band was finished, Mickey hooked up the stereo and everyone danced to the B-52s, English Beat, Oingo Boingo and whatever music was made just for their beach party. Beer was spilled, bongs were spilled, and no one cared because no one could see who did what. Kia floated in and out of the living room, kitchen and backyard. Her friends were here and there and she tried to decide which guy might secretly like her in her now drunken state.

CHAPTER 3

Saturday

The next morning Kia woke up on Ami's couch. She didn't remember getting there. Ami's boyfriend, Nick, was taking a very loud bong hit. She cracked her eyes open to see Ami and Brooke in the kitchen digging through the fridge. Brooke's boyfriend, Brian, came out of one of the bedrooms in his boxers, looking luscious and hot. Kia sat up knowing she was still the third wheel, having not scored a hot guy the night before.

Then she remembered. The left side of her head was sore to the touch. Ouch. That's right, Melissa had elbowed her in the side of the head and made her leave the party. Melissa was dancing in the crowded living room close to where Kia was standing against the wall, and deliberately elbowed her. She remembered Melissa's face in a snarl saying, "Get the fuck out of here, you little poser!"

Kia's eyes welled up with tears, picturing herself stumbling alone to Ami's house and curling up on the couch.

She looked at Brooke, Ami, Brian and Nick wondering if they could sense her embarrassment. She slowly sat up, wincing from the pain in her head.

"Bong toke?" Nick offered from the other couch, holding it out to her.

"Sure." Kia grabbed it and lit up the bowl, holding the smoke down in her lungs until it came out in a billowing cough.

"So what happened to you last night?" he asked casually as he repacked the bowl. Kia turned red.

"Melissa attacked me," she blurted. Her chest heated up with anger. "Fucking elbowed me in the head," she said rubbing the side of her head. The bong hit had given her an out-of-body sensation. Nick passed it back to her and relaxed into another hit.

Ami turned to them from the kitchen with a slice of processed cheese hanging from her fingers. She tore it into pieces and shoved it into her mouth as she spoke.

"So, Kia . . ." Ami paused as she fixated on the remaining cheese pieces attached to her fingers. Kia sat on the couch waiting, watching Ami, hoping she'd say something in her favor and not Melissa's. Hoping she'd have her back like she always did with Brooke and Vienna. Her friends knew that Melissa would pick on her for no reason. They ignored it, mostly because

Melissa was popular and Erica's best friend—except for Brooke.

Brooke met Kia in the morning when she got off the school bus and gave her diet pills so she would be amped up and ready to fight if Melissa was to come after her that day. But Ami and Vienna did nothing. Maybe because they were both the kind of girls who don't take shit or maybe because they were relieved that Melissa's hostility wasn't focused on them.

Nick turned around to Brian who was kissing Brooke in the kitchen.

"Bri, let's go check the surf," he said.

Brian removed himself from Brooke and put on his trunks. Within minutes they were out the door on their skateboards to find out if it was a good day for waves.

Kia arose from the sofa and moved to a barstool in the kitchen where Ami and Brooke were. Ami hopped up on the counter while Brooke leaned against it, putting cottage cheese on Wheat Thins and plopping them into her mouth. She washed it down with Tab. Neither mentioned Kia getting sucker-punched the night before.

Kia decided to complain.

"Fucking Melissa hit me last night," she said.

"What?" Ami acted as if she didn't know. "What happened?"

Brooke only glanced up from her diet breakfast.

"She elbowed me in the head on the dance floor and called me a poser." Kia's eyes flicked back and forth between the two, crestfallen. "You guys didn't see?"

"Um, no, I didn't," said Ami. "Did you Brooke?"

Brooke shook her head no, putting more cottage cheese on a Wheat Thin.

"God, how embarrassing." Kia's eyes filled with tears but her anger hadn't subsided.

Half-perplexed, half-irate Kia exclaimed, " Why does she not like me? Fuck! This sucks so bad!"

Ami shrugged. "I don't know. Maybe you should talk to her. Or stand up to her . . ." she trailed off'. . . anyway, until you do something it will just go on."

Finished with the subject she jumped off the counter and went into her bedroom to put on a bikini. "Let's go to the beach," she ordered from the bedroom. Kia watched her disappear down the hallway frustrated once again by her lack of loyalty.

On the way to the ocean, a car rolled up next to them. Vienna was sitting in the passenger seat making a funny face at them. Brooke was first to the window. She leaned in, followed by Ami then Kia.

"What are you guys doing?" Brooke asked Dave and Vienna in her sweet little voice.

Vienna rose up in her seat nose to nose with Brooke and said,

"We are going to Vegas to get married." Then she laughed. The three girls looked at Vienna and Dave, waiting for them to say more.

"No! We really are!" she replied in her usual sassy way. "I'm going to cruise by my house and pick up some stuff. You guys wanna go?" Vienna asked.

"No shit!" Ami exclaimed, "Fucking really?"

Dave had a cigarette in his mouth and slurred, "Yeah, really." His eyebrow raised in reluctant submission.

Vienna screeched, "Let's party!" The car started to pull away. "Meet me at my place!" Vienna yelled out. The girls watched the car roll down the street toward Vienna's house.

"Fuck yeah! said Ami. "I guess she's not moving."

Brooke cooed, "I wonder what she'll look like with a little baby."

Kia was thinking about how she could finagle her way to Vegas.

"Come on Brooke, let's go to my house and grab some clothes." Ami twisted around to Kia challenging her with a smirk, "Kia, are you going?'

"I'll have to see if I can lie to my parents," Kia replied.

"We'll meet you at Vienna's if you can go," Ami said before pulling Brooke back down the street to her house.

Kia turned and walked home. Her brain was working overtime to come up a good scenario to tell her parents so she could go to Vegas. She didn't want to miss this.

Her mom was at work as an ER nurse and wouldn't be home until late that night. Her dad was usually at home since he had been unemployed for two years. To make money he'd been selling at the swap meets, so their house had all his junk stacked up in the corners. The apartment always smelled of pot and incense. He was on the couch asleep with a newspaper spread across his lap, snoring loudly from his 225 pound frame.

Kia smiled, realizing it might be easy to sneak out if she could leave a note behind with some feasible story about where she'd be for the next few days. She went to her bedroom and quietly closed the door behind her. Her room with its unmade bed, clothes all over the floor and spilling out of her closet, suddenly felt suffocating. She felt a vague loneliness having to pack up by herself when she knew Ami and Brooke were probably together laughing and having fun without the burden of lying to their parents to take off for Vegas with Vienna and Dave. Brooke practically lived with Ami. Besides Erica, Brooke had three brothers and sisters and they all just did what they wanted most of the time. It's too hard for their parents to have them all home all the time so they let them run free.

Ami and her brother live with their single, alcoholic mom who's a cocktail waitress and loves to party. She'll sometimes take off for days to go on "vacations" with her "boyfriends." She'll leave money for them, and basically treats Ami and her brother as friends instead of her kids.

Kia looked around on the floor for clothes that might be clean. She ripped open the dresser pulling out anything cute. She'd never been to Vegas. What should she bring? Fancy clothes? Shorts, tanks, bathing suits? She called Ami's house to see what she and Brooke were packing. The phone rang six times. No answer. Frustrated, she grabbed some shorts, tanks and Levis and shoved them into her backpack. Now what to write on a note?

"Mom and Dad,

Me, Ami and Brooke were invited to spend the weekend at Ami's Uncle John's house in Huntington Beach. I know it's last minute but he's got a boat and wants to take us sailing. I will call you from his house.

Love, Kia"

Satisfied, she grabbed her backpack and quietly went into the living room listening for her dad's snoring. There it was, loud. She left the note on the dining room table and opened the front door, shutting it gently behind her.

She hurried the six blocks to Vienna's house wondering if she should have gone to Ami's house first so they could all go together. Even though Vienna is her friend, she's not her super-close friend and they'd never hung out alone. Kia turned onto Vienna's street and when she got to her house there were no cars in the driveway. She opened the front gate, walked to her door and softly knocked. No answer. She knocked louder. No answer. She turned and jogged to Ami's house. Maybe they were waiting for her there.

She kept a lookout for Dave's car, but there were two streets they could have taken out of the area. She got to Ami's and knocked on the door. Ami's little brother answered.

"What's up, Kia," he said lazily.

"Are Ami and Brooke here?" she sputtered out apprehensively as her eyes looked over his shoulder into the living room. Beads of sweat ran down her face from her unexpected jog over there.

"No, they left like five minutes ago," he began to shut the door.

"Oh, do you know where they went?" she reached out and placed her palm on the door.

"Said they were going to Vegas, left with Dave and Vienna," he muttered before he closed the door to get back to his unsupervised teenage life.

"Oh." (Huh. Maybe they went to pick her up. Shit! They'll wake her dad!)

"K. Thanks," she said to no one in a confused daze.

She ran home, her backpack flopping against her. Breathless, she got to her apartment, opened the door and her dad wasn't on the couch. She heard the toilet flush and he appeared from the bathroom.

"Kia," he flinched surprised to see her, "I thought you went to Huntington Beach."

"Ummm, did Ami and Brooke come by here?"

31

"No."

Fuck. "Oh, I thought I was supposed to meet them at Ami's house," she said more to herself, then asked again, hopefully, "they didn't come by here?"

"Still no." He went to the kitchen and poured a cup of stale coffee from the pot and proceeded to drink it cold.

"Well," he said, "I don't think your mother would appreciate you running off like that and leaving a note. You know how she is. Who is this Uncle John? Have we met him?"

Kia was caught in a lie she would have to perpetuate, but she was confused and mad, not knowing where her friends were. Did they really just leave her?

"Oh, he's Ami's mom's brother. He came to visit and wanted to spend time with her and invited her friends to go. I guess they left without me. Maybe I was supposed to go to Vienna's. Maybe they're waiting for me there. Can I go if I promise to call you when we get to his house?"

Her dad hesitated. She could tell he was debating whether to deal with his wife or his daughter.

"Vienna? I thought it was Ami and Brooke?"

Fuck. She was so anxious to get to Vienna's she used her name.

"Oh, Vienna's going too. I forgot to write that, I guess. Please, Daddy? It sounds like fun. Everything is alright." Kia pleaded.

"If they are waiting for you at Vienna's you can go. But you have to call home as soon as you get there."

"OK! Thanks!" Kia hurried out the front door.

"Dammit! Where are they?" She ran back to Vienna's in a craze. Maybe when she went by earlier they were picking up Ami and Brooke and they are waiting for her now?

She got to Vienna's again, gulping for air and still no car in the driveway. She knew for sure they'd left without her. She sat in the driveway catching her breath. She decided to wait to see if they'd come back. She sat for 30 minutes. Feeling defeated, she walked home.

CHAPTER 4

Sunday

The next morning Kia woke up and stayed in bed letting the sun bake her in her covers through the window above. She'd been up till 3 a.m. watching TV and smoking pot after her parents went to bed, trying to sleep. She cried then screamed into her pillow. Then she got depressed before finally drifting off. She still felt depressed. "I thought they were my friends," she kept thinking over and over. They were probably having so much fun. She figured they were laughing at her. She hoped not. Thinking about it made her stomach ache. She just stared at the ceiling.

She could hear her mother's voice in the living room chatting to her dad. Her mom talked a lot, all the time. Kia put her hand over her eyes pushing it down her face. "Fuck. Fuck. Fuck." She flipped over, grabbed the remote and turned on the little TV by her bed. She switched it to MTV. Madonna's new video for "Like a Virgin" came on and Kia stared at it, wishing she was Madonna on a gondola writhing around in a wedding dress. She was so beautiful and cool and tough. She didn't seem like she'd take shit from anybody. Kia was so engrossed in the video, pretending she was someone else, that she didn't realize her mom had entered her room.

"So Kia, what is this about an Uncle John?" she snapped at her sharply with one hand on her hip, eyes squinted in her usual disappointed way.

Kia snapped out of her reverie, "Nothing, mom."

"Well you know I don't appreciate you just leaving a note, anyway. You know that is not acceptable." Her mom hovered over her.

"I know, mom. It was last minute." Kia waved her hand through the air, "Doesn't matter anyway."

"It does to me!" She paused, and with her head on a swivel she surveyed the room. "Now get up and clean this room. And for future reference, notes aren't an acceptable means of communication in this house regarding your whereabouts, especially if you are going off with people I don't know. You know I work very hard to support this family and that's just not how I expect you to communicate with me." She added as an afterthought, "Or your father."

Kia looked at her and said nothing. She was dead inside. What did it matter now?

"Now get up! And clean this room. Now!" She left shutting the door.

Kia turned back to Madonna, who was also done with her, and MTV went to commercial. She stayed in bed for another hour, watching music videos until her mom returned and shut off the TV, threatening to remove it from her room if she didn't get a move on.

Kia did what she had to, shoving her clothes into her closet and forcing the doors shut to hide the mess inside. She made her bed and threw everything else underneath it. She put on her bathing suit and a pair of boxers rolling down the waistband till they hung just below her belly button like she had seen Madonna do. Then she tied her hair in a knot like Kristen did and went into the kitchen to get something to eat.

Her mom was on the couch with the news on the TV. She was doing embroidery on some pillow as her dad rummaged through his junk in the corner of the dining room. Kia shuffled to the fridge grabbing some leftover potato salad and a fork and declared that breakfast. She stood against the counter quietly finishing it off before throwing the container in the trash and her fork in the sink.

"Your room clean?" her mom asked from the couch over her shoulder.

"Yeah," Kia replied.

"Can I check it?"

"Sure, it's picked up."

Her mom went back to her embroidery.

"I'm going to the beach to lie out. By myself," she added in a hurt tone of voice. Feeling victimized and sorry for herself she grabbed a towel from the bathroom and her beach cruiser from the dining room area.

Kia rode her cruiser over to Hueneme Beach for a change of scenery. She was sad. She figured everyone was probably in Vegas. Everyone who was anyone. Ahead of her in front of the snack bar she saw Zane on his skateboard hanging on the counter talking to the old man who worked there. She parked her bike and walked past him to the left side of the pier hoping she was invisible. She figured the beach would be deserted. She went to the usual hangout spot and saw some towels, but no people. She noticed Brian and Nick in the water with a couple other guys she didn't know. Must be no waves at Strand today.

Zane and his bandmates walked down carrying their skateboards and dressed in Dickies shorts and T-shirts. Not the typical surfer guys, just in board shorts, but grungier. That was OK, they were in a punk band. She sat on her towel and pulled her knees up to her chest. They sat by her but ignored her as they ate chili fries and hot dogs. She eventually took off her shorts and reclined on her towel to tan. She closed her eyes listening to the waves crashing, the tide going back out, and Zane, Eddie and Henry eating. The sun felt good on her stomach.

She turned her head to the right and slowly opened her eyes to see Zane staring at the surf, or surfers.

"Yeah, Dawg! Good one!" he said loudly. He wiped the crumbs off his hands and crumpled the empty food bag before throwing it on the sand next to his skateboard. Kia looked him over from his black Converse sneakers and his very white socks, to his grey Dickies shorts, black Angry Samoans T-shirt and the top of his shaved head. She couldn't decide if he was cute. No, he wasn't really cute, he was . . . interesting. Dark eyebrows, brown eyes, smallish nose and a dimple in his right cheek when he smiled. Cutish, but roughish, too. Kia turned her head back to the sky and closed her eyes, wondering who was in Vegas. She was obsessed. A slight wind picked up, and it felt good. She sat up and checked out the surf. There were maybe five guys surfing. She saw Christian and Mickey, and some guy she couldn't make out, waiting with Brian and Nick for the next set. She looked down at her body hoping she was getting good color. Because she was blonde and blue-eyed she took longer to tan than Ami, Brooke and Vienna. At least she could work on it while they were in Vegas. She still couldn't believe they were in Vegas without her. She fought back her tears.

Zane took off his shirt and laid back in the sand closing his eyes. Eddie and Henry got up and walked back toward the snack bar.

Within minutes, Kristen and Erica appeared and set their towels down on the other side of Zane. They applied baby oil and got positioned on their towels not saying a word. Kia laid back down, too, and shut her eyes. She slowly breathed in and out. After about 20 minutes she turned on to her stomach and rested her head on her hands staring up the beach at the condos in the distance. Her mind was blank.

38

Zane turned over, too, and turned his head toward her. She could feel him staring at her. She looked over and he winked at her and smiled. She smiled back at him. Then he put his arms under his head for support and closed his eyes. She did the same. Every few seconds she opened her eyes slightly to find him looking at her, then closing his eyes when she caught him.

What was going on here? She decided to keep her eyes closed and just feel him staring at her. She smiled. She felt good inside like it was only the two of them lying on the beach having a moment.

She felt water droplets hitting her and sat up to see Christian shaking his hair and body over Kristen. She squealed all cute, of course.

"Christian!" Kristen shrieked.

"Ha! Ha!" he laughed, "What? You don't want to get wet? You looked hot."

He smiled that brilliant white smile of his. Zane didn't move, his eyes were closed and he was smiling. "How does your head feel?" Zane whispered toward Kia. She looked down at him embarrassed. He must have seen Melissa punch her.

"Oh, it's OK," she said quietly, lying back down.

"She hit you pretty good. I think she's a bitch," he whispered.

"Yeah, me too," she whispered back so Kristen and Erica wouldn't hear her. She peeked over at them but they were busy chatting up Christian.

"I don't remember much, I was pretty drunk," she whispered again.

"I know," he replied, "I walked you out after she attacked you."

"You did?" Kia was embarrassed once again. She didn't remember that.

"Yeah, I told you I'd walk you home but you pushed me away and took off."

"Oh. Sorry, I was embarrassed I guess." At this point, Kia thought he was staring at her because of what a stupid girl she was. Zane sat up and turned toward the surf to watch his friends. Kia put her head down and closed her eyes, mortified as usual. Then she heard him laughing.

"Christian! Look over at the pier!"

Kia looked and saw Eddie and Henry hanging over the side without their shirts, shoes and socks, ready to jump.

"What fuckers!" he laughed.

"Go for it shitheads!" Christian yelled, "Watch out for the pylons!"

Before he finished yelling, they jumped, arms flailing looking scared shitless. Kia couldn't help but laugh. The group stood up and stared waiting for Henry and Eddie to pop up in the surf.

"Oh, shit," Erica gasped, "Are they alright?"

First to be seen was Henry swimming toward the beach. Then

Eddie popped up under Brian's surfboard grabbing it and pulling Brian into the water. Everyone laughed.

Kia sat back on her towel. She looked over at Kristen who brushed sand off her perfectly tanned butt. She was almost in a G-string. She had a perfect body. Kia looked at Erica who was wearing the cutest floral bikini, a little more modest than Kristen's suit. She was pretty fair-skinned compared to the other girls. Even Kia was tanner. But it worked with the slight dusting of freckles across her face, her big blue eyes and "beach wavy" blonde hair halfway down her back.

Erica sat down and put on a big straw hat like the lifeguards wear to protect themselves from constant sun exposure. Kristen strutted a bit more, even had Christian check her ass for sand. Kia looked at Zane who also watched Kristen. Kia sighed to herself. Of course he was. Everyone looked at Kristen.

Kristen bent at the waist, gathered her hair and twisted it into a loose bun. Kia absentmindedly touched her own hair to make sure it was still on top of her head. Then she undid it and let her hair fall onto her shoulders and back hoping it would have a nice wave to it. She didn't want Kristen to think she was copying her.

Kristen finally sat back down and put more baby oil on. Christian peeled off his wetsuit to his board shorts and sat next to the older girls. Zane returned his gaze to the surf to see his friends walking back toward them, wet and laughing.

"Ha, ha, dude." Henry said.

"Fuck! I almost ate it on one of the pylons," Eddie laughed.

They both shook off directly onto Zane. "Hey fuckers!" Zane said, shielding himself. Henry and Eddie sat in the sand.

All was quiet again for a moment as the guys watched the surf, and Kristen and Erica sunbathed. Erica had her straw hat over her face, protecting it from the sun.

"So," Kristen said still lying down with her eyes closed, "Dave and them went to Vegas?" She turned her head toward Kia opening her eyes, directing the question to her, Kia assumed.

Kia dug her toes in the sand, "Yeah, I guess. I think so. That's where they said they were going."

"How come you didn't go?" Kristen asked.

"Umm, they left before I could go," Kia replied, feeling childish.

"Oh," Kristen turned her face back to the sun closing her eyes.

"We're out," Zane announced as he got up and wiped the sand from his shorts. Henry and Eddie followed grabbing their shoes.

"Later," he said to the group. "Later, Christian." They slapped hands.

Kia briefly watched them walk toward the parking lot. More people showed up, surfed, laid out, drank beers.

CHAPTER 5

Late in the afternoon Kia rode home. She thought about how Kristen and Erica privately joked about Vienna and Dave going to Vegas. She got the idea that everyone was secretly laughing about it. Kia felt a little better now about not going. But she also worried about Vienna. Was she really going to be married at 15? Was that even legal? Who knew, maybe it would work out. They would definitely have a cute baby.

Kia unlocked the door to find nobody home. She headed to the kitchen to scrounge something to eat. She grabbed Wheat Thins and cottage cheese—the diet lunch. There was no diet soda. The only thing to drink was Tang. She mixed it with water from the tap and threw in some ice. She kicked back on the couch and turned on MTV and chilled for about an hour before becoming bored. With her friends gone who else could she hang out with? She refused to sit around waiting for them to come back. Fuck that. She turned off the TV, put her dishes in the sink and headed for her bedroom. She changed into Levis, pegging them at the bottom, threw on a shirt, put her hair up, grabbed her skateboard and headed for Ocean Street. Maybe she'd head down to the beach to see if anything was happening. She skated barefoot down to the lifeguard jetty, but no one was there, maybe only two cars. On the side of the lifeguard tower someone had written in big block letters with spray paint:

"IF YOU THINK YOU CAN JUST PULL UP AND PADDLE OUT YOU'RE WRONG. OUR LOCALISM IS STILL IN FULL FORCE"

She saw legs hanging off the side of the tower. She picked up her skateboard and walked over to see who it was: Zane, Henry and Eddie. They were watching the couple of guys out in the surf catching the 1- to 2-foot sets rolling in at dusk.

"Hey, what's up?" she asked looking up at them.

Henry looked down, "Waiting for these Valley fuckers to get out," he said with conviction.

Kia looked back to the ocean where two guys were sitting on their boards looking back at the tower every few minutes.

"Oh, yeah?" she said.

"We are gonna fuck them up when they get out!" Henry laughed.

Kia climbed up the ladder and sat next to Zane on the far end.

He was chewing on beef jerky and had a crazed look about

him. His eyes were bulgy and he smacked on the jerky like he'd just snorted cocaine or something. She knew he was straight-edge but he was all pumped up.

Eddie turned toward Zane, "Let's go break their car windows and jack their shit."

"Nah, let's wait till they get out," Zane grumbled, possessed.

"Kia," he said, not taking his eyes off the water, "go get Christian and whoever might be at his house and tell them to come down here."

Kia, thankful for a role to play, grabbed her board and skated to Christian's house. When she got to his place the door was open. She knocked and yelled "Christian!"

"Come in," she heard from the kitchen.

She went in to find Christian, Ramsey, Erica, Kristen and Melissa in the kitchen. Immediately Melissa said, "What the fuck do you want?"

Kia stammered, not expecting to see her there. "Umm . . . Zane wants you guys to come to the lifeguard tower. There are some Valleys out in the water."

"Oh, you're fucking Zane now?" Melissa sneered.

"Uh, no . . . " Kia's face turned red. Fuck Melissa! Why me?

Erica touched Melissa's arm, "Melissa, come on."

"No! Fuck her." Melissa glared at Kia.

"OK, well . . . " Kia jumped on her skate and headed back to the lifeguard tower.

In a couple of minutes Christian and the crew rolled up in Christian's Ford Falcon. They got out and stood in front of the lifeguard tower looking toward the surf.

"Fuckers!" Zane yelled.

Christian walked to the shoreline, his hands up in a "come on, let's fight!" stance.

Ramsey joined him in heckling the Valleys. "Get out pussies! Go home!"

The sun was low and it was getting dark.

"They have to come out soon," Melissa said with evil and hatred in her voice. "Maybe you can go home with them," she shot toward Kia.

Kia stood there shocked and embarrassed. She was tired of all the crap. Her friends left her, Melissa harasses her . . . her chest got hot and tears burned her eyes.

"What are you going to do, cry baby?" Melissa taunted her.

Kia looked around her. Christian, Ramsey, Eddie and Henry were looking at the ocean oblivious to what Melissa was doing. But Kristen, Erica and Zane were watching and wondering.

"Fuck, Melissa! What the hell is your problem?!" Kia yelled before she could stop herself. Now everyone was looking.

"You're my problem, you little bitch!" Melissa sneered. "Thinking you're all high and mighty."

"What?" Kia was confused.

Erica stepped toward Melissa, but Melissa moved closer to Kia's face.

"You are a little bitch!" Melissa yelled at her.

Kia tried not to let tears fall, she was so embarrassed and confused, but then something switched in her and she finally got mad. She threw her skateboard into the sand and remembered Vienna's face when girls picked on her. Kia got a crazed look and started breathing hard remembering the high off the diet pills, which she wished she was on now. She lunged at Melissa and grabbed the front of her shirt in her fist pulling it toward her. She could hear it rip. She threw her weight on her even though Melissa was bigger and outweighed her. Melissa threw back getting Kia under her in the sand. Kia dodged the first blows. She squirmed out from under her and stood on her feet, fists up.

"Fuck you!" she screamed.

Melissa got wild and lunged toward her. Kia moved just in time, but Melissa turned back toward her not losing her footing. Somewhere in Kia's mind she heard the guys hollering and laughing.

"Melissa!" Erica yelled, "Melissa!"

Melissa stood across from Kia panting. The guys had temporarily forgotten about the Vals in the excitement of a girl fight.

"Melissa," Erica said, getting between them, "Come on, this is stupid. Kia hasn't done anything to you. You know it."

Kia's heart was so grateful to Erica at that moment. Maybe this would be over. Melissa turned toward Erica, coming to life. The guys realized the girls were gonna be chicks about this so they all looked back to the ocean, except Zane. Kia felt his eyes on her.

"Well, what's this about then?" Kia asked Erica.

Erica shrugged. She wasn't about to give up the secrets between friends.

Kia looked at Melissa pleading with her eyes for some kind of reason.

Melissa stepped closer to Kia and said in her face, "You spilled a drink on me at Steve's party, you little bitch!"

"Huh?" Kia didn't even remember that, and then realized it's just an excuse she made up. "Oh, I did?" Kia searched her mind, "Well, I didn't mean to, Melissa."

Kia did her best to look remorseful for something she didn't do. She wanted this to be over.

"See Melissa?" Erica said gently, "She's sorry. Let's stop this.'

"Fuck, Erica, you're such a goody-goody." Melissa purred with a look in her eyes that Kia observed was in a worshipful way.

48

Melissa, the hard-ass bitch, had a thing for Erica. Kia saw them looking at each other and she knew in her heart, it was over. Thank you Erica. Goddamn, thank you.

Erica put her arm around Melissa and directed her back to where the boys were standing waiting for the Vals to get out of the water. Kristen looked at Kia and gave her a mischievous grin before joining them. Kia stood there completely relieved and mystified. Then she looked toward the ocean, thankful other people would be getting a beat down, not her.

The Vals ended up paddling as far away from the tower as they could. Everyone followed them down the beach. Kia walked behind the group still anxious Melissa might flip out on her. Eventually the Vals paddled in, resigned to their fate. They took off their leashes and grabbed their boards heading to the parking lot. The five local guys blocked their way.

"What the fuck are you doing surfing here, bro?" Henry sneered at one of them, "Go back to the Valleeee! Kook!"

The two just tried to keep walking.

Christian stopped in front of one, and Henry and Ramsey stopped in front of the other.

"Hey, man, we're leaving," one said to Christian.

"Too late, man, you already surfed our spot," Christian retorted.

"No one was out," the other said.

"Don't matter," Ramsey growled. "You never, never, never surf here. Can't you read?" He pointed to the tower.

The two Vals followed his finger and didn't reply.

"Can you read, I said?" Ramsey repeated, louder this time.

Christian went up to one guy and shoved him. He stumbled back but held his board. Kia felt sorry for them. They looked horrified.

Melissa, of course, egged it on. She needed a fight.

"You stupid pussies," she said walking toward one and attempting to grab his board. He pulled it back out of her grasp. Christian stepped forward and clocked him on the jaw. The guy crumbled in the sand still holding his board. His friend's mouth hung open, scared shitless. Christian grabbed the guy's board and the dude didn't resist.

"You rich little fuckers can buy new boards," Christian said. With that, Ramsey grabbed the other guy's board—there was no resistance. Kia could see Melissa smiling, Kristen looked bored, and Erica appeared pensive.

Henry, Eddie and Zane took off running to the parking lot. Henry ran up the lifeguard tower and grabbed a bat for what had turned into a standoff between the locals and the Vals. Kia turned and walked toward the parking lot. She grabbed her board and skated in circles in the lot, not really wanting to be part of it, but not leaving either.

Henry took the bat and swung at the passenger window of the

50

Val's car. Crack! The window broke. He unlocked the door and scrambled inside, looking for wallets. He retrieved them and a couple of jackets. Eddie and Zane laughed.

Kia watched this then turned to see the group walking up from the beach, the two Vals in front followed by Ramsey and Christian carrying their boards. The two Vals saw their car and grimaced.

"Fuck!" one of them yelled. That made Zane, Henry and Eddie laugh like a pack of hyenas.

"Get the fuck out of here kooks!" Henry yelled.

"My fucking car," the owner said.

"Hey, you want more?!" Henry yelled raising the bat and smashing it down on the trunk.

"Shit man, stop!" the Val yelled

"Dude, let's just go," the other said.

"It's my dad's car . . . he's going to kill me."

"Have him buy you another one Valley pussy," Christian said and then clocked him in the eye for good measure, still holding the dude's board.

The guy fell to the pavement in his wetsuit. He scrambled up, undid his wetsuit, and they both got in and started the car while the group surrounded them.

As they drove away and out of reach, the other guy hung out

the passenger window and yelled, "We'll bring our crew back to kick your asses!"

"Oh, brave now aren't you!" Melissa shouted after them.

Christian looked at the two hijacked boards and said, "Looks like firewood to me. Bonfire at the Dunes tonight." He then strapped the two boards to his Falcon and the group got back in and drove away.

Kia stood there with Zane, Henry and Eddie. Zane turned toward Kia, "What are you going to do now?"

Kia shrugged.

"Got food at your house?" he asked her. Kia thought about it. Not really.

"Come on, let's go," Zane decided and they all skated to Kia's house.

CHAPTER 6

Kia opened the door to her apartment praying her dad wasn't home. She knew her mom was at work. The place was empty, thank God. The boys rushed in behind her. Eddie went for the fridge, Zane plopped down on the couch and Henry started messing with the junk her dad had laying around the apartment.

"There ain't shit to eat," Eddie exclaimed looking through the fridge.

Kia went over and looked. There was a carton of eggs, some cheese, half of a loaf of bread, and some leftovers from . . . who knows.

"Umm," She stammered, "I can make scrambled eggs with cheese."

Zane exclaimed from the couch where he was working the remote, "Get to it, woman!" The boys laughed.

She pulled out the eggs and attempted to make something.

"What is all this shit?" Henry asked, picking up random bits of electronic equipment.

"My dad sells that stuff at swap meets," Kia laughed it off, trying to make it not sound so lame.

"Your parents smoke pot?" Zane asked.

"Umm, yeah," Kia replied puzzled. Why would he care?

"Break it out," he said, still looking at the TV.

"OK," Kia went to her parent's room and found their stash and pipe. She returned, handed it to Zane. She stood there looking at him. She could have sworn he was straight-edge. He took the baggie and shoved it into his pocket.

"What are you doing?" Kia queried taken back, her palm still outstretched.

"For later," he replied, dismissing her.

"My parents will know I took it," she stammered.

"So?" He looked up at her to see if she would stop him.

Kia just turned and went back to the kitchen while Eddie and Henry messed with her dad's stuff.

Kia made eggs the best she could, nervous about her dad coming home, about what her parents would say about the missing pot, and why Zane was bossing her around. But she

54

didn't want to do anything to upset him. She had a feeling he liked her. At least she hoped he did. She wanted him to think she was cool.

She put all the eggs with cheese on three plates. There was none left for her. The guys grabbed them and scarfed the food down. They left their plates on whatever furniture they saw fit. Kia picked them up throwing them and the pan in the sink.

"Let's go to the Dunes," Eddie said.

"Yeah, bro, let's go," Henry chimed in.

Zane got up and turned toward Kia. "Show me your room."

"Yeah, okay."

The other two sighed and sat on the couch. Kia walked to her room with Zane right behind her. She was glad now that her mom made her pick it up. She stood there lamely while he looked around.

"Are you going to change?" he prompted.

"Uh, no, I wasn't planning on it."

"Put on a skirt." He walked to her dresser and started opening her drawers. The first one was her underwear drawer. She came behind him slamming it shut.

"What?" He turned toward her, smiling, standing real close to her.

"That's my underwear!" she said laughing.

"So?" he tried again to open the drawer and she fought to shut it.

He stood there grinning at her and she stared back. She blushed. He leaned toward her and kissed her. It was sweet and he tasted good. He pulled away and plopped down on her bed.

"So, are you gonna change or what?" He leaned back with his hands behind his head.

He looked so good lying on her bed. Zane was on her bed! Without thinking Kia got on top of him and kissed him. It started to get hot and he put his hands on her ass pushing her into his groin. She stopped kissing him and smiled down on him, trying to catch her breath. He flipped her over and got up suddenly. He went to her closet and opened it. Kia flinched at the mess within.

"Damn, girl, this is where you hide your mess? What other skeletons you got in here?" he teased her.

She shoved him out of the way.

"Just like the other night, pushing me away," he teased smirking at her.

Her heart skipped a beat in her chest and she was sure her cheeks looked like ruddy stoplights. But she didn't want him to stop. Not at all.

She flirtatiously looked over her shoulder and grabbed a cute mini out of the closet. "Okay. I'll change. Get out."

"What? I wanna watch."

Kia blushed, again. "No way!"

"Come on." He reclined on the bed.

Kia stood there not wanting to change in front of him. Shit, she wasn't going to do that. She wasn't a slut. Did he think she was a slut? She opened her bedroom door rushing to the bathroom, shut the door and locked it. She changed in a hurry, afraid they might leave without her. She checked herself out in the mirror and rushed out. All three boys were in the living room talking. She dashed back to her room, grabbed her slip-on Vans, socks and a hoodie, put them on and joined them in the living room.

"Let's go!" Henry exclaimed, reaching for the front door. All three left. Zane didn't look back to make sure she was coming. Kia grabbed her skate and followed them down the stairs to the street. They got on their boards and skated the couple miles to the Dunes between Hollywood Beach and Oxnard Shores. Kia skated hard to keep up with them. On the way over she was pretty proud of herself. She felt like one of them. Maybe she'd be Zane's girlfriend. Won't her friends be impressed when they get back? She stood up to Melissa and she's Zane's girlfriend. She's cooler than they realized. That thought made Kia's heart so happy.

They pulled up to the dunes grabbed their skates and started walking in the sand looking for the fire hidden out of range of the cops' radar. They finally heard voices and saw light and smoke. They came upon it and a ton of people were already there. She was thrilled to be walking in with the boys. She wondered what everybody would be thinking. She was the only girl hanging with these guys so she must be cool.

Christian just grabbed one of the Val's boards and threw it onto the fire. There was a loud, "Hurrah!" and laughter. He sat back down with his hoodie pulled up over his head looking dangerous and hot. Of course he sat next to Kristen with her tanned legs in short shorts. She was smoking a clove cigarette and had silver rings on her fingers to match the rings on her toes.

Zane, Henry and Eddie made their rounds slapping hands and exchanging "What ups" Kia was not sure what to do, so she just sat where she'd stood. Melissa was there, but she ignored her.

Kia saw Zane grab a beer which he handed her before sitting down. She felt good again. See? He liked her, she wanted everyone to notice. She could feel his energy next to her. She glanced over to look at him and he was laughing at something he was seeing on the other side of the bonfire. His eyes were shining and his laugh was a little deep in his throat. It was very good. She took a drink of her beer smiling to herself. She leaned back against the dune she was sitting in front of using it like a backrest. She made sure her legs were in front of her crossed at the ankles, and tugged her miniskirt down around her butt. She watched everyone. Some guy came up to Zane and Zane pulled out the sack of weed from her parents and handed it to him. The guy gave him a twenty dollar bill and Zane put it in his pocket like it was his. Kia watched this and it made her angry. She wasn't sure why he had brought it. Maybe to roll a joint for her or something, but that she would be able to put the rest back.

Shit. What a fucker. Now how was she going to explain that? Her mom would be pissed.

She turned back to the fire and away from Zane. She pulled her hoodie up over her head so she wouldn't have to make eye contact with him. It was different for her, didn't he know? Her parents weren't like most of theirs who wouldn't even know or care if their stash was missing. They'd just think they smoked it, or they knew the kids would steal it and didn't care either way. But Kia was an only child and her parents kept track of her for the most part—they definitely kept track of a baggie of weed. It was unspoken that she could take a little now and then. They were both big potheads and saw nothing wrong with it. But they kept her in check and reminded her that good grades were important and they didn't want her running around town all night. She should have left her dad a note before she took off but she was in a hurry to keep up with the boys. Ah well, just another thing she will be in trouble for when she got home.

She finished her beer and played with the empty bottle for a few minutes deliberating over having another. She still felt confident that she came with the boys, though she was pissed at Zane, so she got up to search for a beer. Someone had a keg off to the side, she wandered over to it. Ramsey was standing there, and Christian walked up at the same time she did. They both reached for a cup. He grabbed them first and handed her two of them.

"You hold, I'll pump," he said smiling at her. That came out kind of wicked, she thought. It gave her goosebumps. She nodded and held the cups under the spigot while he pumped the keg. When they were both foaming over he reached and took one of the cups from her, grinning. She smiled back and put her lips to her cup. They both had their hoodies up and looked like they were in disguise or hiding from everyone. He slowly looked away from her and started joking with Ramsey about the Vals from that afternoon. She stood there listening, kind of part of the group, but soon realized she had nothing to add to the conversation. Though she understood the legacy of protecting the local surf, she kind of felt bad about the way those guys were shamed earlier. She decided to walk back over to where she'd been sitting. She pivoted and raised her hand awkwardly as a gesture of farewell. She carefully fixed her skirt as she sat back down. Zane was sitting quietly while Eddie and Henry were singing Suicidal Tendencies' "Institutionalized."

"All I wanted was a Pepsi!" they yelled over and over, laughing.

Appearing out of nowhere, Mickey walked into the group with a six-pack under each arm. He stumbled forward, falling on top of Kristen, beers flying.

"Fucking Mickey!" she shrieked trying to push him off.

He was so drunk he didn't move until he pantomimed dry humping her in the sand.

Everyone laughed while Kristen was pinned underneath him. Eventually she pushed him off and he rolled over and suddenly sprung up in the sand, slightly wobbly on his ascent. He reached down grabbing a beer, rubbed his crotch and grinned stupidly. Kia couldn't help but laugh. Erica wiped the sand out of Kristen's long, sun-kissed hair, smiling. Mickey stumbled off toward the keg where his buddies were laughing.

"Kia," Zane said to her.

She turned her head toward him. "What?" she said plainly.

"What are you doing?" he said quietly grinning and leaning toward her kind of smarmy-like.

"Nothing," she said looking back to the fire, drinking her beer.

"What do you want to be doing?" he said, in a low and seductive tone, leaning on his arm in the sand with his body toward her.

She looked at him with no reply. He ran his finger along the sleeve of her hoodie. She just watched him do it. She knew he was making a move on her.

"How's your beer?" he said with his hand still on her arm, looking up with a smirk.

She looked in his eyes and recognized the look. He was being smooth, or so he thought. In her mind she was still irritated with him for selling her parent's weed, but her heart began to soften at the way he was looking up at her. This tough guy was putting on the charm. She pulled her hoodie off her head and took a drink from her cup which she could now see was little more than foam.

"I could use another. It was mostly foam,' she replied.

"Oh yeah?" he said taking her cup from her and peering inside. "Finish this. I'll get you another."

She did and he stood up taking it from her and giving her a wink at the same time.

Hmmm . . . he was being all nice again. Maybe he didn't know she would be in trouble over the weed. He didn't know what her parents were like. She decided to let it go.

She watched him walk away and decided she liked his butt and the way he walked. He went straight to the keg and started pumping her out a beer. Now it was just the two of them connected. It didn't matter that all of their friends were around partying and acting goofy. It was the first time in a long time she'd been able to relax and not worry about Melissa, who has, thankfully, ignored her the entire time.

He finished, and sat next to her, handing her the beer. She took it and held it. He was closer to her than before. His left leg was right up against her right one. She could feel it and it was "couple-ish." They were definitely together. They both leaned back against the dune. They sat and watched everyone do their thing. Mickey was on a roll, entertaining everyone, talking loud, making jokes and telling stories about surfing. No one mentioned Dave, Vienna or Vegas. Out of sight, out of mind.

Kia felt Zane put his arm around her shoulders and pull her next to him. It was like they're not here, either. A little romance was blooming and it felt like they were invisible. Kia liked that. But if anyone looked their way they would see Zane had claimed her. She took a little sip of her beer.

Suddenly to her right, she saw light, like a bright flashlight scanning the ocean then the sand. It was so quick. Then to her left another light came jerkily over the dunes. She kept looking and saw two cops come over the dunes to her right. She watched Eddie and Henry scramble. She looked and two more cops appeared.

"Hey! Everyone stays where they are!" she heard authoritively to her left.

Mickey threw his cup at the cop and took off running. Two cops sprinted down the darkened shore after him. The two cops on her right came around and told everyone again to stay put.

Zane grabbed her right hand and whispered, "Get rid of your cup."

She slowly flipped it upside down behind her and shoved it into the sand.

The cops came around to where the guys were standing by the keg.

Zane yanked her up and pulled her to the right. He started running, pulling her behind. He reached down grabbing his skate, she barely grabbed hers, and they started running. They let go of hands and ran as hard as they could.

She couldn't even think, she just followed him in the darkness along the shore. She pushed as hard as she could along the wet sand, trying not to lose him.

CHAPTER 7

They ran until they were almost at the end of the Dunes, then he cut right into them and she did likewise. She barely saw him disappear and followed, looking for him. She found him crouched down. She went to him and crouched next to him.

"Shh...', he whispered.

Of course, she thought. She's panting hard and tried to quiet her breathing. They sat there sweaty trying to be quiet. In the distance another cop car had sirens blaring. They ducked down even farther, almost horizontal. Shit. She looked at the night sky with all its stars hoping it's dark enough to protect them.

They waited about fifteen minutes, then Zane slowly rose peering over the Dunes for any cops. Kia laid back relying on him being a dude to check the situation.

"Let's go," he said quietly turning toward her.

They grabbed their skates. Kia stumbled a bit trying to evacuate herself from the soft sand.

"Shhh...", he said again, like she needed to be reminded.

They plodded out to the wet sand and walked along the shore away from the now defunct bonfire party. He grabbed her hand and their free hands carried their skates along. About halfway up the beach they cut through two houses that had a sand break between them. They hopped on their skateboards, flapped the wheels on the quiet street, and skated up away from the shore.

"We need to find a ride," he said over his shoulder as he skated a few feet ahead of her.

She followed him to Harbor Blvd, a busy road, to try to hitch a ride back to Strand. He put his thumb out and directed her to watch for cops. Before too long a man in an old Cadillac picked them up. Zane hopped in front and Kia took the back seat. The dude ended up dropping them off at the Corner Market about three streets from Kia's house.

"You live close by, let's go to your house," Zane decided.

"OK, but my dad is probably home," she said, skating behind him.

"Can you sneak me in?" he said over his shoulder gliding down the street.

She thought about it. She would find a way.

"Yeah, but you'll have to wait till I get in." She pushed her skate right behind him.

They skated quietly, then turned down her street and continued halfway down the block, flipping up their skates to a free hand before walking into her apartment complex.

"There is a garbage dumpster under my window. Wait there," she told him, walking toward the stairs to her apartment.

He headed off to the back. She watched him walk away. "Oh shit, Zane is coming to my room," she thought. She zeroed in on the back of his shaved head and felt a tingle travel through her body. She thought of Ami and Brooke momentarily, realizing she'd done better for herself in their absence. She walked softly up the stairs and unlocked the front door. Pushing it open an inch at a time she saw that the living room was dark and deserted. She went to the hallway and there was no light under her parent's bedroom doorway. She hurried to her room and opened the curtains and window.

"Zane?" she whispered to the darkness.

"Yeah?" she heard his reply.

"Come around, they're not here."

Then she shut the window and slid back into the living room. She could hear him bounding up the stairs. She wished he'd be quiet, it sounded like the noise was vibrating through the entire complex. She saw him coming toward her and said, 'Shhh."

He back pedaled and hunched down, grinning, then glided past her into the living room.

"Got food?" he whispered.

"No!" she said, pushing him on the back toward her room.

She rushed him in and shut the door.

"I don't know if my dad's not here or sleeping,' she whispered.

He put his skate against her wall, then stood there looking around. "I could use a shower," he said. "Join me."

"No! Shhh." she said, thinking he was acting ridiculous. Did he not just hear her?

"Oh well, come here then," he said reaching for her and pulling her close. He kissed her hard.

She dropped her hands to her sides, taken aback, but not resisting. Slowly she put her arms around his neck. He put his arms around her waist and pulled them onto the bed. They made out for a while, entwining limbs and getting heavy.

"Take off your hoodie, you silly girl," he said, pulling it off her. Then he drew her tight to his body and his hands explored her ass, then her chest.

"Take off your shirt," he demanded.

He didn't wait for an answer, but put her on her back straddling her as he brought her shirt over her head. Though she was into making out with him, things were moving fast, and he was ordering her to do stuff.

"Oh," he purred, reaching behind her to undo her bra. She

didn't fight it. She wasn't even sure what was going on, but she went with it.

"Nice tits," he said, kissing her chest.

"Squeeze them together for me," he instructed.

She thought he was getting a little creepy, but she acquiesced.

He ran his tongue along her cleavage while grinding into her pelvis with his groin. She pulled his shirt over his head, and he threw it on the floor. He kissed her neck and soon she could feel him sucking a hickey. She stretched it out for him, enjoying it. She could feel her bare chest touching his as he sucked on her skin. She knew he was "marking her" which meant she belonged to him. She would have a big red mark on her neck tomorrow to show their "love."

But in this moment, all she cared about was that she was with Zane and she didn't even see it coming. Plus, today she was free of Melissa and thanks to Zane fully in the group. She kissed him back hard. She went for his neck but he turned his head and returned his focus to her breasts with his mouth. She decides she would mark him too, just not now.

He reached down and unzipped his Dickies shorts. He took off his shoes and socks, leaving him in nothing but boxers.

This would be her first time. She was the only virgin in her group of friends. She didn't want her shoes and socks on for the first time no matter how bossy he was, but when she tried to remove them he told her, "no," and began kissing her stomach.

It wasn't the way she wanted it but she let it go, inhaling him. He smelled like bonfire and musk. She bent her legs up to enfold him. She could feel his penis inside his boxers, pushing against her panties. He continued to focus on her breasts and folded them into a deep cleavage.

"Do you want me to take my underwear off?" she asked breathlessly.

He didn't answer. He just kept clutching her breasts, pushing them together.

"Do you have any Vaseline?" he asked.

"Maybe in the bathroom," she replied.

"Go get it," he said, rolling onto his back.

She laid there for a moment, topless and exposed. She got up and grabbed his shirt to cover herself. Trying to stay quiet, she opened the door and tiptoed to the bathroom. The light was bright. Before she opened the medicine cabinet she looked at herself in the mirror. Her hair, blonde and almost to her ass, was cute and flowy. Her face was clear and her eyes lighter blue than normal. She looked good! She opened the medicine cabinet: no Vaseline. She closed it and pulled open drawers until finding a half-used, old jar of Vaseline. She took it back into her bedroom trying not to wake her dad, still not sure he was actually home.

She shut her bedroom door holding the Vaseline in her palm like a prize. Zane was naked on her bed lying on his back. His penis was hard. She handed him the Vaseline. He took off the shirt again and smeared some of the lube on her breasts and the space between her breasts. She was confused. Why was he doing that? She was all sticky.

"Push your breasts together," he instructed straddling her.

She was still wearing her miniskirt, shoes and socks. She felt overdressed and awkward, but she did what he said. He then pushed his dick between her breasts. She put her head back on the pillow straining to maintain the position. At this point, it was just a job for her. All she could see was his belly button as he pushed himself against her.

She looked at the cottage cheese ceiling. She kept her end up, pushing her breasts together as the sound of flap, flap, squish, squish resounded in her ears. He went harder and faster. She kept her chin up and off to the side, dismayed. She suffered through it until his cum hit her on the cheek. He shuddered keeping his dick in her face.

"Lick it," he commanded, so she did. Satisfied he rolled off of her. She was covered with goo. They stayed next to each other on the bed for a few minutes. She didn't know what to do next. He was still breathing hard. Eventually she got up to find something to wipe herself off with. She was tempted to grab his shirt but used one of her own that was on the floor in the closet. She wiped down her chest as Zane got up and got dressed. Kia didn't understand what was happening.

"Are you leaving?" she whispered.

"Yeah, I gotta roll," he said, tying his shoes. "You don't want

70

your parents to find me, right?"

She didn't. But it seemed so sudden, and she felt used.

"Uh, no. OK," she said lamely, standing there with a spunk-drenched shirt in her hand and her breasts hanging out while he was fully dressed. She snagged a cleaner shirt off the floor and put it on, dropping the gross one. Zane, fully dressed and ready to go, grabbed the doorknob to her room and gently pulled the door open. He looked out to the hallway to make sure it was clear before stepping out. That was it? Kia thought to herself, disappointed and vulnerable. She followed him out to the living room. He opened the front door with his skate in one hand. She stood there with her arms across her chest. He seemed anxious to split.

"So, see ya later," he said backing away. He turned and scurried down the hall to the stairs disappearing like he was never there.

"Oookay," she stammered to his shadow and shut the door.

CHAPTER 8

Monday

The next morning Kia woke up to sounds in the apartment. She could hear her mom talking loudly.

"What the hell, Alan?" her mom yelled, "I need to know where you are. You think going to the Sea Rounders is helping me?"

Then silence. Her dad had been gone more and more, lately. Sea Rounders? What is that? A bar? Must be, Kia thought.

"I need you home! What about Kia? Or what about finding a real job? Selling this junk isn't helping us! I work my ass off every night and Lord knows what is going on with Kia. Shit baby, this isn't working."

Kia could hear the resignation in her mom's voice. Usually she just yells, this was the first time she sounded defeated.

Kia laid in her bed staring at the cottage cheese ceiling again remembering last night with Zane. What was he doing now? Where was he? Was he at home sleeping or lying in bed thinking about her? She didn't want to go out to the living room. The pot gone, the hickey that is undoubtedly on her neck. Apparently her dad wasn't home so they don't know Zane was there. She turned over and faced the wall staring at the blankness of it. Vienna, Ami and Brooke in Vegas. What were they doing now? Probably having fun. Her life was hell.

After a while she had to get out of there. She opened her bedroom door and checked to make sure she was not seen as she rushed to the bathroom. She quickly shut the door behind her. She looked in the mirror and just as she suspected there was a huge red hickey on her neck. Fuck. She pulled open a drawer to go through her makeup. She found cover up and started applying it over the bruise. She had to spread it to her face to make it look realistic, but it was chalky and looked unnatural. She hoped her her parents wouldn't notice. She put on blush, mascara and eyeliner. When she was done, she realized she looked laughable.

Kia started the shower before trying to figure out her next move. With her head shampooed, she reached for the soap and washed off the residue of the Vaseline. Yuck. She grabbed a washcloth and scrubbed her chest. She felt gross. Then she sat down, letting the shower rain down on her. She had the urge to cry. She felt so unimportant. Her friends had left her, Zane just used her for a titty fuck, and her parents were fighting. She cried. Out of the sobs she realized that her parents' fighting was the worst part. Fuck her friends. Maybe things with Zane would still work out, but her parents—she needed them to be alright.

As much as it sucked that they give her a lot of shit they were real and they loved her. She cried harder. After a while the water turned cold. Kia tried to regain her composure. She'd cried so hard she'd given herself hiccups. She shut off the water, got out and grabbed a towel to dry off. She looked in the mirror. Her eyes were red and she couldn't stop hiccupping, which was just annoying. The hickey on her neck stood out. There was nothing she could do about it. She had heard putting a cold spoon on it helped to make it go away. She would have to go to the kitchen get a spoon and stick it in the freezer, but that was out since her parents were around. She resigned herself to her fate. Wrapped in a the towel, she retreated to her room.

"Kia?" her mom called out as she shut her bedroom door.

She dropped the towel on the floor and got dressed. Just as she pulled her shirt over her head her mom barged in.

"Kia?" her mom said gaping at her.

"What?' she replied quietly.

"What the hell is that?" her mom pointed at her neck, eyes wide.

Kia's hand flew to her neck to cover the hickey then she let it fall to her side. She just stood there hiccupping.

"Kia! What the hell did you let someone do to you?" Her mom grabbed her by the chin cocking her head to the side, eyes bulging. "You look like a tramp."

That burned, Kia already felt like a piece of shit. She didn't

74

need her mom to heap on more degradation. She slumped down onto the edge of her bed hanging her head hiccupping. Tears welled up and fell down her cheeks.

"Well! Needless to say, you're grounded. I will not have my daughter going out into the world with . . . that . . . hideous mark on her neck. Do you know how that makes you look? Your dad is an unemployed drunk and you're . . . you're . . .." she sputtered off. Her mom turned and left her room slamming the door behind her. Kia just sat there hiccupping and silently crying. She heard the front door slam.

After an hour of crying herself to sleep, Kia woke up . She opened her eyes and didn't hear any sound in the house. She felt drugged by her sadness. Her mom thought she was a slut and apparently her dad was a drunk. That last thought confused her. She's never seen her dad drunk. Stoned, yes, drunk, no. She decided to get up and see if her dad was home. She opened her bedroom door and approached the living room. No one was there. She went back into the hallway where her parents' door was open. Empty. She walked back into the living room. She felt deserted. She slumped down onto the couch and just stared out the front window. She could only see the roof of the building across the way. Even though they lived at the beach you wouldn't know it from the inside of the apartment. Ghetto.

So now what? Would her parents divorce? What would become of her? She was scared shitless. Was she going to have to live on her own somewhere? Kia felt utterly unloved. Did Zane care about her? Not likely, not impossible. Yeah, maybe he did. Would he let her move in with him when he realized his girl had nowhere to go? He must like her; he gave her this big hickey. Maybe he's shy, which is why he didn't go all the way with her. Yeah. Hey, Vienna just got pregnant. That's a big deal, she thought.

Kia stared out the window trying to figure it all out. Bored and confused, she turned on MTV. She sat there for hours, afraid to leave the house in case her mom returned. She made some Top Ramen and watched MTV until it got dark. Around 7:30 there was a knock on the door. She jumped up and opened it to find Ami standing there.

"Hey, what's up?" Ami said pushing her way past Kia. "We had sooooo much fun!" she exclaimed plopping on the couch.

Kia just stared at her from the doorway, mouth open. She gathered herself together, shut the door and sat in the chair next to the couch.

"Fuck Kia, you missed it! Ha! Ha! Ha! So, we got to Vegas and got a room at Circus Circus. Then we roamed around and tripped out on all the freaks! We all got drunk and ran around in the casinos. Then, like at some point I was all, hey, let's go find a chapel! And we started asking where a chapel was and Vienna was so hammered she ended up taking off somewhere. We had to go find her and she was with these older dudes at another casino. Dave got pissed and started a fight with those dudes and the cops came. Brooke and I grabbed Vienna and found our way back to Circus Circus. At, like, 2 a.m. Dave came back and said he ran from the cops. Well, Vienna was passed out and Brooke and I were fucked up after drinking everything in the mini-

76

fridge. So me and Brooke left Dave with Vienna and fucking partied in Vegas. Fuck, it was so much fun!" Ami sat back on the couch laughing to herself.

Kia wasn't in on the joke, so she just stared at Ami in disbelief that they completely forgot they ditched her.

"Oh," was all Kia could manage.

Ami finally realized Kia was just sitting there.

"So what the fuck Kia? Where were you?" Ami smirked at her.

"Where was I?" Kia's voice emerged, "Where was I?!" She felt a rush of blood to her chest, then she realized she'd better fucking calm down. She didn't have anyone. "Uh, I guess you guys left before I got there."

"Oh well," Ami mused, "too bad. So, they didn't get married. They got into a huge fight and broke up. The drive home was fucking crazy. Vienna said she's going to get an abortion. So me, you and Brooke need to figure that out, now. Can your mom do it? She's a nurse. Does she do that?"

Kia finally realized why Ami was at her house, to get something from her. It all hit her in a big wave. She closed her eyes to contain herself. Her parents, her friends, Zane, all of them. She has nothing left to give. She was empty.

"No, my mom doesn't do that," Kia said quietly.

"Oh well, we'll figure something out," Ami replied.

Kia couldn't give less of a shit now about Vienna's situation. She didn't give a shit about anybody else right now. Why was everyone else so much more important than her? She sat there depleted.

"Your parents got any stash? Let's get high and go over to Mickey's."

Kia just stared at her.

"Um, no, Zane sold it," Kia replied.

"What? Zane? What do you mean?" Ami asked.

Kia finally felt she could come back from this situation on a high note. Didn't she hook up with Zane and shoot Melissa down while they were gone? She had a story of her own.

"Yeah, me and Zane are together now," she said a bit smug.

Perplexed, Ami repeated, "What?" She sat forward on the couch. Kia had her attention.

"While you guys were gone, Zane and I hooked up—and I stood up to Melissa,"

Kia smiled to herself. She's not as pathetic as they thought. "Yeah, look," she pointed to her neck. Ami's eyes got wide.

"Weird," Ami replied," I just saw Zane and he was with that one girl, you know, that little 14- year-old girl, Jessica? Yeah, they were at the beach together and he was massaging her back."

Kia felt like she was going to throw up.

Ami looked a little pleased with herself. Good gossip is good gossip.

"So, what happened with Melissa?" she asked attempting to change the subject.

Kia was done. She was just done. "Uh, I stood up to her. Like you said," she trailed off.

Her heart was broken into a million pieces. The triumph over Melissa didn't even register.

"OK, well, that's good." Ami started to look uncomfortable."So you wanna go to Mickey's house?" Ami asked, but Kia barely heard her.

"Kia? You wanna go to Mickey's house?" she asked again as if Kia was dense.

"Uh, I can't," Kia said, "I'm grounded."

"Ha! Ha! Your parents are so strict!" Ami laughed, "Well, catch you later." She got up and just left.

Kia sat in the chair, completely defeated. What an asshole Zane was. She looked like a fool, again. Still not one of them. No matter what, she will never fit in. Ever. She really, really wished she had some pot. Afraid to leave the house and afraid to stay. Nothing seemed safe.

CHAPTER 9

Monday-a week later

She was grounded for a week so she stayed home. Her mom came back the next morning after work. Kia stayed in her room for most of the two days her parents were away, which allowed time for her hickey to fade.. Her dad would be home during the day tinkering with his "stuff," but before her mom came home he'd disappear. She spent almost every night alone. No one talked. The separation of her family was close to devastating. She wondered if she should address her mom by her first name since she no longer felt like her daughter, but rather a stranger. She kept her head down and stayed out of the way, mostly in her room watching TV. When the week was up, her mom unceremoniously let her know she was no longer grounded, but she better not get into any more trouble and going forward would have to call her at the hospital to ask permission to go anywhere. Even though Kia's dad was still in the home, he was disregarded as a parent.

The first morning she was free, Kia grabbed her skate and rolled from one end of the beach to the other. She had not heard from any of her friends for the whole week after Ami left her house. She had her hood up and just skated. She felt like a foreigner on her own turf. She had no friends, she had no family. Panting from hard skating, she decided to check out the lifeguard tower. She saw the crew by the jetty partying, playing, and screwing around. She didn't even feel like trying to show herself. She walked along the jetty and went out to the breakwater setting her skate down and staring at the ocean. Behind her to her left she looked back and saw the group laughing and sunning themselves. She felt bitter. She spotted Zane walking into the group alone and her heart jumped. She spied on him. With the hood over her head she felt invisible. She turned away. The wind roughly shoved the ocean back from the shore. She just stared. Somehow her mom never got on her about the pot. She must have thought her dad had smoked it. So be it. She watched the seagulls follow the fishing boats. There were big cattle boats and smaller charter boats coming in. She watched the people swerving and laughing, and the deck hands furiously cutting fish. She decided to skate down to the docks and watch.

When she got there she grabbed a bench and pushed her skate back and forth with her feet.

She spotted Christian. He was laughing with some of the day-trippers. He was covered in fish guts, laughing. That wide, beautiful smile hit her even in her dark mood. She took her hood off, and smiled to herself at seeing him caught in the moment.

She sat there for an hour, smelling the ocean, watching the seagulls swarming, and though it was neat to see all the happy people getting off the boats. She watched Christian.

As the dock cleared, happy fishers left with their cleaned catches and the Mexicans and the Asians left with everything else; fish heads and all. She shivered, yuck.

She watched Christian go below deck and grab his stuff, hoodie and whatever else, and climb the dock. He slapped hands with members of other crews and chatted, she supposed, about the day. Finally he had his skateboard in one hand, a big bag of fish in the other and his hoodie over his shoulder. When he got to the top of the deck, he turned in her direction. She looked toward the harbor, pretending she didn't see him. He walked over to her.

"Hey Kia, what are you doing here?" he said.

She stopped her skateboard between her feet. She wasn't going anywhere.

"Oh, hey," she replied amazed that he actually knew her name, "I'm just checking out today's catch."

"It was a good day," he smiled.

"What ya got?" she inquired looking at his full plastic bag of filets.

"Some Lingcod and Rockfish," he replied holding up the bag.

"I didn't even know you worked on the boats." she said.

"Yeah, for years . . ." he let that hang in the air.

Christian stood there looking at her. She put her hood back on and he grabbed the seat next to her. He smelled of fish. They sat there for a few minutes not saying anything.

Eventually, he turned to her. "So, I'm heading to Mickey's. Gonna barbecue the fish. You going?"

She looked down at her skateboard, swishing it again between her feet, wanting to escape. "No, I don't think so."

"Oh. Why?"

"I'm grounded," though it wasn't true, she didn't belong and she knew it.

"Oh," he said looking at his bag of fish.

"From going to Mickey's?" he asked.

"I'm not really grounded," she confessed under her breath, "I'm just not going."

"Oh," he said.

They sat there staring at the ocean. Why was he still here? Shouldn't he excuse himself and leave?

"Well," Christian finally said, "how about you come to my house and I'll make ceviche. I make the best."

Kia felt a blush race across her cheeks. Why would he want to hang out with her? Then she realized Zane probably told him she was easy.

"Uh, umm . . .," she stalled, feeling like an idiot. "I don't know."

Christian smiled that awesome smile at her, "Come on, I really do make the best ceviche."

She was torn. A part of her, of course, really wanted to go. It was Christian! But another part of her was afraid he was trying to pull something on her.

"Why do you want me to go?" she asked dumbly.

He laughed "I just told you! I make the best ceviche!"

Her face screwed up in a look of mistrust, "Don't you want to hang out with your friends?"

He sat back on the bench, "Is it always this hard to hang out with you?"

"What about Kristen?" Kia challenged, "Isn't she expecting you over at Mickey's?"

"Kristen? Why do you think that?"

"Cuz, you're always with her . . . and stuff."

"Me and Kristen are just friends."

Kia contemplated this. If that's not true then she'd be putting herself in a very bad situation. "You sure? I don't want Melissa to have a reason to go after me again."

84

"I saw how you handled yourself with Melissa," he smiled, "don't worry about it."

Kia still wasn't sure. Christian stood up and faced her.

"Come on," said the boy no girl ever would say no to.

Kia got up despite her ambivalence. They walked out to the parking lot and jumped on their skateboards bound for Christian's house.

CHAPTER 10

Christian lived by himself in a one bedroom across the street from the ocean. He let them in and headed to the kitchen to put down the fish. "Hey, I gotta shower real quick, I'm sure I stink like fish. You want a beer or something?"

Kia shrugged. He grabbed a Mickey's Big Mouth from the fridge and handed it to her. She took it and sat on the couch while he went to shower. "What the hell am I doing here? What does he want from me?" she thought. She looked around his living room. He had a bunch of Surfer and Surfing magazines on his coffee table. He had one longboard and two short boards leaning against one living room wall. There were surfing posters everywhere with the exception of one that showed Kathy Ireland in a bikini.

She gulped her beer and flipped through one of his magazines. His home smelled of fish and Sex Wax. She felt comfortable there, but knew she shouldn't. Her heart started beating fast all of a sudden. She's in Christian's house, alone, with him in the shower. Should she just get it over with? Go to the shower and give herself to him? Isn't that what he expects? Why else did he invite her over?

She heard the shower turn off. She froze. So much for that idea. She crossed her legs and took another swig of beer. She heard him leave the bathroom and go into his bedroom and shut the door. She returned her attention to the magazine.

He emerged from the hallway in board shorts hanging deliciously low on his hips. My God! He was ridiculously hot.

"How's your beer? Need another?" he inquired pausing before entering the kitchen.

"Umm no, I'm good," she replied showing him her only half-empty bottle.

"OK, so come in here and keep me company, you're so far away in there."

She got up and found a counter to lean against. He grabbed the bag of fish, ripping it open, rinsing the filets under the faucet.

Seriously, she wondered, what was she doing there watching this God-like man making food to share with her? She went to the living room and took off her hoodie, plopping it onto the couch.

"Your bathroom?" She pointed to the hallway.

"Yup," he said concentrating on the fish, "Oh! Forgive the mess," he smiled.

She went into the bathroom closing the door behind her. It was all steamy from his shower. She went to look in the mirror to check herself and saw that Christian had written "Hi Kia"on it with his finger.

She stood back, incredulous, but pleased. She peed, washed her hands and tried to check her reflection in the steamy mirror not wanting to clean away his message to her. How did he know she'd see it?

She traveled back to the kitchen, picked up her beer and didn't say a word.

He was cutting fish, squeezing lemons, and smiling.

"So," he said facing her, "Where ya been? Haven't seen you in a while." He turned back to his ceviche.

"I, uh, have been at home. Got in trouble. My mom is kinda strict," she said, immediately embarrassed. Would he laugh at her about it like her friends do?

"Oh, really?" he stopped preparing the fish, knife frozen in the air, "Well that's a bummer. What did you do?" he turned looking her in the eye standing perfectly still.

"I, uh . . ." Didn't he know? Didn't Zane tell him? Isn't that why she was really here?

"You don't know?" she asked.

"No. That's why I asked," he laughed, returning to his task.

Kia didn't know how long she should have to play this game. She actually started to get a little mad. She's tired of being made the fool.

"Look, Christian," she started, "I don't know what you expect from me, or what Zane told you, but if you invited me here because you heard I'm easy or whatever, it's not true," she gulped. "Uh, you're hot." She blushed. "But I'm not going to do this. I just don't think . . ." Kia couldn't help it. Dammit, the tears were coming. He stopped what he was doing. Kia turned to leave the kitchen. She wanted to leave, She rushed to the living room to grab her hoodie and get out. He scrambled after her and grabbed her arm.

"Hey! Wait!" He turned her toward him.

Her head was down and all she wanted to do was grab her skateboard. Fuck this! Fuck everyone!

"Hey..." He touched her chin and lifted her face to his. "I don't know why you're upset or anything about Zane. Of course you can leave if you want. I just, uh, I've always kinda wanted a chance to spend some time with you. I've always thought you were a cool chick." He let go of her face and stood back. "Hey, friends, OK?"

She felt stupid instantly. Whoa. Cool chick? Like Kristen? Friends? She can be friends with him like Kristen? OK, get it together Kia, she told herself, gathering her inner strength and smiling at Christian. "Sorry, it's been a hard week."

"It's cool, little lady," he smiled. "Come on, let's hang."

Kia's headspace did a 180° and she returned to the kitchen.

"How about another beer, dude?" she chirped chugging the rest of her bottle.

"Sure thing, doll," he said getting her another.

They ended up having a really nice day. He really did make the best ceviche! After they ate they grabbed more beer and sat in the two chairs on his front porch across the street from the ocean. She was having a good time laughing (he was really funny) and listening to the waves crash on the shore.

"So, Christian," she inquired, feeling relaxed, "Tell me about your little self."

"Oh, so now I'm little?' he laughed.

"Got to keep you in your place," she giggled.

"Oh, OK," he smirked. "Well, born and raised here. Nardcore!" He looked at her and grinned stupidly. "Umm, two sisters and three brothers. Love 'em to death, by the way, and love fishing. You?"

"Me?" Huh, she thought, what's my story?

"Born in Santa Cruz, lived there till I was 12, then my dad was transferred to Oxnard. He was in the hospitality business. General manager. We used to vacation in some pretty awesome places. My mom is an ER nurse. Crazy. Then my dad lost his job," she got quiet, "and my mom has been supporting the family the last couple of years. I, uh, had a little sister, Bennie, but she died when she was three. She died before we moved here" Kia again became choked up. Why was she telling him this? She hadn't told anyone. "I'm sorry, I, uh, she . . . fuck, why am I telling you this? Anyway, so we've moved here and, well, here I am." She thought she could joke about it and realized it was time to shut up. It was getting dark, she should call her mom.

"Can I use your phone? I'm still on probation," she joked.

"Uh, yeah, go ahead." He gestured to the living room.

"Thanks," she said, and went inside. OK, call your mom, she concentrated. She dialed the hospital and told her mom she was at Ami's and would be home in an hour. Her mom was busy so it was a one-way conversation. Good. Kia went to the bathroom again. The message on the mirror was barely visible, but still there. Get it together, girl, she thought, being too hard on herself as usual. She went to the kitchen and got two more beers for them. Friends. She could do this. Be cool. She took her seat and handed Christian a fresh beer. They sat quietly for a bit. Kia loved being there listening to the waves crash over and over.

"Well," Christian started, "sorry about your sister. Hey, Kia, I wanna tell you something."

She opened her beer slowly and stared down at it.

"I, uh, don't know you very well, but, I've noticed you. I think you undercut yourself with, I don't know, your friends and stuff, and, well, I think you're very pretty."

Her face turned bright red. Me? What? Huh? Me?

"Me?" she blurted.

"Yes, you," he said.

Wait! Wait a damn minute.

"OK," she said after drinking more beer, "shut your face." She
sat back in her chair squeezing out a sarcastic laugh. "You! You
and Kristen! You're fucking with me again!" Kia wanted to leave.

"Okay Kia, I already told you, if you don't believe me . . ." he
sat back in his chair frowning.

She felt sorry. Is he for real? Okay, throw out some more shit
at him she thought.

"So! Christian, you didn't hear about that asshole Zane?"

"No, Kia, what happened with Zane?" He was resigned.

What would she say? Fuck this. They're all the same.

"He took advantage of me. Not, you know, all the way, but . .
." Why was she telling him this? Shouldn't she just go?

"Kia, Kia, Look at me," he pleaded, facing her.

"What?" she said defensively.

"Look, I don't know what is going on with you, but it's fucking
heavy. I just wanted to hang out with you," he said. He leaned
across his chair toward her and moved the hair in her face behind

her ear. She slowly met his eyes, his face was showing genuine concern. His sky blue eyes looked into hers just as a breeze off the ocean blew her hair back over her face like a curtain.

"I'm sorry Christian, I don't know what is happening anymore. My parents, my friends . . . and now you want to hang out with me after I've been feeling . . . used, by Zane, I'm so confused."

Christian sat quiet, then said, "Zane is an asshole. If he had a shot with you and blew it, well, he's an asshole."

She looked over at him, her heart couldn't help but melt. "Thanks Christian, that means a lot to me. Cheers."

They clinked glasses and turned toward the ocean. Really? Wow, she thought. What? Her mind and heart were exploding. If he was for real, what then?

He was staring across the street. She reached over and grabbed his hand. He smiled and squeezed her hand back. They sat there holding hands quietly sipping their beers. When it got completely dark she figured she should go home. She didn't want to, but thought it would be for the best. She was still worried about what was going on at home and finally having such an amazing day after so long was empowering.

"Hey, I should get going,' she said and stood up.

"Oh, alright," he said getting up, too. He walked her inside, took her empty beer bottle and tossed it into his full trash can. Bachelor, for sure. Ha! Ha! She put on her hoodie and he walked her to the front door where she grabbed her skate.

"Hey, hug?" He stood there arms out.

She went to him and he embraced her. Wow, it felt incredible. Her fingers touched his bare back and his smooth skin. Yum. She pulled away to leave and he snuck in a kiss. It was electric. He smelled so wonderful and kissed amazing. It was a beautiful moment. Her knees actually got a little weak.

"Oh, wow," she muttered after he pulled away, "you kiss all your friends like that?"

"No, just the ones I want to be more than my friend," he said, looking into her eyes.

Kia was floored.

"I want to take you on a real date. You OK with that?" he asked sheepishly. He even blushed! This Adonis, the most gorgeous man she'd ever laid eyes on, blushed asking her out!

"Um, sure, yeah," she shrugged, downplaying her excitement without somehow fainting at his feet.

"Give me your number. I'll call you tomorrow."

She did, then she skated home, though her wheels never actually touched pavement.

CHAPTER 11

Christian called her that night. He said he'd just stayed home and practiced playing his acoustic guitar, instead of going to Mickey's. As they were talking though, Kristen, Melissa and Ramsey stopped by so he had to hang up. Kia wondered still if he was sincere. Why didn't he want to be with Kristen? Why was he interested in her? She stood in front of the full-length mirror behind her door, checking herself out. Maybe she wasn't so bad. Maybe she should stop comparing herself to other girls and just like who she was. She had a good heart, she cared about others. Maybe she didn't have the "perfect" body or the best clothes, but if the hottest guy she'd ever seen thought she was a cool chick and pretty, maybe she should take another look at herself.

Tuesday

Kia got up the next morning feeling happy with herself. She cleaned her room without being told. She went to the living room where her parents were having coffee at the kitchen table, poured a cup and joined them. They seemed to be doing alright. Her dad was in good spirits, and he'd been home when she returned from Christian's yesterday. She could hear the TV on in her parent's room.

"So ladies," he said, "I have an interview tomorrow."

"What? Where?" her mom asked as her head snapped up from the newspaper she was reading.

"Well, not in the hospitality industry, but I know a guy who works for the county in the sanitation department."

"The sanitation department?" Kia and her mom said in unison.

"Yeah, I know. It's not being a trash man, it's a managerial position. It's a good opportunity. I'll be in charge." Her dad smiled.

"Well, that's great, honey," her mom replied, as her face softened for the first time in ages. "That's really great."

"Yeah, good luck Dad!" Kia smiled.

Things are really getting better, she thought. If her dad got the job then her mom might not be so pissed all the time.

"Where do you know this guy from?" her mom asked taking a sip of coffee.

"I, uh, met him at the Sea Rounders. His name is Jim. He gave my name to his boss and they scheduled an interview."

The mention of the fact that he met this guy at the bar made her mom visibly tense.

"Oh," was all she said. Then she got up and put her cup in the sink. "Well, I'm going to lie down for a bit. I'm still really tired. We had quite a night in the ER. There was a big accident caused by a drunk driver and we ended up losing a little boy whose family he plowed into." On that note, her mom went to the bedroom and shut the door. Kia and her dad sat in silence, both understanding what that dig was about. Her dad looked at the table, his happiness gone. He picked up the newspaper and started to read, or pretend to read.

Kia stared at him with a sad expression, then got up and put her cup in the sink. The joyful moment had disappeared and heaviness had returned to their home, once again.

"Well, good luck Dad. I hope you get it," she told him, reaching to give him a half hug before heading to her room.

"Thanks, baby," he said as she walked away.

Kia tore apart her closet and dresser looking for something cute to wear. She hoped, of course, to see Christian that evening, but then she froze. It seemed as though every time she was hopeful and happy, something bad happened. She decided to dismiss her mission and lie on the bed instead. She stared at the cottage cheese ceiling reliving all the terrible things that had transpired. She thought about Bennie. Bringing her up to Christian was surprising even to her. She had not dared to think about Bennie for years. God, her baby sister was beautiful. She longed for her now and it broke her heart. She turned toward the wall and replayed what happened. She clamped her eyes shut remembering the accident.

Her dad was driving their family back home down Highway 1 from Big Sur where they just had an awesome weekend at a cabin on the river. One of the perks of her dad being in the hospitality industry was that he got discounts everywhere. He was a general manager at a hotel on the beach in Santa Cruz. They were driving the twisty, narrow highway where the cliff descended hundreds of feet to the ocean, which she could see to her right. She recalls being scared to look out the window. It was so far down. Her mom turned around to tend to Bennie who was getting restless and whiny in her car seat. Mom was trying to give her a graham cracker or something. Then the car suddenly swerved to the left out of its lane. It was sudden, but slow at the same time. Kia's heart froze in her chest. Her mom was still facing backward and she slammed against the window. The car skidded a little bit, and then corrected itself, and the impact from the other vehicle hit the left passenger seat where Bennie was strapped in. Kia woke up at the hospital sore, bruised and with a broken left arm, clearly traumatized. Her mom, who was bruised and had a neck brace on, rushed to her side. She looked very scary, not at all like her mom. Her mom held her and they both cried. Kia didn't realize at the time that her mom was crying because her sister was dead. Kia wanted her daddy and her mom told her he was in surgery. Her dad made it through, and after a couple of days for Kia in the hospital, and two weeks for her dad, they were all home again—without Bennie. Kia remembers crying and crying and wanting her little sister.

Her parents decided to move and her dad found a way to

98

transfer to a hotel in Oxnard. Her mom found a position at the county hospital, and they left their life and friends in Santa Cruz. Kia never went back to school or said goodbye to her friends. They moved into a nice house in Oxnard Shores and her parents never really talked to her about it. After a couple of years her dad lost his job which brought them to the apartment in Silver Strand where they lived now, solely on her mom's income.

Kia opened her eyes once again staring at the wall. What would they be like now if it had never happened? She would still be in Santa Cruz with the friends she grew up with, Bennie and her mom and dad. She would be happy. It had been really hard since they moved. She had to make new friends but the new friendships weren't the same. She had gone to a private school up there with all the same kids since kindergarten. Her school was small and everybody seemed to know each other and there was no fighting.

When she moved to Oxnard she had to go to public school in a very "hard" area known as Colonia. They bused the kids from the beach to integrate with the poorer, Latino kids. Blonde, blue-eyed girls were definitely in the minority. She didn't make many friends. Most of the kids grew up together and stuck together. She eventually found two girls that she played with, but she was shy so she spent a lot of time alone. She didn't meet Ami, Brooke and Vienna until junior high, and she was so grateful they accepted her into their group. She just tried to fit in to get back what she'd had with her friends in Santa Cruz, but there's always been something missing. She was always the "new girl" given that the three had known each other since first or second grade.

Kia began to realize why she had struggled so much. The need to fit in was a coping mechanism, a way to forget what had been taken from her. Her family had never been the same and she desperately wanted to feel like she belonged—somewhere, to someone. It had been a long time, but now, it was coming full circle for whatever reason. She guessed life was just that way..

Feeling the burn of loss, she decided to get up and go out after all. She got more dolled up than ever, shooting for stunning, but she'd settle for different. Bye Mom! Bye Dad! She was out! She stayed put to try to hold onto some kind of semblance of how they were as a family, but that was a long time ago. She knows she's on her own, now.

She changed into "Zane Gear," short skirt, tight top and flip flops and walked out the front door. Fuck' em. Seriously, fuck' em. She felt like "one of them" now, the kids whose parents don't give a shit.

She walked to the Corner Market to see what was happening. Wouldn't you know, Zane and Henry were sitting on their skates on the curb right in front.

"Hey, what's up?" she said on approach.

"Hey, Kiiiia," Zane drawled out.

She felt feisty, and impenetrable.

"Want some 'shrooms?" Zane laughed.

"Yeah, I do," she retorted.

He handed her the baggie. She swallowed two caps and handed the baggie back, though she considered pocketing it. Then she fixated on getting the baggie back from him to make up for taking her parent's weed. She stewed on it and the 'shrooms hit her. She grabbed pavement next to them, yawning. They laughed.

"Hey asshole," She turned to Zane. He slowly turned to her.

"You're a dick," she slurred.

"Oh, really?" he laughed.

"Yeah," she said, then her body got hot and she stared across the street toward Pepe's Mexican Food stand.

"OK," he laughed again.

"No, really," she slammed his shoulder.

"Chill out, Kia," he said quietly.

"No! Really! What the hell, Zane? Hickey?" she slurred still staring across the street, knowing she's talking but not really caring what she's saying. Her mouth felt gummy and dry.

"Whatever," he replied.

Suddenly she knew she didn't belong. "You don't care!" she said getting up, straightening her skirt.

"No bitch, I don't," he smirked.

"Fine!"she teetered, and walked off down Ocean Avenue.

Screw them! She thought, especially him!

She half expected he would come get her, but he didn't. She was halfway down Ocean Ave before she realized it. Where was she heading? Christian! Yeah. She floundered along the first part then felt the 'shrooms hitting her again and slowed down. She really didn't care if she got to Christian's. Maybe check out the sky and the waves, instead. She cut right toward the sand and crawled until she found a spot she liked.

Ahhh, beautiful, she thought. She settled into the sand and stretched her toes. She laid on her back looking at the clouds and feeling everything.

Bennie. Bennie. Bennie. Beautiful Bennie. Her little face and her laughter. Stop it! Painful. Stop it! Christian's laughing face. Better. Where is he? With Kristen? Stop! Oh, fuck it. Let God come in and wash over her. All her pain. Trying to not think of anyone, she let the tide grab her mind.

At some point (she'd lost all sense of time), she heard Zane walking up the beach.

"Kia! Kia!" he shouted.

She responded feebly, "Here." Damn, why did she do that?

Zane and Henry spotted her and flopped down next to her. Zane got creepy with her right away. "Kia," he said putting a hand on her breast.

"Eh," she responded, too high to move it. "Stop," she whispered.

102

He kept his hand on her right boob as they all looked at the clouds.

"You're an asshole,' she repeated.

He ignored her.

They sat quietly in the stillness of the night for a while, though she was uncomfortable and unable to move his hand.

Henry got up to run to the ocean, but instead planted himself on her other side and put his hand on her left breast.

No! "Fuck you guys," she tried to get up but couldn't.

"Yeah," Zane said, "fuck us."

"No!"

She tried harder to get up. Henry tackled her. She struggled and fought, then laughed. It was stupid and she was high. There was no fight left in her. All hands remained on her chest.

They must have all fallen asleep because she woke up cold and in the dark. Zane and Henry were passed out. She removed their hands from her body stood up, shook off the sand and trudged home.

Opening the door to her apartment, she found her mom sitting on the couch and she didn't look too happy. Kia wanted to pretend the wrath wasn't about to be unleashed. She just couldn't take it anymore. Still a little trippy from the 'shrooms, she sat in the armchair and looked at her lap.

Her mom was quiet too. Kia was so tired of all this gloom. "Mom?"

"Yes?" she replied quietly.

"I'm really unhappy," Kia confessed.

Her mom looked over at her with a blank stare. "Me too."

"I can't take this anymore," Kia gestured around her, "it sucks."

Her mom patted the seat next to her on the couch. Kia got up and sat next to her.

"I don't feel safe," Kia mummered.

"What do you mean?" her mom grabbed her hand. Kia felt surprised and a bit relieved. She thought her mom was going to blow up on her.

"You and dad, my friends, everyone is fighting and I feel so alone."

Her mom sighed. "Yes, your dad and I are having difficulties. But you know, no matter what we both love you and we are worried about you."

"I'm worried about both of you, too," Kia said staring ahead out the window, her eyes welling up without her permission.

They sat in silence for a few minutes.

Kia leaned her head back. "I don't feel like I really have any

104

real friends here and I'm thinking a lot about Bennie and I miss our life in Santa Cruz."

She looked at her mom and tears were sliding down her face and her eyes were closed. Then she started to really cry. Kia didn't know what to do because her mom was always so strong and hard. So she just sat there willing herself to hold back her own tears. Her mom really let loose, so Kia got up and grabbed some Kleenex to give her because she didn't know what else to do. Her mom accepted the tissue and attempted to reel in her emotions.

Kia hugged her and they sat there in silence holding each other. As they pulled apart, her mom wiped the tears from her face and said, "We should have gotten counseling after losing Bennie. Your dad and I did not know how to deal with it. We still don't. I'm sorry.. I miss her too, every day."

"What about you and dad?" Kia asked anxiously, fearful her mom might say something that could change her life for the worse, yet again. "Are you getting divorced?"

"No, we're not there yet. Maybe it's time to get help, for your dad and I, and then the three of us as a family."

"Yes," Kia said looking her mom in the eyes.

Her mom smiled and hugged her again, then shook her head like she was clearing an Etch- A-Sketch.

"So, what is going on with your friends?" she asked.

Kia told her mostly about feeling left out of Ami, Brooke and

Vienna's inner circle. She omitted Vienna's pregnancy, Vegas and anything else that might implicate her. She glossed over what happened with Zane, leaving the story off at the hickey, and not mentioning him being in her room. Then she told her about Christian and hanging out with him and telling him about Bennie, which got her thinking about it again. Talking about Christian was the only thing she revealed without filters.

"Oh, Christian called for you a while ago. He left his number. It's by the phone. He sounds a little old for you. You said he's 19 or 20?"

"He's 20. I'll be 16 in a week," Kia said trying to keep the whiney tone out of her voice.

"Well, maybe you should just be friends," her mom said with a touch of that familiar concern in her voice.

"We basically are," Kia replied, "except for the kiss. But I'm not rushing into anything. To be honest, I don't understand why he wants to hang out with me."

"Just be careful Kia, you are beautiful, smart and a caring girl. Probably for those reasons you don't feel like you quite fit in. Your friends always seemed a little too grown up to me," her mom cautioned.

"I will mom, and thanks." Kia hugged her again " And another thing, maybe I should go back to being Lisa. I think changing my name was a way of trying to start over, but Lisa was Bennie's sister, not Kia."

Her mom seemed like she was going to cry again, "That sounds good. You are a wise girl. I love you." She kissed her on the forehead.

"I'm going to call Christian." Kia put her chin down and looked up at her mom the way she did when she was little. "You OK, Mom?" she asked.

"I'm OK, funnyface," she replied using Kia's childhood nickname.

Kia grabbed the phone and Christian's number into her room, shutting the door.

She was finally ready to be "herself." The first step would be to tell Christian her real name.

She dialed his number and he answered immediately.

"Christian, it's Kia. Well, really it's Lisa. Do you have time for a story? I have a lot to tell you." She blurted out.

"I have all the time in the world to hear a story, beautiful. Just make sure it has a happy ending." he replied.

She finally felt that it would.

CASA TROPICAL - CITY OF OXNARD

"Nardcore is a hardcore punk movement that began in Southern California in the early 1980s, in Silver Strand Beach and Port Hueneme. One of the first venues to regularly host punk shows in the Oxnard area was Casa Tropical." — Wikipedia

Author's note: This was one of the first places I can recall attending a punk show. Rich Kids on LSD was the headliner. To be honest, I wasn't drawn there for the music. I was there to see a boy with a shaved head who rocked the hell out of suspenders and Dr. Martens. I was 14. As usual, my hormones paved the way.

CHAPTER 12

Anthony Zane, 19

Wednesday

As he waited for the bean and cheese burrito he'd ordered, Zane peeled off his shirt and sat on the table outside Pepe's burrito stand. After he and Henry woke up on the beach to find Kia gone, they went over to Mickey's and crashed on his couches for a few hours. There was a chick passed out on one who was cute enough, so he lay next to her and felt her up while she slept. She awakened to his hand cupping her crotch. Ha! Ha! He smiled to himself remembering her face as she opened her eyes. Disoriented, she sat up, looked around, got up and left. He just stretched and went back to sleep.

It was around 9 or 10 a.m. he guessed, squinting up at the sun. After coming off the 'shrooms he did the day before with Henry, he was starved. He didn't know what made him decide to do them. He'd been drug free for three years after deciding to stop doing coke at 16. Fuck it. It felt good to let go and trip out.

"Zane! Bean and cheese!" Javier yelled from the pick-up window. Zane grabbed his burrito and scored a free Pepsi after bullshitting with Javier for a few minutes.

Henry came back from the Corner Store across the street with a sandwich from their deli. They sat in silence as they chowed down the grub.

"Hey, I wanna do some more 'shrooms," Henry spit out between bites, his mouth full of meat.

Zane continued to shove his burrito in his mouth, slurping his Pepsi. The breeze hit his face, his nose felt sunburned.

"Ya, OK," he shrugged. "Why not?"

They sat in silence again watching the cars go by. He saw Kristen park her convertible Karmann Ghia in the Corner Store lot and strutted inside.

Zane's penis twitched. Damn, she was hot business. He'd be saving her for later. He finished his burrito and threw his trash on to the table. At the same time Henry wadded up his sandwich wrapper and added it to the pile.

"Fuck!" Zane said, stretching again, "I haven't done 'shrooms in so long."

-Flashback to three years ago-

110

Out of nowhere Aliah's face came into his mind. She was his girlfriend three years earlier. He thought she was "the one." She was a beauty, an innocent. They did so much shit together mostly because she grew up around the corner from him. He thought back to when she was only nine. She was a scrawny, dark-haired, green-eyed little shit who used to make mud pies and bring them to him and his brothers. What a nuisance. But he always liked her. She was special. She radiated even back then in her stupid little hand-me-down flowered tank tops, and shorts that barely gripped her skinny waist.

At 12 they had their first kiss in the field by Surfside Homes. He and his brothers would go there to play basketball and she and her little brother, Evan, would follow them and sit and watch. She was such a little protective mother to Evan. He was only 10 back then and would try to get in the game and mix it up with the big boys, but Aliah would yank him back to the sidelines trying to keep him occupied with some other activity. She used to try to get him to do cheers that she'd learned in school. The poor kid was forced into some girly mimicking of what Aliah was into. But he would always scramble onto the court and get in the way of one of Zane's brothers as they dribbled along. That's how he lost one of his front teeth. It was an accident, but Aliah had bruises on her arms from her dad the next day, anyway.

When they were 13 and in junior high together, they both started hanging out with older kids and smoking pot; no big deal. But Aliah sometimes had a black eye or bruises on her thighs. That pissed Zane off. She wouldn't talk about it, even to him, but he knew. Her dad was a drunk. Zane had seen him quite often in their front yard with Aliah's uncles in their dumb lawn chairs drinking beers and yelling at the kids to shut up and go away. The mom was a pathetic mouse who seemed to be pregnant all the time.

Sometimes Aliah would sneak into his room at night and hide under the covers until morning. Sometimes she would bring Evan, and Zane would make him a bed with comforters and an extra pillow on the floor between his twin bed and his brother Jared's.

By 14, they had tried cocaine together for the first time. That was also the first time they had sex. It was crazy and not as special as he'd hoped. He'd just started playing guitar with some guys from high school in a punk band called The Degenerates. They had a gig at an abandoned warehouse in Hueneme off Hueneme Road where all the hookers and drug addicts roamed. It was a shady spot that had no electricity and they had no right to be there. So one of the dudes in the band brought his dad's generator and they hooked it up. It was a crazy scene with kids arriving from L.A. How they knew about it was a mystery, but The Degenerates and two other bands somehow knocked out a show. By the end of it all the windows in the place were broken, some dude had his head bashed in, and some chick with a mohawk thought she could push Aliah around because she wanted to fuck Zane. Aliah was a guard dog, so she and that ugly chick went into the parking lot and Aliah took out all her rage. It was the only time Zane remembered seeing her angry. She was kicking the chick in the ribs until Zane heard about what was happening and pulled her away.

They had just done coke about an hour or so before and he

lifted her, like the feather she was, away from there. He didn't want that from her, but at the same time, he was impressed. He kept her in a corner while he packed his equipment and they caught a ride to his house from a friend. He walked her right through the front door that night, and hand in hand they made their way to his room. They pushed a dresser in front of the door to block his brothers from coming in then stood there looking at each other for a long time before they both cracked up laughing and he pulled her to him muttering that she was his and his alone. Then he stripped her down and both lost their virginity on his smelly, unmade bed.

After that, they were inseparable (as if they weren't before). Sex was now whenever and wherever they could: the park, the girls' restroom at school, his bedroom, empty bedrooms at parties, bathrooms, etc. They were in love.

By 15 he was playing a lot more shows with the band. Aliah attended when she could, but when she couldn't get away, he would do more coke and make out with other chicks. It didn't matter. He didn't care about them. He was in a band. It was expected. At one of his shows he met a chick called "Tiffany from the Valley." She was blonde, rich, two years older and had a convertible Mercedes. She wanted him badly. They fucked in the bathroom of the shithole dance club he played at, and she had great coke. He really didn't remember much about it except the great coke.

She gave him some and he shared it with Aliah the next night in his room. They got so high he put her on the handlebars of his beach cruiser and rode the 12 blocks to Hueneme Beach. They stayed up all night looking at the moon and writing their names over and over in the sand. When the sun came up they were loopy, and the tide had washed away their late night declarations of love.

He rode her back and they slept in each other's arms in the darkness of his room all day. He never told her about the other chicks because they didn't matter. When Aliah wasn't by his side, life wasn't real anyway.

Tiffany kept at him through the next year. Anytime he played a show in L.A. or the valley that Aliah wasn't at, she was there.

He crashed at her pad once. This only happened because his bandmates split on him and he didn't realize it till he was in the parking lot high as fuck with all his equipment before realizing the van was gone. They were all dopeheads, too, and had just forgotten him.

Tiffany put the top down on her convertible and said she would take him home the next day and to throw his equipment in the back. What else could he do?

Back at her parents' pad in Sherman Oaks she brought him into a quiet house, parents asleep, gone, whatever, and they got naked in the jacuzzi. No condom, of course, in a jacuzzi. They fucked a couple times, did some blow, drank some tequila and passed out in her frilly room.

As promised, she brought him home the next morning to his sad single-story Hueneme tract house on C Street. He didn't feel embarrassed. He was punk rock and gritty living was cool when

114

you're punk rock. Fuck her stupid, lavish Valley life.

As she dropped him off, Aliah turned the corner walking toward his house. He grabbed his equipment without saying goodbye and walked into his house. Tiffany sat there for a while looking at Aliah, as Aliah looked looked back at her, and they knew.

Zane put his shit down and looked out the front window watching them have a conversation. Acting superior, stupid Tiffany flipped her hair and drove off. Aliah stood in front of Zane's house for a few minutes before turning around and walking back up the street.

He was too tired to deal with it just then, but anxiety kept him up.

That's when he made his decision. Nobody was going to control how he felt. He was a star. He was hot. He would not feel hurt. Aliah would get over it. She would. Damn, he was 15 playing in a band and that's just what you did. Bitches meant nothing. He stayed home that night, fucked up, and hung out with his brothers and the family. That's what's real.

Zane woke the next morning feeling good. For the first time in years, he didn't worry about Aliah. He didn't actually see Aliah for a week. That was weird. He went by her house and just rode by on his bike since the dad and uncles were being dipshits in the front yard. He did that twice, otherwise he was taking calls from Tiffany. She wanted to see him again. Fuck it. She was easy, Aliah wasn't.

He did start to worry about her after three days, though. Where was she?

His next show was at Casa Tropical, which was an old Quonset hut turned bar near Oxnard Airport. Big bands came to play. His band was an early opener. They were playing with RKL, Aggression, Stalag 13, Ill Repute. Shit, this would be a show. He showed up earlier than even he would expect.. They played their set and stepped off.

As he was milling in the background chatting up supporters, Aliah came into his view. He didn't hesitate approaching her and putting his arms around her. She shrugged him off. She was with another dude! Some hanger-on, bullshit motherfucker who unfortunately turned out to be Zane's friend, an OK guy named Joey from another band. Fuck!

Aliah looked weird—hazy, lazy but not high. Zane immediately pushed Joey and pulled him outside.

"Dude! No!" Zane protested, "You can't. That's my girl."

"Uh, no," Joey tapped Zane's chest, "she's not."

"Fuck if she ain't!" Zane pushed him again.

"Um, no," Joey dismissed him, and went back inside. Four dudes puffed up their chests at Zane as Joey walked away.

In a panic Zane rushed after him, but Joey was in a better band and had fuckers protecting him. Aliah! Aliah! He thought as he saw her slumped in a corner. She looked haggard, his babygirl.

He turned and went to the bathroom. He pulled out some coke, slurped a couple of lines and got ready for battle. "Fuck Joey! Fuck him! What a dumb fuck! Aliah! Aliah! I'm here to save you," he thought.

He headed straight for Aliah who was so small he almost didn't see her tucked back in the corner. Joey was on stage setting up with his band. Zane grabbed Aliah by the elbow, yanking her to her feet.

"Let go," she said weakly, trying to sit back down.

He lifted her up again.

"What's wrong with you?" he spat.

Her head rolled around on her neck like it was going to snap off and roll away.

"Shhhut up," she slurred. Her eyes were slits and her mouth barely seemed to work.

His friend Henry appeared and was also watching Aliah.

"What's wrong with her?" he asked, peering in.

"I don't know, she's on something," Henry saw that familiar crazy sheen in Zane's eyes. He was about to go off on somebody. He'd seen that look too many times.

"Hey dude, let me use your car," said Zane. "I'm going to lay her down in the backseat." Zane's palm suddenly appeared in Henry's line of sight.

"Uh, yeah, OK. Just don't take off in it," he reluctantly gave up his keys.

Zane hooked his shoulder up under Aliah's and half-walked, half-dragged her through the club to the front door.

Joey spotted them from the stage where he was singing and, still singing, jumped off the stage into the mosh pit where he pushed Zane from behind. This resulted in Aliah falling to the floor and almost getting trampled by aggressive skinheads.

Zane turned around and clocked Joey in the jaw. Joey threw down the microphone and they went at it as Aliah remained on the floor getting kicked periodically until Henry was able to get into the fray and pull her to safety. He set her on the floor next to a wall and ran back to the pit, jumping into what was now a dog pile of fists and Doc Marten boots.

Zane went crazy hitting anyone near him. He didn't even know if he was still fighting Joey. All of a sudden he felt a huge pull from behind catapulting him out of the dogpile. Two of Joey's friends had him from behind, one had his forearm across Zane's neck pulling him to the door as Zane kicked and elbowed the guys behind him.

They got him outside and pushed him to the asphalt. Zane felt the side of his face scrape along the gravel.

"Get the fuck out of here!" yelled one very big motherfucker.

"Fuck you!" Zane yelled, spitting blood out of his mouth.

The big motherfucker rushed toward him and knocked him

118

out with a blow to the jaw.

Zane awoke bouncing around in the back seat of Henry's big old car.

"Eh, uh," he muttered trying to lift up his head. He cracked open one eye. Eddie turned around from the passenger seat looking back at him. "He's alive."

"What the fuck? What . . . shit," he sat up. "Where are we?"

Eddie turned back around. "Heading to your house."

"Where's my equipment? Where's Aliah?"

"Dunno," Henry replied from the driver's seat, "We had to get you out of there because you were knocked the fuck out and the cops were coming down the street."

Zane fell back in his seat, "Fuck!" he screamed.

Henry and Eddie parked in front of his house and they all went in.

Because of that night Zane lost his guitar and amp to the destructive hands of Joey and his friends. This resulted in Zane getting kicked out of his band The Degenerates. Aliah was gone. She disappeared that night. He heard she got in a car belonging to some people up from from LA. No one heard from her or knew where to find her.

CHAPTER 13

For his 16th birthday, two weeks after Aliah disappeared, Zane let Tiffany pick him up, along with Henry and Eddie, to celebrate at some underground club called The Cavern in Hollywood. They parked her car in a lot down the street and did a couple lines of her good blow.

The Cavern was dark and had only purple and red lights roaming the walls. There was a band of four skinny dudes singing old British music that was a mix of punk and ska. The place was filled with mods, skinheads and punks.

The four of them went straight to the bar for rum and cokes. The boys hoisted their drinks and walked away leaving Tiffany to pay for them. They found seats in the darkness against the farthest wall from the stage. Tiffany found them and sat down beside Eddie because Zane made sure there wasn't a free seat next to him. He wanted to check the scene without her stupid face in his. She looked pissed but turned and talked to Eddie instead. Zane smirked to himself.

They sat there for a while, got a couple more rounds of drinks and made jokes about some of the weirder weirdos.

Zane got up to find the john and take a leak. He went down a dark hallway and bumped right into Aliah. She and some girl had their arms around each other and were feeling the walls.

"Aliah. Hey, Aliah," he touched her shoulder to turn her around.

She turned slowly and looked right at him, then looked back to the chick she was with. "I must really be tripping out. I think I just saw my ex-boyfriend," she said.

"Aliah," he turned her toward him again, "What the fuck? It's me."

She looked at him again, her beautiful green eyes so wide, and started laughing. "Oh, shit! Zane!" she exclaimed hugging the life out of him.

He grabbed her into his arms and pulled her off the ground. She weighed nothing. "Where have you been!" he demanded putting her back down.

"Uh, I don't know. With some people? This is Heather," she said turning to the girl next to her who had now wandered off down the hallway, "Shit, she disappeared,"

"Zane , Zane, Zane," she said hugging him again. "Hey! I

got some acid. Take this," she ordered, shoving the tiny paper through his lips. He took it and grabbed her hand.

"Come on, Henry and Eddie are here. Wait! I have to take a leak," he pulled her into the men's room and had one hand on the front of her shirt, keeping her near while he pissed. He wasn't going to let her slip away. No one in the men's room cared. He wasn't even sure it was all dudes in there. Some of the guys were wearing makeup and looked pretty feminine.

"OK, let's go," he said zipping up and pulling her back into the hallway and over to their table.

"Hey, Henry!" He said as he took a seat with Aliah on his lap.

Henry and Eddie both looked surprised. Tiffany glared at them.

Zane wrapped his arms around Aliah's waist and pulled her tight against him. She fell back onto him and then reached forward to the table and grabbed a drink, finishing it in one chug. The band was done and it was just flashing lights and talk everywhere and the sound of The Who's "Magic Bus." Tiffany got up and chatted with some other people but Zane saw her glancing back at he and Aliah. Soon the acid kicked in and he was tripping. Everything was a blur. Aliah was on his lap talking to Henry and Eddie and laughing, then he would see Tiffany come get in his face and he would laugh. There were more drinks, but he couldn't remember how much he'd downed. Then Tiffany pulled Aliah up and they danced. He followed and put his arms around both of them. He recalled Henry making out with Tiffany on the dance floor and Eddie having his arms around Aliah, so

Zane grabbed Aliah and sat back down.

They tripped out on the lights, and the people, and the music, and he was happy that Tiffany was on the dance floor making out with Henry and Eddie.

The next thing he remembered was being squished in the backseat with Aliah and Eddie. Henry was in the passenger seat of Tiffany's car and they were going somewhere.

"Where are we going?" he yelled leaning forward with the wind in his face since all the windows were down.

"The harbor!" Tiffany yelled back.

She took them to her parent's boat in Marina Del Rey near Santa Monica. They stumbled out of the car as he held Aliah's hand. They tripped out on the stars for a while before Eddie ushered Zane and Aliah down the dock to the boat.

Once on the boat, Tiffany pulled out some more coke. She, Henry and Eddie sat below doing lines while Zane and Aliah snuggled under a blanket on the deck looking at the stars.

He held Aliah tight until the sun rose and he and Aliah were damp from the cold dew. They stumbled down below to find Tiffany, Henry and Eddie passed out on the bed together. He and Aliah sprawled out on the sofas near the table and Zane closed his eyes again.

Sometime later he was awakened by Eddie moaning. He sat up to see Tiffany jerking him off.

"Hey! Dude!" Zane barked, "Keep it down dirt-bag."

Eddie stopped moaning and started laughing.

Soon Zane heard Henry mumbling, "Where's mine?"

Aliah sat up. With her hair matted and her makeup smudged under her eyes, she was an adorable mess. She looked at Zane and smiled. They sat perfectly still for a few moments locking eyes, feeling whole again, before breaking into exuberant laughter.

Before long, they were piled back into Tiffany's car heading up Pacific Coast Highway toward Hueneme, with Eddie sitting in front this time.

Aliah stayed with Zane through the whole next night.

In the morning his mom insisted she go home. Zane fought with his mom about it but she insisted they couldn't keep her there. He walked her home holding her hand. When they got to her house, her dad stumbled out of his chair, grabbed her arm and yanked her inside. As soon as her mom saw Zane she slammed the door in his face.

He stood there hurt and embarrassed. He felt helpless like a child. He sat on her porch seriously afraid for Aliah. What could he do? He heard them shouting inside and he decided that he would sit there all night if she needed him. But after 20 minutes he went home.

The next time he saw her was two days later. She came in his window at night with a backpack. She woke him up and asked him if he would leave with her. He held her in his arms and said

124

he would.

In the morning he packed a bag and had Henry drop them at the Greyhound bus station in Ventura. It was Aliah's 16th birthday.

They were going to L.A. to see if they could stay with a friend he knew from the scene. They ended up talking to two dykes for most of the trip and shared a pint of vodka with them. At one point Aliah stumbled to the bathroom with one of them. When they returned, she fell over Zane into her seat. She was groggy. He was still talking to the other one and didn't pay it much attention, figuring she was tipsy from the vodka.

When they got to L.A. he had to help her up. He was a little irritated with her being so helpless. He needed to get them to a pay phone to call his bro they were hoping to stay with to see if he could pick them up. He put her and their stuff on a bench. She lay down while he went off to find a phone.

After working it out with his friend he came back to find her passed out. Fuck. He shook her but she was limp. He couldn't wake her up. He shook her again to no avail. Was she dead? She was fucking dead!

He laid her down and immediately felt sick. His stomach churned and his heart clenched. He sat there staring at her. She was the only person on this earth that he loved, and he'd always wanted to protect her. She died in his care trying to help her escape from bad things and bad people he thought were hurting her. But, being with him was what killed her.

He sat back on the bench and gently placed her head on his lap. He stroked her hair and cried. A man walking by and looked at them. Zane pleaded through his tears, "Can you call the cops? She died," he gasped.

He lowered his face back to Aliah and wrapped his arms around her little body, holding her to tight while he rocked back and forth. His heart broke into a million shards, over and over and over.

He realized she must have shot up in the bathroom on the bus. She was so close to freedom! He, on the other hand, would be held hostage by her memory for the rest of his life.

CHAPTER 14

Back in the present

Wednesday

Zane came back to reality as he felt the sting of tears once again behind his eyes.

"Henry, let's go get 'shrooms."

They skated over to Mickey's house to see who was there and who might have 'shrooms. Ollie was kicking in the backyard, smoking a joint. He was always "holding" cause he was a total shroom freak.

"Dude," Zane hit him up, "got any 'shrooms?"

Ollie looked at them from behind red eyes, handing him the joint and digging into the front pocket of his shorts for a baggie.

"Here," he said, handing them the bag, "30 bucks. These are good ones," he said, baring his yellow, unbrushed-for-a-decade teeth. Every group needed a dude like Ollie who was always holding, even if Zane thought he was a dirty hippie freak.

Zane threw him the money and inspected the baggie. It was a good eighth of an ounce. He split it with Henry and they chewed the mushrooms as they sat in lawn chairs watching some grommets skate the ramp.

Henry got up and grabbed a couple of beers which they chugged while waiting for the 'shrooms to kick in.

Ollie slowly turned to Zane, "Hey dude, I thought you were straight-edge."

"We were," Zane laughed, "Fuck it."

"Welcome to the Other Side," Ollie grinned.

"That freak doesn't know shit about me," Zane thought. He looked over at Henry and rolled his eyes. Henry started to yawn. Zane laughed. Then he yawned, too. The 'shrooms were kicking in. Zane's eyes got filled with light and his head with sound as he sat back in his chair and gripped the arm with his left hand.

"Whoa," he whispered, "These are strong."

He heard Mickey's voice behind him in the living room. He also heard the B-52s blaring from the living room speakers. Mickey opened the sliding glass door and Zane turned his head, very slowly he thought, to see him.

128

Mickey looked at him and smiled. He did a crazy dance and loomed in and out of his vision.

"Zane! Zane! You trippin'?" Mickey laughed.

"Yeah dude, cut it out," Zane retorted with a very big smile.

"That's my little bro! Good for you," and Mickey slapped his shoulder.

"Hey Ollie! Give me some of that joint!" Mickey said walking over. He was a compact little motherfucker, Zane realized. He was wearing just board shorts and a top hat. Zane tripped hard on Mickey's hat.

"Dude, let me see that hat." He muttered rising on wobbly legs with his arms outstretched.

Mickey took it off his head placing it on Zane's. It seemed heavy, but he felt like he needed to wear it. He was now "The Ringmaster."

He turned to Henry laughing and pointing at his hat. Henry looked lost until Zane got his attention, then he busted out laughing.

"I gotta skate," Zane said to no one as he walked over to the ramp. He grabbed a board that was just sitting there. He got onto the ramp as the grommets skated past him and put his hands out to stop them like he was going to perform some great feat.

"Ladies and gentlemen," he announced.

"There's no ladies here!" Mickey shouted.

"Ladies and gentlemen," Zane continued, "You are about to witness greatness!" Then he climbed to the top of the ramp. He kept trying and falling backward. He finally got up and stood on top of the ramp, board ready to roll. The ramp was now the ocean. He was going to surf the ramp. It was huge.

"I hope I don't drown ladies and gentlemen!" he shouted.

He looked again. It was clear. There was a big set coming in! He could do it!

"OK! Here I go!" He dropped in and lost the board, fell on his back and his hat flew off. He sat on his butt in the middle of the ramp, looking around and hoping the wave wouldn't drown him.

He reached for the wayward board and placed it under his back. He laid down on it looking at the sky, forgetting what he'd been doing a minute ago. One of the grommets leaned over him and pushed him off the ramp.

Zane landed on the grass behind the ramp and reorganized himself, laying there looking at the sky. He could hear them resume skating and it was music to him. He could hear his friends talking and laughing and it was music to him. The top hat lay next to him by his head so he grabbed it and held it above him toward the sky. That didn't make sense so he tossed it somewhere nearby. The trees he could see were breathing and it was beautiful. Why did he stop doing drugs? He felt so at peace. He just laid there tripping out for a while.

He sat up feeling suddenly lonely. He looked over at the patio and realized a bunch of people were there. He reached for the top hat and stood up putting it on his head. He wanted company and he wanted to drink! He stumbled past everyone while glancing to his left, seeing most of his friends in a blur as he went for the fridge in the kitchen.

He reached Henry and leaned down, " Bro, bro, wanna beer?" he asked.

Henry looked at him and laughed, "Where you been?" His eyes were super glassy. He pulled Henry up, ignoring everybody else and they escaped to the kitchen.

"Hey!" he conspired, leaning into Henry who stumbled into him, "If there's beer, we're good."

"Yeah, if there's beer we're good," Henry repeated.

They paused before the fridge. What if there was no beer in there? He looked back at Henry who looked at him.

"Do it," Henry encouraged.

Slowly Zane opened the fridge. There was beer. Whew!

They grabbed as many as they could carry and went back outside.

There were more people than Zane realized. He and Henry sat on the concrete and put their beers out in front of them like chess pieces.

Zane leaned over to Henry, "We should drink the pawns first, save the king and queen for later."

Henry just nodded.

They each picked a beer and twisted it open. Zane hoped they picked the right ones, don't want to use up the king and queen right away.

"Hey fucker, knock it off!" said a voice that sounded like Kristen's.

Zane looked over at her. Shit, his friends were still there.

Kristen got up wearing very short shorts. His eyes were on her tan legs as she swished past him into the kitchen. Next he saw Kia walk by in a mini-skirt. Ah Kia, he thought, you saucy bitch. She was sexy and didn't know it. She was the best kind of girl, so easy to get on.

He stood up with his dick leading him to the kitchen. He bounced through the door and felt his top hat almost fall off, forgetting it was even there. He put it back on and approached them as they bent over in front of the fridge. He first butted Kristen from behind, then Kia.

"Hey asshole lay off," Kia said angrily.

"Calm down bitch," he slurred back.

Kristen turned around and smiled.

"Hey Zane," she purred, looking over at Kia. "Um, nice hat."

132

"Yeah, wanna see what's under it?" He challenged, touching his penis over his shorts.

Kia grimaced but Kristen moved closer, "Oh yeah, are you the ringmaster?"

"I am!" He replied stunned that she knew.

"Maybe you could give us a show," she giggled.

"Hell yeah," he answered immediately dropping his shorts.

He pulled his penis from the opening of his boxers and started stroking himself. Kia, the prissy bitch, tried to leave immediately. Kristen grabbed her back.

"Come on Kia, Zane has something to show us." Kristen then whispered something in Kia's ear.

Zane didn't care, he just wanted to fuck one of them.

"OK," Kia said touching Zane's shoulder, maybe reluctantly, he didn't really know.

"Let's go upstairs," Kristen teased.

Zane's shorts were around his ankles. Eager to follow the girls upstairs, he stepped out of them.

Kristen took his hand. Her ass in those shorts was mind-blowing. "Both of them? Shit!" he thought, wondering if he was dreaming or tripping. Ollie's face came to mind for no apparent reason other than the mushrooms. He imagined those yellow teeth. Did he ever get action like this? He shook his head vigorously to get the image to leave.

Zane followed Kristen through the living room to the stairs grabbing Kia by the shirt behind him, making sure she was coming. He might fuck her now. He hadn't stuck it in a girl since Aliah, because he hadn't been able to. But these two chicks? Hell yes!

As they went upstairs Kristen threw open Mickey's bedroom door. Kia pulled back from Zane and removed his hand from the front of her shirt. She turned around and disappeared.

Zane turned around to see her running back downstairs. Kristen looked out the door for Kia.

"Forget her," she said with menace in her voice, "She's a nobody."

She grabbed Zane and pulled him toward her kissing him. He shut the door behind them with his foot.

They began to make out heavily but Zane wasn't into the kissing. He felt like his tongue belonged to someone else, like it was alien from his horniness. He pushed her onto the bed ready to finally fuck. The 'shrooms made him forget why he hadn't for so long. He had been making out, titty fucking and fingering girls for years in his sobriety. All because in his mind, he was haunted by the memory of Aliah. Now, he no longer cared. He wanted to get laid. Kristen was perfect. Wow, drugs opened back up the world of pussy!

Mickey's bed was dank and stinky. Like a dog pissed all over

134

it claiming its territory. He couldn't get past it.

"Hey, get up." He pulled her off the bed, "It stinks in here."

She looked surprised. She probably liked the smell of other men, lots of men.

"I can't fuck you in here," he said grabbing her hand and looking for a different place in the house.

Surprisingly she followed him out without talking. Maybe this was his queen from earlier, the beer chess pieces.

"Hey, want a beer?" he asked her.

"No! We gonna fuck or what? Come on," Kristen replied opening the door to the bathroom.

It smelled better than Mickey's room. He caught a glimpse of himself in the mirror.

"Whoa, who the fuck, oh, it's me," he laughed at himself, eyes wide and bloodshot.

She jumped up on the sink checking the height, then jumped down facing him and kissed him while removing her shorts and thong. She jumped back up spreading her legs.

"Fuck me," she demanded.

The sink was the perfect height but he wasn't hard.

"Get me hard," he whispered in her ear and leaned down to give her a hickey, but then decided he wasn't interested in that stupid game anymore. She kissed his neck and reached for his cock, pulling it toward her. He played with her breasts freeing them from her bra under her shirt, her nipples were hard and he started to get excited.

"I've wanted to fuck you for so long, Zane," she whispered into his ear sucking his earlobe. "Fuck me then," he said putting himself inside her, now hard, grabbing her ass and thrusting. Eyes closed he immersed himself in the feeling of her wetness. Then he barely opened his eyes with his head looking over her left shoulder into his reflection in the mirror. He imagined her as Aliah, back in their time until his face contorted; his eyes rolled back into his head and began to cum inside her.

She violently pushed him away from her when she realized what was happening.

"Fuck! Zane! What are you doing? Did you just cum in me?" He face looked at him like he was the biggest idiot on the planet.

He didn't know what was happening. He refocused on the chick in front of him and it wasn't Aliah, it was Kristen. He stood there with his dick hanging out.

She jumped down off the sink and grabbed toilet paper wiping his semen out of her. She threw the toilet paper in the trash and put her thong and shorts back on.

"Asshole!" She shouted as she stormed out.

Zane looked into the mirror again and his face melted. He thought what happened was beautiful. "Aliah, I'm here baby,

Kristen was the vessel, but you're my queen! I miss you so much, thank you for coming back and letting me fuck you again." He was delirious.

He sat on the bathroom floor with his boxers around his ankles and hugged his knees. For this moment he wasn't alone, he wasn't a loser. He was a king, feeling once again what it was like to be with his queen.

Eventually the bathroom door opened. Zane lost in the melodrama of his imagination, looked up surprised to see Christian standing there.

"Dude, what are you doing?" Christian asked.

"Huh," Zane replied through red eyes. He just realized he had been crying.

Christian walked in and shut the door.

He crouched down, " Hey man, you OK? You may wanna pull up your boxers your dick is hanging out." He said, standing back up.

"Uh," Zane looked down grabbed his boxers and pulled them on. He thumped back against the wall losing his balance a little bit. Christian grabbed his arm to steady him.

He asked again, "You OK?"

"Uh, yeah, yeah, I'm cool." Zane answered.

"Kristen came down all pissed and grabbed the bottle of

tequila and Kia told me she had been up here with you."

Zane tried to remember. Was it Kia, not Aliah, who was here with him?

"Here, I grabbed your shorts from the kitchen," offered Christian.

Zane took them and put them on.

"Kia was up here with me?" he asked Christian, confused.

"No, Kristen was up here with you."

Zane tried to remember, but couldn't. He was with Aliah.

"No dude, I was with Aliah but she disappeared," Zane smiled at him. "Is she downstairs?" He asked pushing through the bathroom door.

Christian followed him out to the hallway to grab him and straighten him out, but Zane rushed down the stairs certain Aliah was outside.

He ran out into the backyard looking around for Aliah. Everyone stopped talking and looked at him.

Henry started laughing and walked over to him. "Dude, where were you?"

"Where's Aliah?" Zane asked looking from person to person.

Kristen sat with a bottle of tequila glaring at him. Kia stared at him with her mouth open.

138

Henry stood in front of him with a puzzled look on his face. "Aliah?" He looked around behind him and turned back to face Zane. "Aliah's, dead, bro."

Zane stood there as anger began to spread across his face. He pushed Henry, "No, she's not! Where the fuck is she?" He demanded as his fists curled up into his palms.

Christian got behind him and grabbed his right shoulder. Zane turned around and socked him in the jaw. Mickey jumped up and rushed over to hold Zane back as he was about to punch Christian again. Christian warded off the next couple blows then punched Zane in the stomach. Mickey got between them, holding each at arm's length. Zane was doubled over catching his breath. Everyone was quiet as they watched it all unfold. Zane got up and turned around. He walked over to Kristen and grabbed the bottle of tequila from her. He coughed chugging it down, then threw it across the yard smashing it against the concrete wall then stumbled back into the kitchen, out the front door and into the night.

CHAPTER 15
Thursday

A shiver jolted Zane awake before dawn. He found himself on the beach again. He slowly hoisted himself up on his elbow and stared at the waves rolling in.

What happened? He remembered nothing. His brain felt like it was still asleep and his eyes seemed to have opened independently to take in the surroundings.

He looked back over his shoulder at the deserted beach before returning his gaze to the ocean quietly rolling in and out.

He felt like he was in a thick fog. His tongue was thick and his eyes were crusted from the heavy sleep rewarded to those inebriated beyond their limits. He closed his eyes and rested his head on his arm. As the breeze off the ocean blew across him, he focused on the sound of the morning tide coming in and off the shoreline. Then a stillness descended and everything was eerily quiet. He fell back into a hazy darkness and pictures began to appear in his mind that were out of his control.

Aliah's face laughing in the sunlight as they were snuggled in his bed hiding from the world. Riding her on his handlebars to the beach and staying up all night playing in the sand. Aliah helping his mom do dishes in the kitchen one of the nights she stayed for dinner, and his mom hugging her and stroking her hair. Her face underneath his as he fucked her, all gaspy and out of breath, and how she would hold him very, very tight when they were finished.

That sparked the memory of the night before and being with Kristen in the bathroom at Mickeys. Zane squeezed his eyes tight, replaying the evening, now vividly. He was so stupid. How could he have thought Kristen was Aliah? He fucked someone else! The bond was broken! He was so mad at himself. She was no longer the last girl he'd been with and he'd never have that back.

He hated himself—even more than he already had.

In his despair he felt that maybe it would be easier to die. If he died, he could be with Aliah again and not have to deal with any more pain. He'd spent the last three years being an asshole, anyway. He wasn't making anyone's life better. He started to imagine how he'd do it. Various images flashed through his mind; driving off a cliff, gunshot to the head, maybe a bad heroin shot like Aliah. But then he saw himself paddling out for one last session and drowning. He played the scenario over and over again in his head, one huge wave rising up to crush and grind him, like life has.

Yea, that's it! That was how he'd do it. He rolled in the sand to rise up. Surging with a new purpose he ran up the beach toward Christian's house to lift one of his boards. The streets were completely deserted as his bare feet pushed against the pavement, his destination getting closer by the minute. Spotting Christian's pad he slowed down to catch his breath. He sauntered up to the front door and silently twisted the knob, pushing into the living room. Nobody appeared to be awake. He tiptoed over to one of Christian's longboards and clumsily bumped it against the coffee table turning it around to get it out the door. He stopped and listened for any movement, anyone alerted to his presence. Down the hallway he heard someone snoring. He waited a few seconds to make sure before hauling the board out the door and down the street to the end of this life. He didn't even bother to close Christian's front door because that's the kind of dick behavior he was about to rid the world of.

He hurried along the street holding the board snug to his side. He walked onto the sand back to the spot where he'd woken up. He dropped the board and glanced down at it hoping it wasn't one of Christian's favorites. He was sure it would wash up to shore after he drowned, but it would always be known as the board Zane used to kill himself. God, he was such an asshole.

He scanned the beach break looking for a good place to paddle out. Mother Nature must have wanted him dead, too, because it was sizing up to be a pretty good day. He ripped off his shirt, grabbed the board and paddled out.

142

The board split through the frothy water as he made his way to the incoming sets. He felt the urgency to do it as quickly as possible before the morning patrol of surfers showed up.

But as he was getting ready to paddle for the next wave, a tingly feeling came up through his stomach and filled his chest. He was paralyzed by it and the images in his head changed. He was not directing what was happening. A tickling of the rage he'd harbored for so many years started to burn up his belly straight into his heart. His heart felt like it was on fire. He closed his eyes to return to his death scenario and squeezed back burning tears.

A wave built up in his mind as if behind his brain. He saw himself sitting on his board looking to the horizon waiting for the deadly set to come in and take him out. But instead of a rolling wall of water he saw a man walking toward him, on top of the water. The man was laughing and threw his arms up to the sky smiling at Zane. Zane felt he was supposed to be in on the joke but didn't know what was so funny. A wave began building behind the man who looked back at it and then looked at Zane. Zane watched the wave lift and carry the man. The foam was barely touching the bottom of his feet, carrying him like he was a king and the wave was only there to serve and amuse him.

Zane now cried tears cool to the touch. The fire in him was melted by the cooling waters of forgiveness. It was time to forgive himself. Zane watched the man go on and on, down the beach with the wave never ending until he couldn't see him anymore. The image left his head and he opened his eyes. His chest was still tingling and he didn't feel sad anymore. All of a sudden, just like that, he felt hope enter his heart. He knew who that man was. He realized Jesus was the first surfer ever, the "Man Who Walks on Water." If God made his only Son a surfer, then Zane now felt forgiven for not saving Aliah, for hiding in his pain. He could still feel the sensation of being overcome physically and he would never forget the vision. Somehow he knew he wasn't ready to die. He smiled to himself. Someday he'd surf with Jesus.

Friday

The next day Zane skated over to Henry's house for band practice. Henry was pounding on his drums in the garage when he walked in. Zane gave him a nod and walked over to his guitar and strapped it on. The two of them ripped through some random jamming until Eddie got there and strapped on his bass. The three of them ran through their set. It felt good to play and scream, he let the music roar through him. He felt at home.

When they were done they roamed the kitchen looking for food. Henry's parents were gone for the night and some friends were coming over later to kick it and listen to them play. They found enough ingredients to make some nachos which they devoured.

Mickey, Christian and Dave showed up with beer. Kristen, Melissa and Erica arrived with more beer. Kristen still gave him the cold shoulder. What the fuck ever. Crazy chick. He leaned back against the kitchen counter drinking a beer and talking to Dave.

Melissa, Mickey and Christian started playing quarters. Kristen walked over to Henry and took his beer out of his hand,

144

smiling at him, flirting. Zane looked away, he didn't care. Sloppy seconds, he smiled to himself. Erica walked over to where he and Dave were talking and touched him on the shoulder.

"Hey Zane," she smiled. She had a great smile Zane thought to himself. "How are you doing? You know, last night and all."

His cheeks flushed. He didn't realize till that moment that he was embarrassed. "Uh, yeah, I guess I was an asshole." He looked at her and shrugged his shoulders.

Concerned, she moved closer to him and whispered in his ear, " I just want you to be OK."

It gave him goosebumps.

Then she stepped back and said, "We all care about you."

"Maybe not Kristen," he mumbled, smiling.

Erica looked over her shoulder at Kristen and Henry flirting with each other. She looked back at him and laughed, "She'll get over it."

Yeah, I guess she will. Maybe I'm not the asshole."

"I never thought you were," she said, her face serious.

He just beamed at her, kind of seeing her for the first time. She was really pretty, he'd always seen that, just not how pretty she was up close. She had light blue eyes with flecks of gold. And she had cute freckles across her nose, and a smile that knocked you on your ass. She broke their stare and looked around. He continued to gawk.

"Hey motherfuckers," Mickey yelled, "I wanna hear some music!"

Zane looked away and smiled at Mickey, "OK, calm down motherfucker, we're going!" and he walked away from Erica glad for the interruption. She was unnerving him. He felt like he was under a spell.

They all filed into the garage and their friends kicked it on the two ratty couches that were facing their equipment. They started their set and Zane tried to focus on playing but he kept getting distracted when his eyes settled on Erica sitting and watching him.

He played the last three songs with his eyes closed.

After they were finished it was somehow decided they would leave Henry's house and go to the dunes for a bonfire. Since Kristen wanted to drive with Henry, and Zane didn't want to be anywhere near her, he drove with Melissa and Erica. Melissa drove so Zane took the backseat and sat in the middle where he could see Erica. He felt excited for some reason, like something was going to happen, something good. He was almost giddy about it, and he didn't know what or why.

When they arrived, they unloaded the wood they'd taken from Henry's house, and grabbed the beers trudging through the sand laughing.

Sitting around the huge fire though, they got quiet. Everyone was transfixed by it. Zane could hear the waves in the distance and he could feel the heat from the flames across his face. He looked up to the sky and it was so clear out that the stars were super bright. He laid back and stared.

He felt some movement to his right and Erica appeared handing him another beer and sitting next to him, leaning back to stare at the stars too.

"Pretty, huh?" she sighed.

"Very," he said quietly. But not as pretty as her, he thought. He had known Erica for years and he knew she was a nice girl. That's why he never thought about her. He didn't have any use for a nice girl—before. But since Aliah returned to his mind and his heart so recently and so hard, he realized he was ready to fall in love again. He closed his eyes fighting back the cold chill of fear, he never wanted to go through that pain again. He opened his eyes and turned Erica. She smiled at him. He smiled too.

"Hi," he whispered.

"Hi," she whispered.

Maybe she's worth it. He reached over and took her hand.

Arnold's Road- Pt. Hueneme

At the end of a long road is a mostly deserted strip of beach called Ormand Beach. No one really went there. It was usually windy and there was the close proximity of the ugly remnants of an old smelter and power generation plant. It was a gritty beach. The balance of beauty and ugliness in one location. Great place to hide.

CHAPTER 16

Henry Petit, 19

Kristen Dewster, 18

Saturday

Kristen woke up next to Henry in his bed. Her mouth was dry, but otherwise she felt pretty good.

He was sleeping on his back, covers half on with his left leg bent at the knee, mouth open. She took her hand and put his knee down.

She wanted something to drink. She slowly got up from bed and noticed she had on one of his T-shirts, the one from last night. She remembered that his parents were gone so she quietly opened his bedroom door and peeked out. It was quiet. She creeps down the hall to the kitchen. There are empty beer cans all over the counter from the after party that followed the bonfire at the dunes. She opened the fridge and grabbed a cold Budweiser since there wasn't anything else and she didn't drink tap water. Grimacing, she drank it. Immediately she felt better because her cottonmouth was gone.

Shit, what a night. She walked into the bathroom to pee. She admired her reflection in the mirror. She was just beautiful. She smiled and crouched over the toilet to pee. She refused to sit on any toilet but a clean one at home. Henry's house was the typical Hueneme tract home filled with his parent's knick-knacks, old mismatched furniture and an obvious lack of housekeeping. She wanted to shower, but after peeking into his she decided against it. All the soap scum, mildew and cheap shampoos and soaps made smelling like campfire and beer a better option.

Regardless of all that, there was something about Henry. She always thought of him as Zane's sidekick, but the other night at Mickey's when he was shrooming, and after the incident with her and Zane, he was really sweet. He was goofy and always laughing and since Christian was up Kia's ass and Zane turned out to be wacko, it was nice to have Henry come sit next to her. She'd been really pissed but his eyes were so wide and with that perma-grin he had she couldn't help but go into a good space with him. He was infectious. She had tried to get back at Christian for hooking up with Kia. Damn, he was such a pussy over her. When did that happen? Melissa should have kicked her ass! She was used to Christian paying her all the attention. It's true they hadn't hooked up in a long time, but still, Kia? So, when she saw Henry again at his house last night it felt natural to flirt with him and see if she could get him. Get him she did.

Henry rolled over to his side, gradually opening his eyes, and he sort of remembered not being alone. Was there someone missing? Kristen? Kristen! Oh, shit, did that really happen? Nah, no way. He sat up looking around. Henry you dumbass, you're still dreaming. He lied back down, smiling. Man, doing drugs and drinking again had really scrambled his brain. He closed his eyes and images of the night before came into view. Playing the drums, Kristen flirting with him in the kitchen, driving to the dunes, she kept touching his leg, bonfire, making out, yup they made out, wow . . ..

He reached down and touched his dick; not sticky, flaccid actually. Where was the morning wood? Maybe he was still drunk.

Then Kristen appeared in the doorway. "Hey," he said, startled with his hand over his boxers.

She looked at him and smirked, then walked over to the other side of the bed.

"All there is to drink is Budweiser," she told him. "Here," she tossed a can onto the bed.

He picked it up and set it on the nightstand since it was all shaken up.

She sat down and chugged the rest of her beer before setting it down on the other nightstand. She reached down and picked up her clothes, setting them on the bed before pulling Henry's shirt over her head. That's his shirt! Henry realized. She had her back to him and it was a beautifully tanned back with bikini string markings. He gazed at her, still wondering if he was drunk.

She stood up to put on her shorts and tank top. Wow, a perfect ass like you see on chicks in Surfer Magazine, he thought. His dick was getting hard.

"Henry," she said, turning around dressed but with no bra, "let's get up, you need to take me home so I can shower."

"Uh, yeah." He couldn't get up quite yet. He looked down and grabbed his shirt, but sat back down for a minute to get a grip and open the beer. He took a big gulp and set it back on the nightstand.

He was still hard. It was no use trying to think of something to make it go away with Kristen sitting there looking at him.

He just smiled and shook his head and flipped back the covers to unveil his problem. Kristen looked up at him and smiled a lovely, genuine smile. He grinned back at her and made a goofy face.

"Well, Miss, as you can see I have grown a third leg and I'm not used to walking on it just yet."

She laughed. "You're such a dork."

He flipped his dick back and forth. "He waves hello."

152

"Oh my God Henry," she laughed.

He reached across the bed pulling her into his arms. She rolled onto him. She felt so good on top of him. She was so light and she smelled faintly like chocolate and vanilla.

He put his hands up behind her ears, his fingers falling into her soft long hair, and pulled her close for a kiss. It was soft and slow. Her skin was smooth, and he ran his hands down her back over her hair reaching for that World Class Ass.

She moaned and they kissed deeper. She sat up straddling him and pulled off her shirt.

Henry's eyes widened, Fuck she was gorgeous.

She looked down at him smiling, aware of her beauty.

"God, Kristen," he unwittingly blurted.

He pulled off his shirt in a hurry and she leaned forward, placing her spectacular breasts on his bare chest.

They continued to kiss deeper. He put his hands back down toward her ass to undo her shorts. He unbuttoned them and slipped them off, followed by her thong, until she was blissfully naked on top of him. He flipped her over and removed his boxers. He was out of his mind with excitement.

"Henry, do you have a condom?"

"Yeah," he said, throatily.

He reached for his nightstand digging for the box of condoms he knew was there. He doesn't use them much so he's confident they are in there. He finds one, rips it open and rolls it on.

He leaned down to kiss and suck softly on her breasts and nipples.

She moaned and arched her back.

They kissed again and he slipped it in.

Oh, Lord, that feels good. He starts to push harder.

"That feels so good," she moaned in his ear.

"Yeah," he moaned back.

They went faster and faster as she lifted her legs circling his back. He reached down and lifted her ass off the bed, holding it as he thrust it inside of her, on his knees. He looked down at her and her eyes were closed but her mouth was open and she was panting. It was the sexiest thing he had ever seen in his life and in that moment he fell in love with her.

He closed his eyes, feeling the rush of the orgasm coming, the back of his head getting numb from the crash. He gasped and cried out.

His brow was sweaty, his eyes wide.

She looked up at him, eyes wide too.

"Wow," she said

"Wow," he nodded..

154

He laid back down next to her and pulled her into his arms while he caught his breath.

They remained there for a few minutes before she whispered; "Now we both need a shower."

Eyes closed, he smiled, "Wow, you already to go again in the shower? How will we get clean while we are getting dirty?" he joked.

She replied in a naughty voice, "We'll use lots of soap," then hesitating she added, "but let's go to my shower at my house."

Henry ended up just dropping her off at home. He said he'd just go surfing to get clean. Kristen thought it was because her mom's car was in the driveway and she got the feeling Henry wasn't ready for that. No problem she thought as she opened the door to their huge house on Hollywood Beach. No one was in the kitchen or living room so she climbed the stairs to her bedroom. It felt good to be in her beautiful room again. Light filled the room from the windows facing the ocean. She went to the window and looked out over the sand to the ocean. There was a slight offshore breeze blowing the spray back over the waves as they crashed on the shore. What a beautiful day, she smiled to herself. She headed to the bathroom. It was blissfully clean thanks to the maid. She turned on the hot water over her deep tub and switched on the shower. She undressed and got in, sighing with pleasure as the hot water washed away last night's smoke and grime and Henry's sweat. Henry's face filled her mind when she closed her eyes.

"Henry," she laughed out loud, "Henry . . .."

As her expensive soap and shampoo filled the steamy room with the delicate smell of coconut and chocolate, she remembered looking at him when she woke up. Henry with his bleached blond hair in a tangled mess all stiff from whatever crap he put in it to have it stick out from his head. He had a cute boyish face with full lips and light brown eyes. His body, on the other hand, that part needed work, she thought. He was in good enough shape and all but he needed a tan badly. If she decided to be his girlfriend he would need a makeover. Christian didn't ever need a makeover, he was perfect. Too bad it didn't last between them. He just kind of stopped calling and found excuses not to hang out. He would still flirt with her around everyone but didn't want to be alone with her. It was so frustrating. The thought of it, began to upset her. And now he was with Kia, or Lisa, or whatever the fuck her name was. She thought about it as she rinsed out her hair. She pictured Kia/Lisa and kind of surmised that she's cute in a young, innocent way. She never paid her that much attention until Christian did. She just thought of her as part of that little girl crew with Ami, Brooke and Vienna. She never in a million years thought Christian would ever like her. Guess he likes them young and dumb, she smirked. But Kristen knew she was hotter, no doubt about that. She could have anyone— except Christian, apparently. She angrily turned off the water and stood in front of her full-length mirror. Maybe she needed a deeper tan. And maybe more highlights, too. Yeah, maybe. She had Henry, now, but maybe she wanted Christian back. Maybe.

Henry pulled on his wetsuit while checking out the surf. It was small but doable. He stood by the bathrooms at Hollywood Beach where some of his local buddies were suiting up, too. He glanced over at Morgan and Gerard and they looked ready to go so they headed out together. Henry didn't surf Hollywood Beach often so he was somewhat comfortable paddling out with two locals. It was very territorial. There were only so many waves. As he got out he saw two chicks, one on a sponge and one on a real board. When he got closer, he saw it was Kia on the sponge and some chick he didn't know on the board. They were talking so he guessed they knew each other. Kia was cute. Damn! Her butt in that wetsuit was amazing.

Kristen lounged on her bed looking through the latest issue of Cosmo with MTV playing through her television and flipping through articles like "Sexual Moves That Will Blow His Mind" and "How I Got My Ex Boyfriend Back." The sexual moves were noted but the article on getting an ex-boyfriend back was devoured. She finished the magazine and threw it aside. Suddenly she was bored with being inside on such a pretty day and reached for her phone to call Erica. No answer. Then she called Melissa. No answer. Where were they? She stood up and looked out the window again. It was a perfect day. She put on one of her tiny bikinis and brushed out her hair before applying some make up. She grabbed a towel and headed to the beach to work on getting a deeper tan.

CHAPTER 17

Henry, Morgan and Gerard surfed for a couple of hours. Hunger set in so they agreed to head in and hit up Mrs. Olsen's Coffee Hut. After scarfing down burgers, Morgan suggested they cruise over to Breakers Apartments to see if Big Bob was home. They piled into Henry's big ol' jalopy. Morgan and Gerard headed across the street to Gerard's house to drop off their suits and boards. Big Bob was on the deck working on his small barbecue. He smiled when he saw them pull up and waved them over.

Henry found Zane and Erica sitting on the couch drinking beer. He had his arm around her and they were laughing. Henry hadn't seen Zane so happy in a long time. His eyes were sparkling and he was just fucking happy. He jumped up and gave Henry a half-hug before sitting back and putting his hand on Erica's leg. He finally got himself a good girl. Henry was happy for him. There was a case of beer sitting on the floor so Henry helped himself. He went outside to chat with Big Bob who was in the local punk band Dumptruck Babies and they have played shows together.

"How's it hanging, Bob?"

"About 12 inches," he bellowed with laughter.

"So when are you guys playing again?" Bob asked.

"We're playing at the Olympic next month, August something," Henry replied tipping back his beer.

"Oh yeah, I think we are too."

"Right on."

Zane came outside to join them. He leaned back against the railing his eyes darting over to Henry.

"So what's going on with you and Kristen?"

Henry immediately blushed. Then he smiled looking at the ground.

"Oh, really?" Zane teased.

Henry looked up smiling from ear to ear.

"Yeah, I hit it."

Zane drank his beer, "I hope it turned out better for you than it did for me."

"Well she did want to shower with me after we did it."

Zane laughed, "Probably to wash off your funk."

Henry laughed, too, "Fuck you dude!"

Then Zane got serious, "Be careful man, don't get attached."

"Uh, yeah, no worries," Henry mumbled.

Then Henry started wondering why he said that. Does he think I'm not good enough for her? She's the hottest chick from all around. Does he think he's the only one who's hot shit? Nah, Zane was his bro, so he asked, "Why did you say that?"

Big Bob grabbed his meat off the barbecue and went inside.

Zane said, "Cause she's a slut, man."

Henry felt his face flush with anger. He decided not to say anything. Instead he turned around and looked out over the railing. He spotted Christian's Ford Falcon pulling up and saw him get out with Kia and that chick from earlier.

Zane put his hand on Henry's shoulder and saw Christian, Kia and some chick walk over.

"Just be careful is all I'm saying." Then he turned around and went inside.

Kristen had been sunbathing for an hour and she was bored . She applied Hawaiian Tropic oil to her entire body and sat up to survey the beach from all directions. There were surfers hitting the waves up and down the shore. Ahead of her some guy was getting out of the water. He was at least 6'2" and she noted that he was in great shape as he peeled off his wetsuit. He had long hair that he shook back and forth before bending over to expel the water from his ears. He grabbed his board and headed up the beach in her direction. She didn't want to be caught staring so she laid back down and closed her eyes. She could hear him to her left so she turned her head, noticing that he positioned himself on a towel a few feet away from her. He pulled a sandwich from a cooler and ate it while watching the waves. He had not looked her way once. That wouldn't do so she turned over on her stomach to show off her awesome ass. She put her chin on her hands and looked up the beach toward her house with a sigh. Damn, that guy was hot. Who was he? She had lived on Hollywood Beach her whole life and had never seen him. She figured he was probably from the Valley. She peeked over at him again to see that he was still staring at the ocean. He had light brown hair with blonde streaks from the sun, and from his profile she could see he had a handsome face. Maybe Hawaiian? Not the typical pasty Valley. He was dark and tanned. She watched him finish his sandwich and brush off his hands before reaching into his cooler when he finally noticed her and caught her looking at him. He smiled and did a little head nod. She quickly closed her eyes, embarrassed that he caught her. Guys usually checked her out, not the other way around.

Christian bounded up the stairs with Kia and that other girl behind him. Henry greeted them with "What up," and noticed the other girl he hadn't realized was kind of cute. Not in a Kristen way, more in a cute tomboy way. They all went inside the living room and Christian headed for the kitchen to chat up Big Bob who was cutting up a steak and eating it. Oingo Boingo's "Only a Lad" was playing on the stereo. Zane and Erica were still on the couch being all googly-eyed in their own world, and Kia and the other chick were sitting on the floor looking a little out of place, glancing at the beers but not taking any. Henry decided to do the honors.

"Ladies?" he said reaching in and handing them each one. Kia looked relieved and thanked him as she accepted the offer. The other chick took one without meeting his eyes.

"Henry," Kia said, "This is my friend, Natasha."

"What's up?" Henry said clinking beers with her.

"She's from Huntington Beach, she just moved here."

"Hey," Natasha said shyly.

"Hey," Henry responded.

He took a seat in the recliner and drank his beer while everyone else talked. He wasn't all that curious about what Kristen was doing at that moment because Natasha looked interesting.

The guy on the beach walked over to Kristen, but she figured him for some Valley kook so she'd have to get rid of him. She wondered what Henry was up to. (Probably thinking about her.) He was sweet and in her band of friends so she'd keep him for a while, at least until she got Christian back.

"G'day!' the guy said, standing over her, "You local?"

She slowly turned over looking bored and bothered, "Yeah."

"I just moved here from Australia, are the waves always this small?'

Oh shit, that accent! Kristen was immediately interested. She'd better make her home beach appear cool.

"Oh no, it's just small today," she replied having no idea if it gets bigger at all. "Soooo when did you move here?" She looked into his gorgeous green eyes.

"About a month ago. My cook was from here originally and she missed her mob. She's eight months pregnant."

"You moved here with your pregnant cook?"

He laughed, "Language barrier. Cook is slang for wife. Mob is her family."

"Oh." A pregnant wife. Bummer! He only looked around 22 or so. "That's nice."

"Yeah, too right." He trailed off. Kristen watched him shake his head again that long hair reaching down to the middle of his back. Damn, he was fine.

"So you grew up here?" he instigated.

"Yes, I did," she sat up, "great place to raise kids," she added, disappointed about where the conversation was heading.

" Want a tinny?" he asked handing her a can of beer.

"Would love one," she smiled. What the hell, she was bored.

Henry watched Natasha. She had blonde hair to her shoulders, light brown eyes and a cute face. Her body was small—small tits, small ass—but her smile was huge.

"So Natasha, when did you move here?" he asked leaning forward. He realized his beer was empty and got up for another one while she answered.

"A little over two weeks ago. Lisa is the first chick I've seen in the water so far," she said looking back at Kia.

"Lisa?" Henry blurted.

Kia looked sheepish. "Yeah my real name."

Henry looked at her quizzically.

Kia explained," My given name is Lisa and when I moved here I wanted a fresh start so I changed it to Kia," she blushed.

Henry grinned leaning back in his chair, "Cops after you? You a wanted woman, Kia? I mean Lisa."

She glanced over at Natasha who was hearing this for the first time also. Kia gulped air and fiddled with the top of her beer can.

"It's a long story, but in short before we moved here from Santa

Cruz because my little sister was killed in a car accident and it was a painful time. I just wanted to start fresh." She continued to look down messing with her beer.

Henry didn't know what to say, luckily Natasha did.

"Oh wow, that's sad. What made you decide to go back now?"

Kia glanced over her shoulder back at the kitchen, "Umm, I ended up telling Christian about it, and once I did it helped me talk to my mom about it and I decided that I needed to go back to the name Bennie knew me by, that's my sister, to not forget her, ya know?"

Natasha put her hand on Kia's leg and kind of patted it.

Henry had no idea that she went through that. Honestly he really hadn't talked to her much, or any of the girls for that matter. He drank from his beer and still didn't know what to say so he sat there quietly. He glanced toward the couch and noticed Zane and Erica staring at Kia. Lisa. He had to remember to call her Lisa.

Erica opened her mouth, "Wow, that's so sad Kia, I mean Lisa. How old was she?"

Kia met Erica's eyes, "Three. Um can we change the subject?" she pleaded.

"Sure, of course hon," Erica replied.

Zane sat back and pulled Erica close so he could put his arm around her.

Natasha turned to Henry, keeping her hand on Kia's leg.

"So, umm, how are the breaks on the other beaches here? I've only surfed this beach so far."

Henry was relieved to change the subject and then got into a detailed discussion about the different breaks and the best places to go out at Hueneme, Strand and Shores. He advised her to always lock her car.

Kristen drank the beer the hottie gave her.

"Sorry, where are my manners? Eh? My name is Mark."

"Kristen."

"Kristen, so ah, what's it like living here?"

She thought about what to say and decided to make it seem fabulous. Even if he was married with a pregnant wife she could tell he was interesting and cool, if only because he was gorgeous like her.

"Oh, it's great," she enthused, "parties all the time and stuff." That's really all she could think to say. He was obviously older, and from Australia, what could she tell him? She hangs out with high school kids? She wished she was in her 20s.

"Parties, eh?" Mark smiled, "How old are you?"

She was 18. Stupid 18. "I'm 22. Why how old are you?"

He leaned back on his elbows, "I'm 23."

"And already married? Wow. How did you meet your wife?"

"My wife came over on a holiday backpacking around Australia with her sister. I met them at the bar I worked at."

Kristen pictured two young American girls roaming around Australia and finding Mark in a bar. She decided to taunt him by reapplying the tanning oil. She put down her empty beer and slathered the coconut-scented oil on her chest, stomach and legs.

"Can I have another?" she asked, handing him her empty one.

"Sure, Spunk," he said as reached into the cooler.

She hoped the fragrance of the oil would remind him of Australia. Maybe he would imagine meeting her there. He started to hand her the beer but she couldn't take it because she was still busy oiling up her legs. So he let it hang in the air in her direction while he watched.

"Oh, thank you," she said, putting down the oil and taking the beer. Then she proceeded to ignore him pretending to watch the waves. He continued to admire her for a minute before turning his eyes back to the ocean.

Right in the middle of his discussion with Natasha, Morgan and Gerard showed up. They grabbed beers and flopped on the couch next to Zane and Erica.

"You guys want a tab?" Morgan asked, pulling a baggie from his pocket.

Henry looked around the room for takers. Morgan stood and began handing them out. Everybody was in except for Big Bob who had things to do later in the day.

"OK, you guys can't stay here and trip out, though," said Big Bob, I've got to leave soon."

With that, the gang said goodbye to Bob and regrouped downstairs near Henry and Christian's cars.

"Where do you want to go?" asked Christian.

"Let's go down to Arnold's Road,"suggested Zane.

"How are we going to get there? I'm not driving," Henry replied. Christian also seemed reluctant.

"I have a VW bus," Natasha chimed in. "I'll drive, come on, I live just down the street."

CHAPTER 18

They moved as a group following Natasha. Henry walked beside her as they continued to talk about surfing. She wore an ankle bracelet with a bell on it, and when she walked it sounded like Tinkerbell or something. She mentioned the good spots in Huntington Beach and the OP Pro that happened there every year.

After a couple of blocks they turned right into the condos where Morgan also lived. They walked to her parking space where there was an orange VW passenger van with the words "Rasta Bus" painted on the driver's side. On the passenger side was a Jamaican flag with the silhouette of a guy with dreadlocks smoking a joint. It was the coolest thing Henry had ever seen.

"Cool bus," he remarked as Natasha climbed in.

"Yeah, it's very incognito," she laughed.

They drove off Hollywood Beach toward Arnold's Road in Hueneme. As Henry gave Natasha directions he could feel the tab kicking in. It seemed like it was taking forever to reach their destination. By the time they arrived at the secluded beach at the end of the road, everyone was high as fuck. They all piled out and onto the beach and one by one they plopped down into the sand. Henry fell back and looked at the sky as he ran his hands through the sand. His body felt as though it was vibrating. He could hear Kia and Erica laughing. He wouldn't remember to call her Lisa, today. He thought about what a trip her story was. Wow, her little sister dying in front of her. Henry started to feel sad and wanted to cry. He wondered if anyone ever cried on Ecstasy. A tear tumbled down his cheek. Embarrassed, he turned away from the group. He looked across the ocean and made himself focus on its calm and blue. He took some deep breaths to relax. "Shit, I need to get happy," he thought. But temporarily forgetting he was among other people he just stared at the ocean and tripped out. He had no idea how long he was doing that before he heard Zane calling to him.

"Henry! Henry! Turn around!"

Henry turned around and all his friends were petting Kia's hair.

"Come here, feel Kia's hair."

"It's Lisa," she laughed.

Henry decided it was a good idea and walked over. Zane reached up for his hand and moved over. Everyone moved out of the way so Henry and Zane could experience Kia's hair together.

170

"Dude, isn't that soft?" Zane said, turning to him. His pupils were so huge that his eyes were almost completely black.

Henry looked at the back of Kia's head and ran his hands through her hair. Just the three of them sitting there reminded him of when the three of them were lying on the beach on 'shrooms, Zane and him with one hand on each of Kia's breasts staring at the sky.

"I love you guys," Henry said, feeling really close to them.

"Yeah, I love you too," said Kia, reaching her hands back and grabbing theirs. The three of them hugged each other for a bit. Henry sat down and observed his friends. Christian was standing up staring at the ocean with his hoodie on. Morgan and Gerard were sitting a few feet away conversing intensely. Erica was on her hands and knees crawling toward them. Natasha was on her back staring at the sky.

Henry got up to sit beside her. He took her hands and pulled her up to face him. They sat facing each other with eyes locked.

Kristen wanted to keep the conversation going as she and Mark stared at the ocean. His accent, his looks, everything about him was HOT.

"Sooo..," she trailed off not quite sure what to say next. He looked over at her and grinned. She gazed at him with his beautiful long hair, gorgeous face, fit body and wished he wasn't married. She wanted him. She wanted him to be single. Other girls would die if they saw her with him. He was a hunky, older Australian—so much better than the hood rats she had to choose from. Better than Christian, even. Way better than Henry. Why did he have to be married? She decided to dig in. "So how long have you been married?"

He leaned back on his elbows, "Oh, about three months."

She was surprised. "Oh, isn't your wife eight months pregnant?"

"Oh, ya, but it's all part of my plan to become a citizen here."

Huh? So he doesn't love her? She was intrigued. "You just married her because she's pregnant?"

He drank his beer looking a little ashamed. "Yeah, well, that wasn't the plan, but you know, I'm a good bloke so I did."

He turned on his side facing her and she could see in his eyes and his grin that he was flirting with her.

"Oh," she replied, feigning disinterest. Maybe she'd be able to steal him. She would bring him to all the parties. Forget Henry. She wondered if it would it make Christian jealous. She pictured herself introducing Mark to her friends, the girls would be jealous for sure, but would the guys try to kick his ass? He surfed and he was Australian, maybe he would be accepted, like having Occy in their crew. Yeah, maybe.

"You know in Australia, Sheilas lay out topless," he said, eyes fixed on her chest.

She was feeling a bit drunk and reckless.

"Yeah?" she replied, looking around as if she might actually do it.

"Yeah, it's quite normal Kristen."

She actually considered doing it. Maybe that would show him that she's worldly.

"Hey, hand me another beer, Mark."

Henry looked at Natasha and reached out to touch her face, but pulled his hand back. She smiled and touched his hair. He put his head down like a dog to be petted so she patted it on the spiky points that he had slathered in Ajax and egg whites for extra stiffness.

"Like a porcupine," she whispered.

Smiling, Henry lifted his head and grabbed his hair, making it stick out even further.

She didn't laugh at the silly face he made, but instead gave him a serious look.

"Natasha?" He stopped smiling.

Suddenly she backed away from him and started breathing hard.

"What am I doing here? Who are you?" she gasped.

173

He wasn't sure what to do. She looked around and seemed panicky. His eyes were wide as he watched her trip out and realizing that he didn't really know her. Was she freaking out? What should he do? He looked for Kia or Erica. Maybe one of them could calm her down. Kia and Christian had disappeared. Morgan, Gerard, Zane and Erica had their heads in a huddle and their arms around each other and were swaying back and forth making tribal moans. Maybe that was where they needed to go. He didn't want to be alone with her.

Natasha's eyes were wide and she was anxious.

"Sshh," he said to her, "look we are going over there." He pointed behind her. She didn't look. "Natasha," he whispered gently, "everything is OK. He stood and extended both of his hands to help her up. She didn't look up but raised her arms for him. He helped her over to the group.

Henry felt as if he was carrying a casualty from the war and could see that his friends were oblivious to the situation. Let us in, he thought, she's wounded. He tapped Zane on the shoulder. Zane was the crew's General. They were really going strong at this point with their arms around each other swaying in a circle, chanting and moaning. Natasha leaned harder into him as if she was going to pass out. Henry forced Zane and Erica apart, putting himself and Natasha between them. Morgan and Gerard were across from them and everybody's head was down, eyes closed. Henry sat next to Erica and she put her arm around him, he responded in kind and guided Natasha into the circle. Henry closed his eyes and swayed with them as colors exploded behind his closed lids. Who knew how long they remained entranced before Natasha started chanting, "Love, love, love!"

Soon everyone followed her lead chanting, "love," until all of a sudden it was over. The all felt as though they had completed something.

CHAPTER 19

Gerard sprung up and looked around. "Fuck! I'm thirsty!" he shouted and ran toward the ocean. "Shit man, you can't drink the ocean," Henry thought. Before he knew it they were all up to their knees in the water looking for Christian and Kia. Henry held Natasha's hand and pulled her along the water as they looked for their missing friends. But now it was beautiful. No one was worried. Erica jumped into Zane's arms and they fell back into the water. Henry, in slow motion, saw them get up laughing, and it was alright. They all trudged on. Where are Christian and Kia? Now, it was a mission. They stopped and huddled together like a football team before the next play.

"So," Morgan said, "Where did they go?" He was giddy.

"Don't know," Zane replied as though he was about to get the next play from the quarterback.

"I say we get out of this fucking water and search the beach,"

Morgan was serious.

"I think we're turtles," Gerard chimed in.

Mark handed Kristen a beer but halfway through it she remembered who she was. She wasn't about to take her top off for some married guy. She was Kristen! Not some dopey girl who was vulnerable to the power of his suggestion. She smirked to herself, confident that she wouldn't fall for that bullshit.

"Well, chicks may do that in Australia, but here it's illegal. I think," she retorted.

"Oh, what a shame my wife has no problem with it. And her breasts are so full and spectacular from being pregnant. You don't have to worry about being embarrassed in front of me," he said, looking back at the ocean.

Well, his wife was a pregnant, fat chick, Kristen thought. Then she smiled, why not give him a thrill? His wife is fat and pregnant. He was probably is dying to see her with her top off. Poor gorgeous guy.

"What's it worth to ya?" she flirted.

"It's no big deal. I'm used to topless girls on the beach." He turned his attention away from her and back to the ocean sipping his beer.

I'll show him, she thought as she reached back and untied the various strings keeping her inside her top then laid back and

177

closed her eyes. The sun felt good and she was a little buzzed, so it seemed natural to lay there without a top on. Without opening her eyes she knew he was staring at her. She wouldn't open her eyes to check. She wouldn't. A few minutes went by and then she heard, "Hey, Kristen!" It was not a voice with an Australian accent. Shit. She opened her eyes, sat up and quickly covered herself.

"Oh, hey Mickey." She tried to smile at Mickey and also Ramsey standing next to him, both in their wetsuits holding their boards. They'd just gotten out of the water.

"You don't have to cover yourself up, we already had the view," Mickey smirked.

"Hey, I'm Mark." Mr. Australia reached his hand out but Mickey didn't oblige.

"Yeah, hey man," he nodded up at him then looked back at Kristen, "You all good over here?" asking in his own way if this guy was bothering her.

"Yeah, I'm good. Mark was just telling me about Australia. It's all good." She took one arm away from her chest and used her hand to shield the sun as she looked at Mickey, and nodded.

"OK . . . ." Mickey stepped back. "See you around." He and Ramsey walked away as Kristen watched before resuming eye contact with Mark. He smiled at her. She smiled back.

Henry and Natasha, still holding hands, walked up the sand to her VW bus. He opened the sliding door and they sat on one of the bench seats. His feet and pant legs were wet. He bent down yanking off his shoes then removed his pants. Standing in his boxers he placed his pants over the front seat to dry. Natasha, wearing shorts so only her legs were wet, removed her slip-on Vans as Henry sat back down. He picked up her hand.

"Fuck, this is weird, he mumbled. "I haven't been this high for years."

She was quiet. He looked over to see her staring at the ceiling of the van.

"You, OK?" he asked.

"Yeah, I'm alright, but these fairies won't leave me alone."

"Huh?"

"Wicked fairies," she murmured, "everywhere—and they have fangs. They always bother me."

Henry's eyes grew large and he casually let go of her hand.

"Yeah," she continued, "devil fairies, they follow me."

Henry became increasingly uncomfortable and a sickening, dark sensation rose up through him.

"Huh?" he said, looking around.

She flipped her feet up and rested them on the back of the driver's seat, causing her ankle bells to chime.

179

"I wear these bells to ward them off, but they still follow me," she explained.

Henry felt naked and cold. He looked out the window. Where were his friends? He reached forward and touched his pants hoping they were dry. They weren't. He pulled them down. "Get out," he thought.

She grabbed his left arm and forced his hand between her legs. "Henry, get the Devil out of me," she said with her head slumping to the left, her eyes rolling, and her jaw slack.

"What?!" He stood up and rushed to get into his pants. "What the fuck happened to you?"

"Henry!" she screamed, "Henry! Hairy balls! Hairy head!"

She was tripping hard. She reclined back in the bench seat all the way to a horizontal position and pulled off her skirt and panties, "Fuck the Devil out!" She was naked, but she was crazy. No way! He lost all attraction to her. She was losing it.

"Natasha, no."

He zipped the fly on his Dickies.

She was squirming and panting. Holy shit, what was happening?

Kristen felt hungry, hot, sweaty and somewhat drunk.

"I'm hungry," she exclaimed.

"Sandwich?" he asked, reaching in his cooler.

"No, I've got food back there," she motioned to her house.

"You live there?"

"Yup." She got up and grabbed her towel. She was taking him home. "Come on," she told him as she gathered her stuff.

"You want me to go home with you?"

"For food."

"OK."

He collected his towel, cooler, board and wetsuit. She wandered off toward her home, a little tipsy from drinking beer in the sun without food. Trudging in the sand felt like a hardship. It seemed to take forever to touch pavement. Finally, there was solid ground and she turned left to open the door to her house. She walked into the cool foyer and felt him right behind her. He deposited his belongings there.

She headed to the kitchen. Her face and body felt burned and hot. She opened the freezer letting the cold air blow on her face. The maid stored tons of meals for her mom her and to re-heat.

"What do you want? Lasagna or enchiladas?" She turned around to see him seated at the counter. His face was flushed and sandy. She stopped herself from gazing at his beauty. He outdid her. He was truly breathtaking. She was always the most attractive person in the room. Not this time.

"I'm not hungry—for food." He smiled.

She stepped back losing her footing at what he was implying.

"Mmmmm?"

He got up and joined her in the kitchen. She still had the freezer open. He stood behind her and untied her top, letting it fall to her feet. The air from the freezer makes her nipples instantly hard.

Henry looked at this seemingly crazy girl grinding her ass into the seat, legs wide, screaming for him to rid her of the Devil.

He stared at her, frozen. She began to moan and growl. Henry looked at her open pussy. He hadn't had too many opportunities for sex and this morning he'd fucked the most beautiful girl he had ever seen—and now this. But he couldn't. Something was seriously wrong with her. He turned and opened the passenger door, cold air flew at him. She didn't stop. Zane was right there when he opened the door. His eyes looked at Henry's face and then beyond him at Natasha's writhing pelvis and exposed pussy. Wide-eyed, Henry shrugged with disbelief.

"She's fucking tripping!"

Henry jumped down to the sand. Zane looked past Henry at Natasha who was now yelling, "Get them off me! Fuck the Devil out of me!"

Zane looked at Henry: "What are you doing? Go!"

He pushed him back toward the van.

"Huh? No."

Henry noticed Zane was alone. "Where is everybody?"

"Looking for Kia and Christian," Zane responded, looking over Henry's shoulder at Natasha, again.

"Dude, seriously, she's fucked up."

"You want me to help her?" Zane appeared to be salivating.

Henry looked back at Natasha who was fully naked and screaming.

"Can you help her?" Henry pleaded.

"I can," Zane pushed past Henry jumped in the van and shut the door.

Henry sat on the sand and heard Natasha scream, "Help me!"

His eyes scanned the horizon, his body heavy with fear.

CHAPTER 20

Mark's hands were cupping Kristen's breasts. He began kneading and pulling. He turned her around his mouth searching for hers. They kissed and it was sloppy. Wait! Her mind stopped. He was awful. She pushed him away for a moment, and tried again. He was all tongue and mouth. It was gross. He couldn't kiss. Her dream was fading. How did he get a chick pregnant? She pushed him back again. He grabbed her closer and tongued her again. She resisted,

"You're a terrible kisser," she said.

He became enraged. "No one tells me I'm terrible, you skank!"

His accent was gone. She broke free and ran.

"Come here bitch!" he grabbed hold of her by the elbow spinning her around. "You slut."

What the hell was going on? He was not Australian anymore? "What happened to your accent?" His hand was on her elbow, squeezing, "Oww!"

"Shut up!" He pulled her toward him. She placed her free hand on his chest trying to push him away but he wouldn't let her go and she felt sharp pain in her wrist.

"Stop it asshole!" She screamed.

They struggled and he overpowered her. The pain in her left hand shot up her arm and she winced. She was frightened. This had never happened to her. His eyes were angry and his mouth was set in a hard line, his face determined. He grabbed at his shorts with his free hand, his other hand now around her throat. He slammed her onto the couch while stepping out of his shorts. In all her terror, Kristen couldn't help but notice his perfect penis. But still she struggled to get away from him. He smelled of of sweat and anger, pushing on top of her. Her arm was squished up against the cushions and it was throbbing.

"Get the fuck off me!" she screamed, again, hoping her neighbors or someone could hear her. He removed his hand from her throat and covered her mouth, ripping off her bikini bottoms. She slapped at him but he turned his head to deflect the blows.

He rammed himself into her with one hand over her mouth, the other on the armrest to steady himself.

"Open up you slut," he growled, "you know you like it. Fucking taunting me all day, stupid bitch."

185

He definitely no longer had an Australian accent. Kristen was confused and helpless. She squeezed her eyes shut, tears seeping out the sides. She suddenly thought of Henry, nice Henry. "Come save me!" her mind screamed. Engrossed in fucking her, he released his hand from her mouth. She was resigned to what was happening physically but images of Henry, followed by Christian, came to mind and she wished one of them were there to pull him off her. She should have never talked to this guy, what an idiot. What if he has some disease? Who was this asshole? Obviously not who he said he was. She was really scared. She wanted her mom!

Henry sat outside the van. He could hear Zane trying to talk to Natasha.

"Calm down! Hey! Calm down! You want me to fuck you?"

"Please, fuck the Devil out of me," she whined.

What in the world was wrong with this chick? Henry thought. What was Zane doing in there? Was he really going to fuck her? What about Erica? Come on bro, don't do it.

The van rocked to the side like there was a struggle. Henry couldn't sit there like a pussy. He jumped up and turned toward the door but he couldn't see inside. Fuck it, She didn't deserve this even if she was crazy. He pulled open the door and saw Natasha on top of Zane on the floor by the seat, and she was trying to pull his clothes off. He appeared to be fighting her off.

186

"Henry get her off me! Fuck man, help!"

Henry pulled Natasha back and she quieted down but continued thrashing until she knocked Henry in the eye with her elbow.

"Owww! Fuck!" Henry shrieked, still strong.

Zane stood up. He was wild-eyed. "Hold her!" he yelled, looking around the bus.

"What are you looking for?" Henry struggled.

"A fucking blanket or something!"

Apparently there wasn't one, so Zane grabbed her shirt that she'd flung on the passenger seat.

"Let's get her dressed!"

Natasha turned around like a scared animal and scratched Henry's face. "Fuck!" he cried out in pain, letting her go.

Zane was holding her shirt, frozen in disbelief when she lunged at him. He slapped her. "Get your clothes on you crazy bitch!"

"You're the Devil!" she screeched before jumping out the passenger door naked and running down the beach.

Henry's hand was covering his eye, he was bent over in pain.

"What the fuck just happened?"

Zane looked stunned holding her limp shirt, his head facing the direction she'd run.

"I have no fucking idea."

"Were you trying to fuck her, man?" Henry faced Zane, his hand still over his eye.

"I thought about it, then, I don't know, I just wanted to calm her down and help her. I like Erica I really do." He seemed amazed at the realization. He dropped Natasha's shirt and asked Henry, "You OK?"

Henry looked at him with one eye, "Fucking crazy," he smiled.

Kristen checked out. Her mind was numb, her body was numb, she just wanted it to be over. He grabbed her hair and pulled. She winced, his tongue sloppy all over her mouth. She pursed her lips, revolted. He was in his own world pushing into her. The house was so quiet. Where was her mom? Momma, please come home. He thrusted once more hard, and she felt a ripping sensation in her vagina. So much pain! He gasped and shivered like a total asshole. She wanted him off her but she was afraid to move. He was gasping and she got the feeling he was pleased with himself. He got off her suddenly and she remained frozen with fear. He turned away and bent down to grab his shorts. She thought about attacking him but was too broken and dazed to move. She watched him from the couch as she lay paralyzed and he got dressed.

He put his shirt on very casually never once looking her way. She heard him walk toward the foyer and grab his stuff. The door opened and he left.

Her legs were still open. Her arm throbbed, as she tried to make sense of what just happened. She stayed that way for a few minutes before realizing the door was unlocked. She tried to address it quickly but the pain was distracting. Finally on her feet, she rushed to the front door and bolted it. She stood there fully naked with her hand on the deadbolt and began to cry. She cried out of shock, out of terror, out of fear. Slumping down on the floor, her bare ass on the cold tile her cries became hysterical.

Henry moved his hand down from his face, "How does it look?"

Zane replied, "You're bleeding. She got you good."

"Fuck, it hurts like a bitch."

"A bitch hurt you," Zane laughed.

Henry smiled. "Fuck that was crazy. Where did she go?"

Zane shrugged, "Who cares? Let's go to the ocean and put some saltwater on that cut so it doesn't get infected. Who knows what a crazy chick like that has going on?" He got out of the van. Henry followed him, his hand covering his eye.

They walked silently to the water. Henry squatted in an attempt to throw water on his face; it wasn't working. He rolled up his pants to wade in. He got water in his cupped hand and threw it onto the cut. It hurt! He did it a couple of times and waded back toward Zane who was standing there smoking a cigarette.

"Got another?" Henry asked.

Zane pulled out a pack of Marlboros and handed one to Henry.

"My hands are wet, light it for me."

Zane lit it and put it in Henry's mouth. Henry ran his wet hands down the sides of his shirt squinting against the smoke.

Zane looked around, "Where the fuck is everybody?" The sun was setting.

Henry sat in the sand staring at the ocean, "I'm not high anymore, yeah, I don't think I'm high anymore."

"Yea, me either," Zane replied looking down at him, "Where the fuck is everybody?" he repeated.

Henry looked to his right down the shoreline, it looked as if some people were in the far distance.

"Look over there," he pointed for Zane.

Zane squinted. "Yeah, that must be them. Shit, they went far."

Zane sat next to Henry in the sand, smoking cigarettes, waiting for their friends to come back.

190

Finally their friends came into view: Christian, Kia, Erica, Morgan, Gerard and Natasha wearing Christian's hoodie which covered her to mid-thigh. Erica was holding her hand. Natasha's head was down, hair in her face. Henry watched them approach.

Morgan reached them first, "What the hell happened? That chick was running down the beach naked and screaming!" Morgan looked at Zane then Henry. "What fucking happened to your face?"

Henry touched the throbbing scratch on his face. "She tripped out, ripped her clothes off and wanted me to fuck the Devil out of her, then attacked Zane and when I pulled her off him she attacked me."

"Damn.." Morgan snickered, "Crazy one!"

The rest of the group walked up to them, except for Erica and Natasha who walked to the van.

Christian sat down next to Henry and asked him what happened.

Henry repeated the story for the group. As soon as he was done, Kia walked off toward the van. When she left, Zane started laughing and went into all the details Henry had left out.

"Her titties were flying everywhere, butt-ass naked trying to wrestle me and pull off my clothes. But fuck man, she is strong! If Henry hadn't come in she could have bit off my dick and her mouth would have been foaming."

The guys all chuckled.

Gerard chimed in laughing. "She would have been running down the beach with Zane's dick in her mouth, maybe Henry's dick stuck in her ass," he laughed harder.

The absurdity of that picture was hilarious to them.

"Let's get the fuck out of here, this has been a weird fucking day," Christian said as he stood up, "I'll drive.

The five of them trudged their way to the van not sure what to expect, but each one of them wanted to get the fuck home and get something to eat.

CHAPTER 21

Kristen was exhausted from crying. She sat there dazed, whimpering, trying to make sense of what had happened. It was painful to move. Her wrist was definitely broken or badly damaged; her vagina was throbbing with pain. She laid on her side in a fetal position against the cold, hard tile. The house was getting dark as the sun was setting behind the beach-facing windows. She closed her eyes, and wished for her mother to come home.

Kristen realized she'd fallen asleep when she heard a key in the door and the doors begin to open hitting her in the legs. The house was dark.

"Mom?" she said.

"Kristen? What are you doing on the floor? Move out of the way. What the hell are you doing?"

Kristen tucked her legs up to let her mom in but didn't get up.

Her mom stumbled in drunk.

Fuck, Kristen thought, she's drunk again, just when I need her the most.

"Mommy?"

Her mom towered over her looking down.

"Kristen what are you doing lying naked on the floor?"

"I was raped," she started crying again.

"What?!" her mom shrieked.

"I was raped and I think he broke my wrist," she said between sobs.

Her mom crouched down staring at her, "Can you get up?"

"No."

"Come on," she said scooping her up before falling on her own ass.

"Fuck mom, you're drunk."

"No, I'm not," she slurred.

Kristen cried harder. Her mom clumsily took off her shoes and tried to lift Kristen up again.

"Owww!" Kristen wailed.

194

"Kristen! I'm trying to help you!" Her mom's voice took on a strict tone as she struggled to help Kristen up.

Kristen felt herself be hefted to her feet and they stumbled toward the couch like they were in a three-legged race.

"No, not there," Kristen looked toward the couch with disgust.

"Huh? Here. . .." Her mom gasped as she clumsily placed Kristen in the chair next to the sofa.

She grabbed an afghan from the back of the chair and covered Kristen with it. Then she sat on the couch and pulled out a cigarette. In a daze, Kristen watched her mom. "She's sitting there fucking smoking when she should be helping me," Her mom's head snapped back and she looked at Kristen with glazed eyes.

Kristen was filled with fury . "Call a fucking ambulance, call the fucking police!" she screamed.

Her mom took a drag off her cigarette. "What happened? Did one of your boyfriends do this? Who did this? What happened?" It came out all mumbled. Her mom sat back on the couch staring at her, eyelids heavy.

"Goddammit Mom! I was raped right there where your fucking drunkass is sitting!"

Her mom didn't register, she just sat there smoking. "Let me call Roger." she said getting up and wandering off to the kitchen to call her boyfriend.

Kristen started crying again. Her mom was so useless. I'm her baby, her heart cried, I'm her baby and she can't help me or protect me.

She heard her mom calling Roger and asking him to come over and saying she didn't know but something was wrong with Kristen. She hung up, "Roger is coming over."

Kristen didn't reply, she just curled up inside herself and got quiet.

"Let me get you some clothes. We don't want Roger to come over while you're naked," she warned as she stumbled off smoking her cigarette.

"And call an ambulance," Kristen whispered.

CHAPTER 22

Christian drove the van to Natasha's house. Everyone was completely quiet on the drive back. No one dared say anything, no one wanted to take sides.

Christian pulled up to her parking space and shut off the van. Henry opened the sliding door and they all filed out. Christian turned to Natasha and handed her the keys. She handed him his sweatshirt that she was hugging even after Erica helped her get dressed. She turned without a word and headed back to her home.

They rest of them walked to Big Bob's where their cars were parked.

"I feel sorry for her," Erica mumbled.

"Me too," Kia added.

"I don't," Zane said getting out another cigarette and lighting it. He put his arm over Erica's shoulders.

"Were you trying to fuck her?" she asked.

"What? No! I was trying to help her, babe. She lost her shit! She fucking flipped!"

Erica peered at him and he stood looking back at her, casually smoking his cigarette.

"She was crazy," Henry added trying to help.

"I was helping her, right, Henry?"

"He was," Henry confirmed. "Look Erica, look what she did to my face."

Erica turned toward him and then looked back at Zane.

"She was naked," Erica stated.

"She had a nice ass," Gerard added,

Morgan giggled.

"Shut up you guys," Kia said, "Something is really wrong with her."

"You brought her," Zane sneered.

"She was cool out in the water," Kia replied as they walked on.

"Just forget her. Come on, I'm starving," Zane said.

"Yeah, me too," Christian added grabbing Kia's hand.

They got in their cars, each headed in a different direction. Henry started up his ol' jalopy and drove down the street heading home. He drove by Kristen's and decided to stop in and see her. He parked across the street, walked over and knocked on the door.

After a minute a woman smoking a cigarette answered. "Who are you?" she asked.

"Is Kristen here?"

The lady stood in the doorway looking him over.

"Did you do this to her?" she leered.

"What?" Henry stepped back.

"Henry! Henry! Come in," he heard Kristen's voice.

"Mom, fucking move and let him in. Henry!" she screamed out.

Henry looked past her mother. Kristen was in the distance in a blanket on a chair.

Her mom turned sideways and Henry saw Kristen's hands motioning him to her.

He slowly stepped past her mother.

"Hey," he said, approaching with caution.

"Oh, Henry," Kristen broke out in tears, "Come here."

As soon as he reached her an older man stepped in the doorway.

"Hey, babe," he kissed her mother before leering at Kristen. "What's happening?"

"Kristen says she was raped."

Henry heard this, his eyes shocked looking at Kristen who was nodding her head, tears streaming down her face.

"Did you do this, you little fuck!?" the man screamed at Henry, enraged.

"Huh? What? No!"

"Did you try to touch her you little shithead?" Her mom's boyfriend lunged toward Henry, "She scratched you pretty good. She put up a fight at least."

"What the fuck?" Henry ran behind Kristen's chair putting it between him and what he sensed was an intoxicated lunatic. "I just got here."

"Stop it!" Kristen screamed, "It wasn't him!"

Roger stopped his attack, her mom stood behind him, unsteady.

"What is going on?" Henry said mostly to himself, having walked into chaos. What a weird fucking day it had been. Kristen was crying and howling, and some dude named Roger

200

was staring at her and Henry.

"Cheryl, what the hell is going on?" Roger asked Kristen's mom.

"I came home and Kristen was lying naked on the floor in front of the door and . . . she said she was raped," she burst into tears running into Roger's arms. He held her but looked at Kristen. Henry didn't like that look, he seemed creepy.

"Henry, Henry," she turned behind her pleading, "Get me out of here."

"Yeah, sure," he came around the front of her chair.

"I can't get up," she cried.

"You're not taking her anywhere," her mom said, separating from Roger, "I'm calling the police." She turned toward the kitchen to reach the phone.

Henry helped Kristen up. She was clutching her blanket with her good hand, "Take me upstairs to get dressed."

Her mom was sitting on a barstool looking through a phone book too drunk to remember to dial 911. Roger was standing in the living room watching Henry gather Kristen.

"Now hold it," he said, "She needs me to help her." He swatted at Henry's shoulder. Henry shrugged him off helping Kristen who was crying and not standing steady.

"Look man, knock it off," Henry yelled.

"Fuck you, don't touch her. Come 'ere baby," he tried to push Henry away.

"Don't let him touch me, Henry," she whimpered.

Henry had enough fucking craziness for one day. He let go of Kristen and pushed Roger away.

"Leave her alone!" he yelled.

Roger's eyes narrowed. "Fuck you punk!" He swung at Henry, missing him by inches. Something in Henry snapped. He fisted up and knocked the guy on the jaw. Roger went down, and out cold.

Kristen's mom screamed, "Roger!"

She ran toward him and drunkenly fell on top of him.

Henry looked at Kristen, her eyes pleading with him, "Just take me to the hospital, please."

He helped her step over Roger and her wailing mother, and they went through the front door to his car. He opened the passenger door and helped her in. He ran to the other side, jumped in and started the car. He tore off down the street fishtailing as he roared off.

"Fuck, Kristen, what happened?"

"Just take me to the hospital. My wrist is hurting," she mumbled.

"OK, OK, I'm here," he reached for her hand but settled on

her leg instead.

They drove in silence to Ventura County Medical Center. He pulled up next to the emergency room door entrance and ran inside. He found a nurse and dragged her outside to the car.

"She was raped. She was raped." He kept repeating. The nurse opened the passenger door and spoke quietly to Kristen then raced back to grab a wheelchair. Henry watched frozen and helpless. He went around to the passenger side to see if he could help but the nurse was all business.

She helped Kristen into the wheelchair and as she was rolling her in said over her shoulder, "Move your car." Then she was gone through the automatic doors whisking Kristen away.

Henry jumped in his car to park it so he could go find where they took Kristen. His mind raced as he drove to the parking lot. Raped? Who raped her? What happened? His thoughts were entirely on her as he parked and ran back to the hospital. Unsure where to enter, he had to explain himself a couple of times to find the waiting room.

What the hell? he wondered over and over. Who raped her? He sat for an hour between smokes. As he was sitting, two uniformed cops came and asked for the location of Kristen Dewster. He sat up and followed them down the hall. He shuffled behind them until one of them turned around.

"What are you doing?"

"That's my girlfriend, Kristen Dewster."

"Come with us," he directed.

Henry followed them to a room where Kristen was in bed with bandages wrapped around her wrist. She looked spent. Her hair was sweaty, but her eyes and face were beautiful. She saw the cops then she saw Henry.

"Henry," she whispered.

He pushed through the two cops and stood by her side.

"Did he do this to you?" One of the cops abruptly asked, staring at Henry.

"No, no, that's not him. No." she grabbed Henry's hand.

"Well he looks like he got a good scratch on him," the other retorted.

Henry's hand went to his face.

Kristen turned her head, "Yeah, what happened to your face?"

"Uh, nothing, long story," he tried to change the subject away from his face. He squeezed her hand. She pulled it away, in pain.

The cops looked at Henry like he was a dirtbag.

"What happened?" One of them continued.

"I was at the beach today, minding my own business and this guy," she stopped, "this guy kept harassing me." She looked at Henry and reached for his hand. He didn't give it to her, instead he put his hands in front of his chest. She continued bewildered.

"And he said he was from Australia, like I really believed him, and we talked and he kept giving me beers. I didn't want the beers," she continued her face getting red, "and a couple of my friends—Mickey and Ramsey—came by and asked if I was OK, but they just left, left me there with this psycho. I was scared, but they just left."

"Did they know you were in danger?" an officer asked, writing down Mickey and Ramsey's names.

"Ummm, yeah, I think so," she stammered.

"Why didn't they help you?"

"I don't know," she began to cry.

"So you were on the beach drinking beers, and you were uncomfortable but you didn't leave with your friends?"

Henry looked at her confused. If Mickey and Ramsey were there they would have protected her. WTF?

"Um, yeah, I was scared" she looked down tears flowing.

"So then what happened?"

"I got up to leave and he must have followed me. I went home. I live right there."

Henry pictured this in his mind. His friends would have helped her, that's all he kept thinking.

"And then I walked in my door and he pushed his way in from behind, and then he threw me on the couch and it was terrible. I fought him!" She lifted her bandaged wrist.

She looked miserable, but still pretty Henry thought. Shit, this happened to her while they were tripping on Ecstasy? He felt terrible.

"So he pushed his way in. Did you know him?"

"No, I thought he was Australian, said he moved here with his pregnant wife. I was just being nice."

"What did he look like?"

Kristen visibly gulped and looked at Henry. "Umm . . . long brownish-blondish hair, 6'2" or so."

Henry registered her uneasiness.

"What color were his eyes?"

"Blue, green? Light colored."

"Was he fit, out of shape? Any distinguishing marks or tattoos?"

"He was in very good shape, he was a surfer. I guess you would call him attractive. He kind of resembled Tom Curran, I guess."

"Who?"

"Tom Curran the professional surfer, but better looking."

Henry didn't like the way he was feeling about her describing this guy who attacked her. Why would a good looking guy feel like he had to rape a girl? A guy who looked like she described who seems to have it made in the looks department, like Kristen, have to force himself on any chick?

"Can you describe him to a sketch artist?"

"Uh, yeah, I guess."

"What was his name?"

"He said Mark. But I don't know. When he was raping me he didn't have the accent."

"He no longer had the Australian accent?"

"No."

"We need to do a rape kit and get a sketch artist. Where's your family?"

Kristen looked annoyed and to the side facing the opposite wall, "My mom's at home with her boyfriend, Roger. He's a retired detective." She smirked at the cops. "They are a couple of drunk idiots. "

The policeman raised his eyebrows writing that down. "Does she know you're here?"

"I don't know, her boyfriend attacked Henry so we left."

"Why did he attack Henry?"

"He thought Henry raped me. But he didn't. He came over after it happened."

"Why did you go to her house?" the cop said turning to Henry.

"I, uh, just wanted to come by and say hello. I hadn't seen her all day after I dropped her off in the morning and I was driving home." Henry stammered uncomfortable with where this was going.

"Dropped her off? So you two were with each other last night?"

They both nodded. "Are you a couple?"

"I don't know." Henry replied and Kristen gave a firm "Yes," at the same time.

She glared at him, the cop continued taking notes.

"And where were you today?" the cop asked him.

"I went surfing out at Hollywood Beach after I dropped her off then I hung out with my friends."

"Your friends will corroborate this?"

"Definitely."

"Of course they will," the officer mumbled. "You guys all stick together."

"What?" Henry leaned forward.

"What happened to your face?" The officer pressed.

"Uh, a chick scratched me."

"Why did she scratch you?" The cop stepped closer to Henry

nearly backing him up to the wall.

Henry hesitated as this was looking bad for him. "Uh, see this chick we didn't know was hanging out with us, and she, umm, kind of tripped out and attacked me."

"Why did she 'trip out'?"

"She was on drugs," Henry tried to look the cop in the eye.

"Did you supply her with these drugs?"

"No."

"Were you also on drugs?"

This is where he needed to make a choice to tell the truth or deny everything. Damn. "Nope, just her."

"I see. So," he said turning to Kristen, "you were not in the company of this young man after he dropped you off until he arrived at your house after you were raped by a man you call Mark who was Australian and then not Australian, who looks like a professional surfer, but better looking."

Kristen hesitated, distracted by whoever the fuck Henry was hanging out with that did that to his face. Who was this random chick and what drugs were they taking and who was there? Did her friends see him with this girl? Was he with her?

"I don't know what he was doing this afternoon," she stated with ice in her voice.

"OK."

"It may be we are actually dealing with two cases here. I'm going to need you to come with me," he said, turning to Henry.

"What? I didn't do anything!" he protested backing further up against the wall. The cops reached for him to detain him. Henry reacted by fighting back and getting the hell out of there. No chick is worth this! Are they all fucking crazy or what?

"No man! Get your hands off me!" Henry yelled as they took him to the ground in the hospital room. One of the cops called for backup to retrieve a suspect after they cuffed him and led him from the hospital room as he struggled and cursed.

Kristen was confused and pissed. What the hell were they doing? She was the victim. There was a psycho guy out there and they were focusing on Henry? She was left alone in the gross hospital room with no one to hold her hand and help her through this ordeal. She found the button to ring for the nurse. After a few minutes a nurse came in. Kristen yelled at her, "I need a phone! Can you call someone for me? Please, I'm alone," she cried again surprised there were more tears to give.

"Shhh, it's okay honey," the nurse tried to soothe her. "Do you want me to call your mother?"

"Hell no! Can you call my friend Melissa? Here's her number."

CHAPTER 23

Sunday

Henry sat in lockup through the night. The cops questioned him for a couple hours and got the truth out of him; how he spent his day and everyone's names and phone numbers. He was released to his parents late the next afternoon. He was told that there was no physical evidence of him being with Kristen (thank you, condom) but that was after they took his DNA. He was told not to leave the county pending further investigation. Henry went to his room after the ride back. His mother had asked every possible question while his dad retrieved his car from the hospital parking lot. His mom was an old-school kind of mother from the Philippines. His dad was from Texas and worked on the oil rigs. They met when they were in their 20s. Henry was their only child. They knew he was a good kid, he'd never given them any trouble and so they mostly let him be. They bought him his first drum set when he was five. His mom came from a musical

211

family. They didn't get the punk rock music he played these days, but when he was little his dad played some guitar and his mom sang and they used to have fun playing different varieties of music. They were a cool people, very normal, quiet, everyday unemotional people. Henry had lived in the same house since he was born. It was all he knew; blue collar working family. All good.

He went to his room and shut the door. He flopped on his bed—the same bed he shared with Kristen a little more than 24 hours before. He grabbed the pillow she had slept on inhaling it, looking for the smell of vanilla and chocolate. It smelled only of a bonfire. He put it aside and stared at the ceiling. All the stars and planets and stuff had long ago lost their ability to glow-in-the-dark. Now it was just an old memory, trash really, from when he was a kid and stuck them to the ceiling for their comforting glow. He would fall asleep after staring at the universe he'd created.

He was so tired now. Why did he have to be arrested and sit in a cage for hours? He was just a kid. Only 19 years-old and forced to stay awake in the corner of the holding-cell while vatos from Colonia and blacks from who knows stared him down. What the fuck did he do wrong?

Melissa finally showed up the next day and sat with Kristen while the cops interrogated her again. She was wheeled out for a rape kit and semen was taken from her to be analyzed. It was humiliating.

"When can I leave?" she asked anybody who would listen, over and over.

Melissa tried to bully the staff to let her go home but they had their regulations and rules. She gave a description of "Mark" whose DNA they had since he had ejaculated inside her. She was terrified of having some disease, and they assured her they tested her and she will just have to wait for the results. They told her not to have sexual intercourse until the results were ready, like she was stupid or something. Finally she was allowed to leave.

She was wheeled out with her hair stuck to her head and no make-up— embarrassing. People sitting with their broken loved ones looked at her with sympathy.

"Get me the fuck out of here," she grumbled for Melissa to hear.

"I am," Melissa replied through gritted teeth, worn out from all her attempts to make that happen.

Kristen sat in the wheelchair under nurse's guard while Melissa went to fetch her car. The nurse was silent, tired of the primadonna, though sad for her nonetheless. Rich girl, spoiled girl but still sad she went through the trauma. "Thank God she didn't have kids," the nurse smugly thought.

Melissa tore up the driveway stopping in front of them in her black VW Rabbit and jumped out to open the door, but the nurse beat her to it to get Kristen on her way. Melissa jumped back in the driver's seat and took off before Kristen had her seatbelt on.

"Fucking slow down! Shit!" Kristen said buckling herself in.

On the drive back to Hollywood Beach, Melissa lit a cigarette and said between puffs, "So what really happened?"

Kristen looked over at her annoyed, she already felt gross and humiliated, now she had to repeat herself.

"Oh fuck, Melissa what should I do? It is mostly like I said, for real. I was raped." She tried to cry again but she was over it, she was mostly annoyed. She wanted her bed with the clean sheets, and her expensive bath products, and she wanted to feel beautiful again. Right now she just felt dirty.

"This guy—and let me tell you he was hot—raped me." She felt the truth rise up and confided in the crazy bitch she knew was a lesbian. Damn, she wishes she had called Erica. She was gentle.

"Yeah?" Melissa drove fast to every stoplight just to almost slam on her brakes when it turned red. She couldn't get her home fast enough.

"Yeah, he was gorgeous! And I thought he was Australian, like Occy you know—so much better than Henry or even Christian."

Melissa didn't know who Occy was and didn't care. "So better than Henry, well that's not a stretch," she laughed. "Better than Christian? If you say so."

"I don't know what happened," Kristen trailed off.

"You got raped, that's what happened," Melissa retorted.

"Shut up." Kristen felt defensive. "What guy has ever thought he could touch me unless I let him?"

On that note Melissa concurred she was right, "That's true." She just wanted to drive on in silence, drop Kristen off and go home.

"So they arrested Henry, and I don't know why or what happened to him, but I think I should stand by him." Kristen trailed off again.

Melissa groaned, pretty chicks are so stupid.

"Why did they arrest Henry?"

"He had scratches on his face from some chick who was tripping, supposedly." Kristen got lost in thought wondering what really happened.

"Maybe he's not the nice guy you think he is,," Melissa replied.

"He is. " Kristen affirmed. "He really is."

Henry slept through the day not waking up till dusk. He opened his eyes and took in his room. It was a disorderly mess. His bed stunk, there were dirty clothes on the floor and empty beer cans on the nightstands. His closet was open and he turned his head to look at it, to just look, like he was seeing everything for the first time. It was as though he was taking in his environment as a new person. He sighed. His closet was nothing but broken skateboards, dirty shoes and empty hangers.

215

He looked around noting his old broken dresser, the posters on his wall he hadn't changed since eighth grade. The room had a dusty, dark feel. He sat up and turned around lifting the blinds behind his bed. There was a concrete path facing a brick wall. He saw a couple of old patio chairs and a dirty, most likely broken, barbecue. Mickey had broken it at some point when they were partying there.

Depressed, he sat back down. He'd never felt bad about being poor before, why did he feel that way now? Maybe being in jail, the Natasha incident, and Kristen being raped. His life was brown—brown walls, brown house, brown outside, just brown. He laid back and stared at his feet. He didn't want this anymore. His heart hurt. He wanted change. He turned over and buried his head in his pillow, feeling confused.

Melissa walked Kristen into her house. No one was home. Her mom never came to the hospital. Melissa told her she had to go, hugged her, and left. Kristen shut the door and locked it. She turned around and felt the silence. The house was full of light but she didn't see it. She went to the windows facing the beach and closed the curtains drawing the house into darkness. She turned back around to look at the couch. She pictured him fucking her and how she laid there like a victim. She was pissed at herself and ashamed. She felt so alone.

She went upstairs to her room and shut the door. Her pretty room made her feel a little better. She shut the curtains up there, too. She stepped into her bathroom for a shower and filled the room with steam. She poured her expensive bath wash into her palm it was going to help her feel like herself again. She lathered up and rinsed. She lathered up and rinsed again, filling her nostrils with perfume. She grabbed the shampoo and poured it on her wet hair, taking the lather and rubbing it between her legs, rubbing back the old Kristen, the badass bitch that everyone wanted. Halfway through her fury she sat in the tub and just let the hot water run over her.

Henry got up and started picking up the trash in his room. He went into the kitchen in his boxers and grabbed trash bags. His mom yelled from the living room, "Henry, dinner, eat."

"No, it's OK mom, I'm cleaning my room." He rushed back into his room and started shoving trash into the bag. Then he ripped his posters down and shoved them in, too. He took all his clothes and dumped them in the hamper which he took to the washer. He dumped them in with detergent, turned on the water and slammed the lid shut. He was dazed and delirious but on a mission. He went to the garage and grabbed his dad's sledgehammer. Taking it to the backyard, he saw the broken barbecue and decided to beat the shit out of it. Why not? Everything around him was broken. He started slamming into it making a bunch of noise. His mom came to the doorway to see her son in his boxers killing their barbecue. She rushed back in and his dad came out. He stood there for a minute watching Henry let out his fury before stepping behind him and grabbing the sledgehammer from his hands on a back swing. Henry turned around snapped out of his moment. His dad just looked at him.

217

Henry was panting.

"It's a piece of shit!" he yelled tears coming out of his eyes.

His dad said nothing.

"Everything we own is a piece of shit!" Henry cried now. He sat down in an almost broken chair, defeated.

His dad stood there looking down on his son. He put the sledgehammer against the wall and sat in the other chair.

"Sorry, Dad. I, just . . . fuck!" he yelled.

His dad remained quiet. Henry silently sobbed, his shoulders shaking.

They sat together for a few minutes. His dad took out a cigarette, lit it and offered Henry one. Henry reached over and took it. His dad handed him a lighter. They quietly smoked while Henry calmed down.

"Dad," he finally said looking at the ground, "I want more."

His dad took a drag and said, "You should."

Henry looked at him with red eyes and saw his dad as a man and not just his father.

"What?" he asked.

"You should want more. What are you going to do about it? You hang out with these kids partying, or whatever you do, and now you are in trouble because of it. I do expect more from you and

218

want you to make more of yourself. I'm a redneck from Texas. I was raised poor, your mother was raised poor. We are doing the best we can. When are you going to get your shit together?" He looked over at Henry and Henry detected a slight smirk.

"Really dad? You're smirking?" Henry took a drag.

"Well it's just stupid to me to watch you run in circles."

"What do you mean?"

"Think about it. What do you love? What are you good at? What makes you happy?"

Henry looked back down taking a serious drag off his cigarette and thinking. "I love my friends," he replied sincerely.

"Sure, but have they got you to where you are now, or where you want to go?" his dad replied.

"I dunno they're my bros. My family." Henry replied then righted himself. "You know, not like you and mom and all."

His dad frowned and continued to smoke looking at the sky above the wall.

"I dunno, I like playing the drums. That makes me happy."

His dad nodded and put out his cigarette. "Yes, you are good on your drums, though I don't get the music you play now, when you play you are . . .." He stopped.

Henry looked at him, "What?"

His dad stood up, "you're you." He put his hand on Henry's head then turned and walked back into the house.

Henry sat back smoking and looking at the sky over the wall.

CHAPTER 24

Kristen turned off the shower and watched the water drain from the tub. She hugged her knees till it was all gone and the heat disappeared from the room. She got out chilled. She didn't want to be alone anymore. She grabbed a fluffy towel and dried off. She looked at herself in the full length mirror with the towel around her wet hair. She was beautiful. She was. She checked her front and back, everything was perfect. She took the towel off and blow-dried her hair. Then she put thick lotion all over her body and glancing back at the mirror she decided she didn't even need makeup. She looked like a younger version of herself. She pictured herself as 12, before her parents divorced and her dad and mom used to call her their princess. Well, her dad did. They would go to fancy dinners and her dad always looked at her and smiled. She looked at herself, again. She put her hands on the counter and peered into the mirror. Where did that girl go? She decided she wasn't going to do this. Wasn't going to go there. She opened the door and went into her bedroom. She looked in her dresser for a cute nighty and put one on. She felt pretty, she looked good.

She laid on her bed and decided to call Henry. She wondered if he was home. What happened to him?

The phone rang at Henry's house. He heard his mom answer and then she came to the back door.

"It's Kristen," his mom gave him a disappointing look.

He looked in his mom's eyes and shook his head no. "Tell her I'm not here, or I'm sleeping or something."

His mom nodded, said something into the phone and hung up. She came back to the doorway. "Henry get some clothes on and eat some dinner."

Henry put out his cigarette and came inside. He grabbed some shorts from his dresser and went into the kitchen to get some food from the crockpot. He sat at the counter to eat just as someone knocked at the door. His mom opened it and let Zane and Mickey in. Henry was shoveling food into his mouth as they walked into the kitchen.

"Hey," Zane up-nodded at Harry.

Mickey sat at the counter and asked Henry's mom for some dinner. She fussed around and made plates for Zane and Mickey before going back to the living room to watch TV with her husband.

Zane stood at the counter eating, "What happened to you? Heard you got arrested."

"Yeah," Mickey gobbled down the food then yelled to the living room, "Great dinner Mrs. Petit! So what happened?" he turned to Henry.

Henry stopped eating and sighed, closing his eyes, "After I left everyone yesterday I went by Kristen's to say hi or whatever. When I got there she said she had been raped."

"What?!" Zane exclaimed.

"No shit?" Mickey said with a mouthful of food.

"Her mom was there drunk, and then this dude came right after I got there and he was drunk, too. He thought I did it 'cause this fucking scratch on my face," he lightly touched his face to confirm the raised scratch was still there. "So he rushed me and I knocked him out cold."

Zane laughed. "Hoo hoo Henry!"

"So Kristen was begging me to take her outta there. She was naked and wrapped in a blanket."

"Mmmmm," Mickey mummered. Henry shot him a dirty look.

"So, I drove her to the hospital and cops came and started questioning me about this stupid scratch and how I got it. Kristen was telling them it wasn't me, but they went after me and I fought them too."

Zane snorted.

Henry turned to him, "What?"

"I don't know, you did a lot of fighting yesterday, damn."

"Yeah, so," Henry continued, "they took me to jail and questioned me about who I was with and what happened and wanted everyone's names and numbers."

Zane nodded and continued eating.

"So wait," Mickey finished his plate and set it aside," who did they say raped her?"

"Some guy at the beach. Zane you got a smoke?" Henry replied.

Zane tossed a pack on the counter. As Henry lit his cigarette Mickey spoke up, "Yeah, I saw her yesterday at the beach, me and Ramsey. She was fucking laying out topless next to some dude."

"What?" Henry almost choked. "What do you mean she was laying out topless?"

"Yeah," Mickey continued, "fucking titties out next to some guy."

Henry's brain froze on the picture of Kristen lying out half naked next to the guy she said raped her.

Zane said, "Sorry bro, told you she's a slut."

Henry looked at him then to Mickey, "Tell me what you saw."

Mickey explained that he and Ramsey walked over, asked her if she was OK, she said she was, and they left.

"Did she look scared?"

"Nope. Maybe a little drunk, I dunno."

Henry's stomach lurched into his heart. That lying bitch!

"That fucking lying, fucking bitch!" Henry exclaimed pounding the counter, "She told the cops she was scared and you guys left her there. I knew that was wrong."

"She what?" Mickey exclaimed.

"Yeah, she gave the cops your real names."

"That skank," Mickey muttered.

"Alright," Zane took control, "we are calling that bitch right now and she better have her fucking story straight."

The three of them got up and went to Henry's room leaving dirty dishes behind for Mrs. Petit to deal with. Henry grabbed the phone from the kitchen on his way and stretched the cord to his room shutting the door behind him. It only reached halfway so the three of them sat on the floor.

"Call that bitch," Zane hissed.

Henry looked at the phone then he picked up the receiver and realized he didn't know her number.

"What's her number?"

"Shit, I don't know," Zane shrugged. Mickey shrugged too.

"You know Erica's number?" Henry looked at Zane.

"Yeah, hold on," he pulled out a small black phone book, located Erica's number and called.

"Hey it's me Zane. Yeah hey, yeah hi, so can you give me Kristen's number? For Henry. Yeah. Uh, he just wants to call her. Yeah, I'm at his house. Do you know anything about what happened to her yesterday? No? OK. No, nothing. Can I have her number for Henry? Thanks. Yes, I'll call you later." He hung up and handed Henry the receiver. "Dial that bitch."

Henry stared at the phone, then sighed and dialed her number.

Kristen picked up after the first ring. It was Erica.

"Hey Kristen, I just got a call from Zane to get your number for Henry. How's that going?"

Kristen laid on her bed and smiled. "Good, I think. He's really been there for me after what happened." It felt good to hear from Erica, she could tell her story to someone who would give her sympathy. Erica asked what happened and Kristen gave her all the details, playing up her role as a victim.

"Oh my God, Kristen! How horrifying! Are you OK?"

"No, do you think you could come over? I'm alone."

226

"Sure! I'll be right there. You need anything? Poor baby."

"Maybe some Boone's Farm wine if you can score it. I just want to forget."

"Yeah, sure, I'll try. Be there soon." Erica hung up.

Kristen hung up and kept the phone on her chest. Erica would be there soon. She needed the company and the sympathy.

When is Henry going to call?

Henry hung up, "It's busy."

"Try again," Zane prompted.

"Give me another cigarette," Henry said with his palm out.

Zane gave him another, they both lit up.

"Give me the phone," Mickey ordered."What's her number?"

Zane dialed and Mickey grinned giving the thumbs-up sign.

"Hey Kristen, it's Mickey."

Henry moved closer to the phone so he could hear.

"What's up, Mickey? Ummm, I'm waiting for a call from Henry."

"Yeah, yeah, he's here. So I'm calling to find out what you told the cops."

Henry's heart stopped, the moment of truth.

"Huh? What do you mean?"

"You know, when Ramsey and I saw you yesterday you looked pretty comfortable."

"What? No . . .. then silence. "Uh, no Mickey, I was scared. You know that."

"No Kristen you weren't. You told us to go away, basically. What the fuck were you doing with that poser and then saying he raped you?"

"With your tits out!" Zane chimed into the phone.

"Shut up, Zane!" she yelled into the phone, "you weren't there!"

Zane grabbed the phone, "No but my boy Mickey was and he says you're lying. And fuck you for fucking over Henry!"

Kristen was taken aback. No one talked to her this way.

"Fuck off, Zane!" She slammed down the phone. Shit. She looked at the phone. They hate her. She started crying. She grabbed a pillow and threw it against the wall. Then she screamed and no one was there to hear her. No one was there for her.

Zane put down the phone and looked at Henry. "Fuck her man, she's a slut. I told you." Henry shrugged, but inside he was heartbroken.

"I thought she liked me,' he whispered.

Mickey spoke up. "Don't trip man, you got a good piece of ass," he smiled.

Henry looked up at his two friends. They looked back at him smiling, trying to make it better.

All three of them were uncomfortable, they didn't know how to deal with emotion.

Though inside he was miserable, he didn't want all this attention, and he didn't want his friends to be uncomfortable. But there was a truth he felt that he couldn't suppress and he needed to talk about it.

"Hey," he started, "Thanks guys but," he stopped himself. "I, uh . . .."

Zane cut him off. "Don't. Look, fuck her. Oh wait, you did!" he laughed, "but so did I and a bunch of other dudes. I know what it's like, you know? But she's not worth it. Find a good girl. You deserve a good girl." Zane sat back. Henry knew what he meant.

"Aww, fuck 'em all," Mickey stood up, so did Zane.

Henry followed suit, looking down at the phone on the floor, he understood.

Zane looked around and commanded, "Call Eddie. Let's play some music."

Henry looked at his friend, "Yeah, let's play some music." He reached for the phone again. Music was his girlfriend, now. Music wouldn't fuck him over.

CHAPTER 25

Kristen heard the doorbell. She ran down the stairs and opened the door to Erica standing there with her overnight bag.

"Come in," Kristen said still crying.

Erica put down her bags and hugged Kristen. Kristen sobbed. They stood in the foyer for a few minutes and Erica held her tight. She pulled away and looked in her eyes, "You OK?"

"No."

"Come on." Erica shut the door and took Kristen's hand. She led her into the kitchen and pulled out a bottle of Boone's Farm. Kristen smiled.

"Thank you, Erica."

Erica smiled and opened the wine. Kristen took her glass and gulped it down. She motioned for another. Erica obliged.

"So, what happened, again?" Erica was calm and caring.

Kristen looked up at her and tears poured forth again. She knew she was a liar. She knew she was a bad person. She just wanted to hold on though. Being pretty, being popular was all she had. She was totally alone except for that.

"I was raped," she blurted out.

Erica took a drink. She motioned toward the couch, "Let's sit down. Tell me what happened."

Kristen looked toward the couch, the fear crept into her eyes. "No, that's where it happened."

Erica looked back at Kristen, "Oh, really? OK, we'll stay right here." She reached for Kristen's hand and grabbed it across the counter squeezing it. Kristen drank some more getting her thoughts together.

"Yeah, so, I was at the beach yesterday 'cause I couldn't find you or Melissa," she looked up to Erica meeting her eyes insinuating because they weren't around this happened to her.

Erica twitched, "Yeah, I was hanging out with Zane. I'm sorry."

"He's a dick, by the way, called me a liar. And what happened yesterday? Some chick scratched Henry? What's going on? You guys ditched me and was Henry with some other girl?" Kristen angrily turned the tables on Erica. Maybe she couldn't be trusted after all.

"No, we, well me and Zane were at Big Bob's and Kia showed up with some chick who just moved here. We all ended up at Arnold's Road on ecstasy." As soon as she said it she knew how that sounded.

"Kia!" Kristen yelled, "you were hanging out with Kia!"

"Yeah, well, no, not originally," Erica took a drink.

Kristen was angry. She felt redeemed. Her friends were assholes hanging with Kia while she was getting raped.

"Kristen listen, I was hanging out with Zane, I like him," Erica stammered.

"He's an asshole," Kristen drank and finished her second glass. She grabbed the bottle and poured another.

"Henry didn't do anything wrong," Erica continued. "That girl tripped out and attacked him. He didn't do anything. Are you two OK?"

"No!" Kristen screamed. "Because of your asshole boyfriend we are not. Fuck those guys!" Kristen grabbed her drink and plopped down on the couch oblivious to the fact she'd just told Erica she didn't want to return to the scene of the crime. Erica followed her and sat in the armchair holding her drink.

"OK, Kristen, tell me what happened to you. I'm sorry."

"You know what, Erica, I was raped. You weren't there. I think Zane is an asshole, and Henry doesn't want to be with me because of it," she sobbed looking for attention.

Erica sat back in her chair speechless staring at her friend. She let Kristen cry and quietly drank her wine.

Kristen spilled, "Ahhhhh, everything is a mess. Come here and hold me."

Erica complied.Kristen cried into her shoulder.

"Hey, hey, shhhh. Calm down and tell me what happened." Erica said stroking Kristen's hair.

Kristen finally settled down and pulled away. It felt good to have Erica there, she felt so alone. She just needed Erica to believe her and stand by her.

"So, Henry dropped me off and took off surfing, or so I thought, and I was bored and didn't know where anyone was so I decided to lay out. And this guy started talking to me and he was gorgeous with an Australian accent." Kristen got livelier as she retold her story." And you know I usually ignore guys who hit on me, plus you know, I'm with Henry now, or I was." She looked up tearfully at Erica for sympathy then continued. "Anyway he kept giving me beers and he was talking about his pregnant wife so I was just trying to be friendly because they just moved here, so I was telling him that this was a nice place to raise a family. Oh my God, Erica he was so fine." The corners of Kristen's mouth curled up slightly. "And then because I was drinking on an empty stomach in the sun I was getting hammered. But I still felt safe, you know, he was married. Then he was telling me how girls lay out topless in Australia and I told him they don't do it here 'cause it's illegal' plus I'm not like that. He got aggressive with me after that and I started to get scared. He said I had to take my top off and he showed me a knife he had and said I better or he would hurt me. I thought, 'God, this guy is crazy, and there is no one around to help me.' I was afraid, so I uh," Kristen closed her eyes tight and said, "so I did quickly and laid down with my eyes closed thinking if I did it he would calm down and leave me alone.

Erica gasped, "Oh no, Kristen."

"So then I heard Mickey and Ramsey walk up so I covered myself and I'm sure they could see I was scared, I never lay out topless. Why would I do that? But they didn't help me, they just got their jollies seeing me topless and left. They left me with that psycho!" Kristen starts to sob again, almost believing her own story, caught up in her manufactured drama.

"What? They didn't help you? Wow, that seems weird."

"No, they didn't!" Kristen glared at Erica. "And then that guy forced me home with that knife and of course no one was home, and when we got inside he forced me on the couch and raped me." On that last statement Kristen jumped up from the couch and ran back to the kitchen to sit on a barstool. Erica got up and followed her. She put her arms around her, hugging her hard.

"How did it stop? What happened? How did he leave?"

Kristen truthfully told the rest of the story about him not being Australian after all, and her mom and Roger coming, and Henry coming in and Roger attacking him, and going to the hospital, and the cops taking Henry away.

Erica couldn't believe all that had happened to Kristen. She felt so bad.

"Why did Zane call you a liar?"

"He said Mickey told him I wasn't scared when they saw me that day. He's a liar! They are all liars. All of them! Now everyone hates me and I'm the victim here! Me!" She poured another drink, completely devastated.

"Oh God, are the cops looking for this guy?"

"I don't think so, they were more interested in what happened to Henry, can you believe that? And my mom never came to the hospital. I had to call Melissa to pick me up and she was worthless. That bitch couldn't wait to drop me off at home and just leave me here by myself."

Erica shook her head in disbelief.

"You believe me right? I would never lie to you. You're my only real friend."

"Of course I believe you! You poor thing. What can I do for you?"

"Just stay here with me. And stick by me. And straighten everyone out. I can't believe everyone has turned on me. Zane needs to apologize to me. Hell, everyone does. I thought Henry was better than that especially since I was basically slumming by being with him. But I thought he was nice and I'd give him a chance, you know?" She took a drink catching Erica's eye. She was directing Erica to clean up this mess on her behalf. If Erica

236

believed her everyone else would because Erica just doesn't lie.

"Yeah, of course I'll stay with you. I'll explain it to everyone. It sounds like there was big confusion. I can't believe those guys and Melissa didn't have your back. Wow." Erica was still. "It was a crazy day yesterday. A lot of weird things happened."

"Not weirder than getting raped," Kristen exclaimed.

"Of course not," Erica assured her. "Of course not. Look this will get straightened out. I will go to the cops again with you tomorrow if you want."

Kristen thought about that, "Yeah, maybe. But maybe I just want this behind me, you know?"

Erica tried to sympathize. "OK, but if that guy is out there he could do that to someone else."

"Yeah, I know, I just want to forget it for now and lay in bed with you and drink and watch TV. OK?"

Erica smiled at her, "OK, let's do that."

They grabbed the other bottle, went upstairs and laid in bed together watching TV as Erica tried to keep Kristen calm and figure things out.

Monday

Henry woke up the next morning feeling better. Playing music always made him feel better. That's where his focus should be. He checked the clock and was relieved he was up in time to pick

237

up Eddie and Zane and go surfing. He grabbed his board and spring suit and went to fetch his bros.

Kristen woke up and nudged Erica.

"Hey."

"Morning," Erica replied.

"I'm starving. Let's make some breakfast and head to Hueneme to lay out. I want to be away from this beach."

"Yeah, OK."

They made their way downstairs to get something to eat. No one else was home.

The guys pulled up at Hueneme and got out to check the surf. It looked decent and uncrowded so their put on their suits, waxed their boards and headed out.

CHAPTER 26

Monday

A little after noon, Erica and Kristen parked at Hueneme and brought their stuff down to a spot by the pier to lay out. They noticed Henry's car in the parking lot which made Kristen hesitant about going on from there. She decided if Erica was with her, and those guys tried to give her shit, she would back them down. The previous night, she'd tried to get Erica to break up with Zane. Erica said she would think about it depending on how he reacted when she told him what really happened.

Kristen just wanted Henry back—she didn't tell Erica that, though. She figured if Henry took her back then everyone would believe her and she could break up with him in a couple of weeks if she felt like it.

The guys were out in the water so the girls spread their stuff out nearby and applied tanning oil. Well, Kristen did; Erica always put on sunblock and a big hat. What a dork, Kristen thought.

Henry rode a wave and noticed Erica and Kristen on the beach. He paddled back out to Eddie and Zane.

"Shit, she's here."

"Who?" Eddie turned around.

"Kristen."

Zane turned around and saw Erica and Kristen. "Damn, she's got balls," he replied.

He looked over at Henry who was staring at the horizon with a worried look on his face.

"Henry, don't stress it man. She's just some piece of ass."

Henry wasn't so sure. He didn't think that way. He remembered their morning in bed and how she made his heart jump when she smiled. And she was so beautiful, dammit. Maybe Mickey and Ramsey didn't get it exactly right. Maybe that guy forced himself on her and they didn't pick up on it. Why was she laying out topless next to some dude? He felt anger spread through his chest. He was so lost in his thoughts he didn't see the set rise up before him until he noticed Zane and Eddie paddling out and getting over the lip just in time. Henry wasn't going to be so lucky. The lip slapped him back over the falls and he went under, swirling around in the moving water, swimming for the surface to grab air. He emerged in time to take a breath and go back under as the next set gave him a good pounding. One more time up for air, one more pounding, and he was done. He turned and paddled back toward the beach, his head and heart not into surfing anymore.

Trudging with his board to the shoreline, he reached down and undid his leash and unzipped the top of his wetsuit. He carried his board to the sand and set it next to his stuff. He didn't acknowledge the girls. He grabbed a towel and put it around his waist, peeled off his wetsuit and put on his board shorts. He could feel Erica and Kristen looking at him but pretended he didn't notice.

Damn, he is a cutie, Kristen thought. He was even cuter because he was ignoring her. She needed to get him back. She sat up and looked away from him toward the surf. She looked down at her tanned legs and tight stomach, her breasts barely covered by her bikini top. He's got to want this, she thought. He couldn't get anyone hotter than her. She decided to ignore him too, hoping he would realize she was mad at him for not believing her. Out of the corner of her eye she could see him sit down, staring at Zane and Eddie catching waves. He must have come out because he saw her there. Why didn't he say something?

"Hey Henry," Erica said.

Henry turned toward her, "Hey Erica." He looked at Kristen then looked away.

"So, how are you?" she asked.

"I'm good," he replied still looking ahead.

"So Kristen told me the cops took you in because of what happened at Arnold's Road."

"Yup." Still staring ahead.

"Oh, that sucks. That so wasn't your fault. That's what I told Kristen."

He didn't reply. He reached into his backpack, grabbed a beer and started drinking.

Erica looked back at Kristen and shrugged. Kristen rolled her eyes and laid down. She closed her eyes but inside she was sad. Tears started to come so quickly that she turned over onto her stomach.

Henry turned around and watched her turn over. He couldn't help but notice her perfect ass. Damn.

Kristen turned her head away from them and silently let the tears pour down. It was quiet for a few minutes with just the sound of the crashing waves. The whole situation sucked. She wasn't used to not being in control of her group of friends. She was the one who was untouchable, never on the bottom, always on the top. Fuck! Come on, Erica, talk to him! Her mind screamed. She turned her face toward Erica, tears streaming down, silently pleading with her to do something to fix it. Erica looked over at her and immediately felt concerned.

"Help," Kristen mouthed.

Erica nodded.

"Henry, can I talk to you in private?"

He looked over at her and saw Kristen's face behind her, tears streaming. They looked at each other for a minute before Kristen turned her head away.

He looked back at Erica and shrugged, "Yeah, I guess."

"Can we go for a walk?" she asked getting up.

He shrugged again, "I guess."

Kristen heard this and smiled to herself. She heard them both get up and walk away. She felt a moment of relief. Erica would fix this.

She laid there alone, hoping the nightmare would soon end, but before long she heard people coming. Bags were being dropped in the sand near her. She looked over and there was Kia, Christian, Vienna, Ami, Dave and Ramsey. Oh, what hell was this about, she wondered. She turned over and sat up glaring at Kia. Kia glanced at her and turned away.

"Hey Kristen," Ami said.

"Hey," she replied still glaring at Kia but giving Ami a feeble smile.

At the same time Zane and Eddie were on the shore taking off their wetsuits. Ramsey looked at her and raised his eyebrows.

She glared at him too. She looked farther to her left and saw Erica and Henry walking down the beach.

Vienna put her boombox down and turned the radio dial to 94.7 KMET. Music filled the air while the newcomers settled in. Zane and Eddie walked up to greet Christian and Ramsey while the girls applied suntan oil. Kia sat the farthest from her and watched Christian. That bitch, Kristen thought. Somehow this was all her fucking fault. Ever since she hooked up with Christian shit's not been right. Zane looked her way and smirked. Then he looked down the beach at Henry and Erica. He toweled off and kept his gaze in their direction. Soon everyone was sitting and drinking beers—and ignoring her.

"Henry, what happened wasn't Kristen's fault," Erica stated walking in the sand next to him.

"I don't know," he was skeptical.

"She told me what happened. Henry, she was scared. Did you know that guy had a knife on her?"

Henry walked on, "No, she didn't tell me anything."

"Huh? Didn't you drive her to the hospital?"

"Yeah, but she wouldn't talk about it."

Erica thought about that, "Maybe it was too soon after it happened and she was, you know, traumatized."

"Maybe," he mused.

244

"Look, she really likes you and is devastated by what happened and would like for you to be there for her."

"I was." He stopped walking and faced her. "And I went to jail and then Mickey told me she was, you know, not scared and hanging out topless with some dude. I thought she liked me." He walked on.

Erica got in step next to him, "She does. She cried about it all last night. I think Mickey and Ramsey didn't see what they thought they saw."

Henry didn't say anything. Why would they lie? He continued to think maybe no one thinks he should be with Kristen 'cause she's so hot. Maybe they are just jealous. The only guy she's really been with from their group was Christian (besides that stupid thing with Zane, but he could be an asshole and he treated her badly).

Vienna was laying out closest to Kristen so she turned to her, "What happened? I heard some dude well, you said, some dude raped you?"

Kristen looked at her like she was a piece of shit on the bottom of her shoe, "Who told you that?"

Vienna looked over at the group. "Everyone, what happened?"

"None of your fucking business." Kristen was mad and lashing out. "None of anyone's fucking business because there are some assholes telling lies," she said looking at Ramsey and Zane.

Zane caught what she was saying and started laughing. "You

245

are a delusional whack job!"

Kristen stood up. "What did you call me?"

Christian stood up too and walked toward Kristen. "Calm down," he said to her and then over his shoulder told Zane to knock it off.

Christian reached for Kristen and put his hands on her shoulders. She looked up at him and started crying. He pulled her against him as she placed her arms around his waist. She was sobbing. "Something bad happened and everyone's lying about it."

He put his hand on the back of her head holding her close. She pulled away looking in his eyes, "And it's because of her."

"Who?"

"Kia."

"What?"

"She stole you from me and since then only bad things have happened to me, and she brought that girl that hurt Henry." She hugged him tight glaring at Kia over her shoulder. Kia stared with her mouth open. She started to get up but Ami pulled her back down and shook her head.

Kristen saw that and nuzzled Christian's shoulder. Christian pushed her away looking into her tear stained eyes, "Kia didn't do anything. Stop it, Kristen."

246

"Yeah, stop with your fake waterworks," Zane yelled before sipping his beer.

Kristen stepped back glaring at Zane, "See first she fucks Zane, then you," she said to Christian, "And now look!" Then she started crying again. Christian just stood there helpless.

"Oh, shut the fuck up you slut," Zane yelled.

Kristen turned red and stormed over to Zane and stood over him, yelling, "You have a small dick!" Then she walked over to Kia and shrieked, "Get up! Get the fuck up!"

Kia looked at her horrified and shocked, "What did I do?"

"You know what you did you pasty, fat, little whore!"

Zane stood up and came over to Kristen seething. Ramsey said, "No bro, don't."

Zane looked at Ramsey. "Tell 'em, tell everyone what that slut was really doing and what a fucking liar she is!"

Ramsey then threw his hands up. "I don't want any part of this."

Zane told Kia, "If you want to kick her ass I'll hold her for you, she deserves it."

"Huh?" Kia looked at them and looked around her, "I seriously don't know what's going on."

Ami smiled at Kia. Vienna fiddled with the radio and found a station playing The Go Go's "We Got The Beat."

"Come on, Kia," Zane encouraged, "get up and kick her ass."

Kia looked down then searched longingly for Christian. He was five feet to her right looking at her and shaking his head.

Kristen was ready to beat down but then Erica ran up to join them, Henry was still down the beach.

Erica ran up to Kristen, "What are you doing?"

Kristen looked at her then back at Kia. "Her!" is all she could form out of her mouth.

Erica saw that Kia was obviously confused. Erica knew Kristen was still in love with Christian and was jealous of Kia. She needed to blame someone.

She grabbed Kristen by the elbow and pulled her to the shoreline. Kristen fought but went along.

"What are you doing?" Erica gasped.

"It's her fault," Kristen kicked at the water.

"Look Kristen I just spent the last 20 minutes explaining to Henry how much you like him and what happened to you, and how your mom is never there for you, and now you are fighting Kia for Christian? Really? What the fuck is wrong with you?"

Kristen took that into consideration, realizing she'd fucked up. But thinking for a moment that she might get Christian back made her crazy. She attempted to get herself together and took some deep breaths. Erica put her hand on Kristen's back.

248

Kristen turned toward Erica, "It's just too much, you know?" she pleaded. "It's all too much. And Zane was egging it on. I told you he hates me. I guess because of that night, I don't know." She threw in that dig, suggesting that she had been with Zane. Erica grimaced and took her hand off Kristen's back.

Henry approached them.

"Kristen," he said.

"Hi Henry," she smiled.

"Wanna talk?"

"Yes."

Erica turned and walked away.

"So what is going on?" Henry asked.

Kristen tossed her hair back. "Umm, I don't know. I mean you were there for me after it happened. You saw how upset I was, you know. And now Zane and Ramsey and Mickey, who I thought were my friends, are lying about me." She tilted her chin up in defiance. "Honestly I think they are jealous because they don't want us to be together."

Henry looked away from her down at his feet. "Yeah, maybe I was thinking that too."

Kristen smiled. "Can we start over, I guess?" She reached for his hand. He let her take it. They just stood there holding hands looking at the ocean. Kristen breathed a sigh of relief. She was

249

gaining control again.

It felt good to hold her hand even though he was embarrassed in front of his friends. He looked over at her and his heart jumped. She was extremely beautiful with her hair blowing back in the breeze, her beautiful body, her gorgeous face.

"Let's go for a walk."

"Ok," she smiled at him.

They turned and walked toward the pier and sat down in the shade of the pylons. He put his arm around her and kissed her. It was good, she tasted so sweet. Whatever happened was done. He wanted to believe her and felt like an asshole for ignoring her if she was telling the truth. That was a fucked up day for both of them.

"I guess we shouldn't be apart so I can protect you from all the assholes. I'm sorry about what happened to you."

"I'm sorry about what happened to you, too." She ran her finger over the scratch on his face that was becoming a scar, and took his face in her hands and kissed it. "To make it better," she said. Henry smiled.

"Do you want to be my girlfriend?"he whispered.

"I do. Yes."

He kissed her again and they started making out heavily, oblivious to their friends. It didn't matter anymore what they thought. Kristen was his girl, fuck them.

After awhile he helped her up and they rejoined their friends sitting next to each other holding hands. Zane looked over and shook his head. Henry winked at him and stuck his tongue out. Zane laughed.

CHAPTER 27

As the day wore on the guys went out for another session while the girls laid out listening to music, drinking beers.

"Whoa, who's that hottie?" Kristen heard Ami say.

She opened her eyes, sitting up and following Ami's gaze. And there he was. The Asshole. He was down the beach zipping up his wetsuit. She would know him anywhere, that long hair and ripped body.

"That's him," Kristen gasped.

Erica looked over then looked back to Kristen.

"That's him?"

"Yup," she whispered

"That's the guy!" Vienna said loudly.

"Shhh." Kristen hushed her staring at him.

All five girls turned and stared.

As he reached down to grab his board he noticed the girls staring at him and smiled. He gave a quick nod before heading out into the water.

"Asshole," Kristen said between gritted teeth.

Ami turned toward Kristen, "Damn, he's fine."

Kristen glared at her then let her eyes follow him out into the water, "Doesn't give him the right to rape me."

"No of course not," Ami mumbled.

The girls all watched him paddle out just down from the guys. He sat on his board and shook out his hair waiting for the next set.

"We gotta tell the guys," Vienna said.

"Maybe they will figure it out, especially if he tries to talk to them in his fake Australian accent," Kristen replied.

"If he's smart he won't," Ami chimed in.

"I don't think smart is a talent of his," Kristen said. Inside she was worried. What if he tells them what really happened? No, it was too late for that. She would continue to deny everything and call him a liar. Only Ramsey may not believe her now, and of course Zane. Fucking Zane.

Kia stood up and walked over to Kristen. "Do you want me to go over and steal his stuff?" she said trying to get on Kristen's good side.

Kristen squinted up at her rival. Kia looked incredibly uncomfortable. Good. Let her make amends for all the trouble she'd caused.

"Yea, Kia, would you?"

Kia nodded and walked down the beach to gather his stuff and carry it back. She came back with a cooler and a towel and set them down before handing Kristen a beer.

"Fuck him," she said smiling at Kristen.

"I wish I hadn't," she said taking the beer.

"Oh yeah, sorry, I didn't you know, mean that." She went and sat back down.

Kristen opened the beer and ceremoniously poured it into the sand. At that moment he took a wave and as he turned to paddle back out he noticed his stuff was missing. Kristen watched him scan the beach before noting her pouring out a beer and flipping him off. He turned and paddled in.

He got to shore and ripped off his wetsuit knowing he had an audience.

Henry looked behind him on the shore and watched some long-hair walk toward his girlfriend. That's him. He knew it. He saw Kristen get up and watch the guy approach.

"That's him," he said to Zane, Ramsey, Dave and Christian while paddling furiously toward the shore. The guys all turned their boards around following Henry. Henry got to shore and untied his board, never stopping on his way toward that asshole who was now with the girls and yelling at them. He saw Kristen get up in his face. It was going down.

"Hey, motherfucker!" Henry screamed as he came at him with his fist but missing the guy's face by at least five inches. The guy pulled back and hit Henry on the chin, knocking him to the ground. Zane looked at Henry and ran toward the guy's waist tackling him to the sand. Zane straddled him and punched him again and again. Henry got up shaking his head and looked at Kristen smiling at Zane beating up this shithead. Henry rushed over to Zane and threw his body between them. "Mine!" he yelled.

Zane got off the guy and Henry stood with his fists up.

"Come on, motherfucker!" he yelled.

The guy sprinted up, looked around then focused on Henry. "Come on, mate!"

"Fuck you and fuck your fake accent!" Henry yelled back.

Erica grabbed Kristen's elbow looking back at the action. Kristen's face was alive, she was smiling.

"Come on!" Henry yelled throwing another punch and missing. Ramsey grabbed the guy from behind and held his arms.

"Get him, Henry!" they chanted. Henry shook his head as he quickly checked the guy out. He was over six feet and muscled.

He was a good looking guy.

He looked over at Kristen. She looked at him raising her eyebrows throwing a fist out. "Do it!" She yelled.

Henry tackled him and Ramsey. Ramsey fell back like a turtle on its shell squirming to right itself. Henry went to town hitting the guy in his face as hard as he could. Everyone hooted and hollered and encouraged.

Soon the guy was out. Henry stood over him victorious like a warrior. His hands were in the air. Kristen looked at the asshole knocked out and saw Henry smiling.

She walked over and kicked sand on the jerk on the ground.

"Yes!" Erica gasped surprised at herself. Kia gave her a side hug smiling. Everyone was happy. It was done, Kristen thought, beaming.

They came together when it was important. Yes, that's what friends are for.

"Let's go," she said to Henry kicking sand on the asshole's face once more.

Henry grabbed her hand and gathered their stuff. Triumphantly they walked back to his jalopy and headed home to his house. Their friends could deal with the mess. They were going home for dinner, and hopefully a fuck.

CHAPTER 28

THE BEACHCOMBER TAVERN
Silver Strand Beach, CA

Where you can escape the sunshine. Tiny place of cool darkness, cold beer, and the best Adams Family pinball game. We all spent years in there before we were legally supposed to. Locals Only. *SSL*

Years Later 1995 . . . Reunited
HOLLYWOOD BEACH, CA

Lisa never really stuck. Her friends already knew her as Kia.

Kia walked out of the liquor store clutching her wine, toilet paper and cat food. Home alone yet again to sit in front of the television. Her son was sleeping at a friend's house. She was bored. She was only 25 and still felt like going out and partying.

She hadn't done that since Joey was born. Being a single mom didn't give her much freedom. Maybe she'd go out, but she wanted to be home first and see how it felt.

SILVER STRAND BEACH, CA

Zane finished his beer at The Beachcomber Tavern—he was the only person there. It was kind of depressing to get drunk alone in the dark bar with the sun still out. But he didn't want to go home. He couldn't stand his baby's momma. She was such a bitch.

Kia resigned to watching Friends. Bored. Bored. Bored. She's knew "he" was out there. Or maybe not. Fuck it! With no work the next day she rushed upstairs to tear through her closet for something to wear. She was going out!

Zane ordered a whiskey shot. Maybe that would urge him to go back to the dingy house he shared with that cunt. He looked at the shot asking him to drink, promising to numb his anger. He shot it back and slammed it down. The sad act vibrated throughout the empty bar. He thought about his baby girl's beautiful little face. Damn, she was cute. She had her mother's blonde, blue-eyed looks, but he was sure she had his spirit. As adorable as she was, he could sense that she was a little rebel to the core. They named her Madison, but he called her Lia, her middle name. He and that whore mama fought over names forever. But Zane had the overwhelming urge to name her after a girl from his past, Kia. Her name was both Lisa and Kia, he remembered. So he named her Madison Lia as a combination of those two names. Kia was a pure soul, something about her that he never realized back in the day when they were hanging out, but came to his mind and heart when Madison was born. He was just compelled to do it, and the best part was Madison's mother never figured it out.

Kia didn't dress up much, just changed her shirt. She gulped her wine and put the empty glass in the sink on her way out the door. She walked over to the Rudder Room. As she entered, the overwhelming smell of sewage and sea lifted to her nose. She smiled to herself. It was part of the charm of this true dive bar. The bar was at the end of the street that ran along the ocean with the jetty immediately to its side. It was the last building before the water that broke up the road between Hollywood Beach and Silver Strand. On more than one occasion her friends from back in the earlier days paddled their boards across the jetty where the boats were going in and out, to surf the neighboring breaks, or hit up a party. She sat at the bar staring out of the huge window that faced the beach and the volleyball courts. The bartender placed a vodka tonic in front of her just as she ordered. The ocean air filtered through the open door, and she never felt so lonely.

Zane had finished his shot but still didn't feel like going home. He got up and put money in the pinball machine. He focused his mind on kicking its ass.

Kia looked around at the men sitting at the bar also staring at the ocean. Some salty old locals, she thought. Looked as though most of them had been there all day every day. Her lips curled up in a smile as she pondered how things don't change. She drank her vodka and stared at the sun realizing it was also still holding its place as the backdrop for this world where everyone lived every day, all day at the beach .

She sighed. She would love to find a good man. It had been so long since she had a relationship and having her son with Christian. They'd really had a good thing while it lasted. Kia wondered if she should have stayed with Christian. He was her first and only real love and relationship, even now at 25 years-old. He was still the most beautiful and caring man she'd ever known.

But after five years and a child together, they never got to the idea of marriage. She began to stew about it and looking over her past she wondered if she was broken somehow and if that prevented her from moving forward. Why else didn't he want to marry her?

Since Christian was a commercial fisherman he was gone a lot. When he got his captain's license and was given charge of one of the busiest and biggest boats running out of Channel Islands Harbor, he was gone even more.

She got a job as a waitress on The Landing a seafood restaurant which had a bar upstairs that pushed out hard drinks on locals and tourists. The restaurant sat on the harbor, right in front of the docks with floor to ceiling heavy glass windows. On rare occasions when their schedules collided she would see Christian's boat pull up and she would watch him conversing with the crew and passengers. Her heart flipped every time she had the chance to watch him undetected. His long blonde hair pulled back from his sun-kissed, ocean-sprayed, glorious face. He had the kind of blond surfer boy looks that could grace any publication of Surfer or Surfing magazine in those ads advertising Rip Curl, Body Glove or any type of surfing apparel. He was almost too good looking, and she never quite wrapped her head around why he chose her over someone as stunning as Kristen. They looked like they could sell the hell out of anything together.

She thought maybe that realization had plagued their relationship. She always felt she'd ended up with Christian by accident. She never felt like an equal, she never grew to become one. Instead she imagined herself as perpetually the fifteen-year-old girl he confessed his feelings too. She didn't want to break the magic that somehow convinced him he wanted to be with her when she wasn't even a whole person.

She'd moved in with him when she was 17, into the cute little house across from the ocean. Her parents let her because they liked Christian and grew to trust him. She got pregnant at 19. It wasn't on purpose, but it wasn't an accident. They were just careless.

Since he gently took her virginity on her 16th birthday that was an area of their relationship she did grow into. Her shyness dissipated over time and she enjoyed the carnal knowledge he shared with her. She began to appreciate the voluptuousness of her full breasts and how he grabbed her hips just below her small waist exclaiming his approval of her womanly shape. She loved lying in bed together afterwards in the quiet moments, when he'd lay on his back panting, with his hand splayed over her flat stomach. The move made her feel his ownership over her. Every feeling as a woman she had making love to Christian she owed to him .

After giving birth to Jake, that connection between them had less and less time to recover. Between Christian's long hours on the boat and Jake's erratic sleeping schedule, as well as the responsibilities of mothering, they became two people doing what they were supposed to do instead of what they wanted to.

The summer she turned 20, she'd already felt old. She had been playing the role of a grown woman for years as a young mother. She had more responsibilities than she was ready for. She also felt more like a person navigating that role alone than in a partnership. It wasn't Christian's fault that he worked so much. It wasn't her fault that her time was divided between work and caring for Jake.

Then, somehow she was pregnant again. In one of the rare moments that they found time to sleep together, between sleeping, one of his guys found its way in to suggest life, and the thought of becoming indentured to yet another child loomed. This time she wasn't excited or even the least bit happy. As much as she adored Christian and Jake, she also resented the fact that she had no time for herself. She came home from work, picked up Jake from the neighbor, and spent the evening just with him most of the time all alone. She no longer roamed the streets on her skateboard or woke to the expectation of catching some good surf before going home to knock back some beers and enjoy the best ceviche. The choice her heart had made at 15, had worn her down to a numbness five years later.

She couldn't face doing it again. She didn't reveal her condition to Christian. He would never know because she wasn't going to keep it, and she wasn't going to keep him either.

She scheduled the abortion to happen when he would be gone on one of his many week-long commercial trips. She still didn't have any real friendships outside the circle of Christian's friends, which were mostly guys. Every once in awhile there was a barbecue that Kristen, Melissa and Erica attended, but as she knew, they weren't her friends. Vienna, Brooke and Ami had fallen off her radar not long after the summer of '85. She'd been so into Christian that she hadn't cared, anyway. But here she was now wishing she had some friends conspiring on her behalf on how to get rid of this unwanted pregnancy. There was no one she could tell who would help her without Christian finding out. But after some serious fretting, she came up with someone: Natasha.

About a week after that day at Arnold's Road she'd checked in with Natasha. She went to her house to see if she was alright. They sat in her living room while Natasha explained the mental illness she had been trying to contain, and how it had been a factor in her leaving Huntington Beach. She'd moved to Ventura County to receive outpatient treatment through Camarillo State

Hospital. She definitely wasn't supposed to take drugs, but she wanted to fit in with her new friends. She called Kia by her real name, Lisa, and explained that she'd never really had friends. Kia understood. She really, really understood. They stayed friends and surfed together when they could. Kia never brought Natasha around her other world again and never mentioned their ongoing friendship.

Natasha provided transportation to and from the clinic the day she aborted her and Christian's second child.

When Christian came home again, Kia told him she wanted to break up. He was understandably confused, sad and then angry. Where was she going with his son? Why was she taking his son from him? Wasn't he a good supporter, a good dad? The words "a good boyfriend" never escaped his lips. She knew she was right to leave. Not to take his son, but to find herself and be on her own. The two had never had a serious fight before, mostly because she never had a strong opinion, but this time she spoke up for herself and the woman she searched to become. Taking Jake away wasn't an option. Christian would never let that happen. Once they cooled down and sat together and spoke reasonably she conceded to share responsibilities. She wondered how he would manage it since he was always gone, but he assured her that if he was gone when it was his time, he had a huge family who would help raise Jake. Where was his family when she was working and spending all her free time alone as a mother? He stated that his family respected their choices and would not step in unless asked. Maybe she should have asked sooner. Maybe it wouldn't have come to all this. But it was too late now, she did something she could never tell him—or live with him knowing.

264

She moved back into her parent's apartment. Her mom was more help than she'd anticipated. She always delighted in being a grandmother but now she took hands-on control. Apparently her parents also respected their decision to try and do everything themselves.

Now Kia had some breathing room. There were more hands and hearts involved in Jake's rearing than just her own. She used that experience to spread her wings more than ever.

She began work at a new harbor restaurant soon after. There was a guy who she noted was a happy hour regular there. She learned his name was Zac and he was a tattoo artist from Brazil. He had the good looks of a man who was self-confident. He was cocky and sure of himself and terribly exotic. He even had an accent that made her strain to understand when she stopped by the bar to pick up drinks for one of her tables. It took a couple of weeks before he noticed her, too. After that, every time she came to the bar to fill an order he would stop talking to whomever he was engaged with—man or woman—and turn his chair to face her direction, smiling. She would always blush and smile grabbing her order and trying to be as professional as possible. He was older than Christian, probably in his 30s—a real man. His tanned face had small lines around the eyes and mouth when he smiled. At the time she thought, "This man has lived," unlike her. Soon he managed to talk her into a ride home on his motorcycle. She remembers climbing on the back of his bike and putting her arms around his waist, holding tight as he sped her through the sandy streets. The smell of his leather jacket filled her nostrils and her body hummed with the knowledge she would soon show him what part of her was a woman (thanks to

Christian).

The first time they fucked was at his house on Santa Cruz Street in midtown Ventura. She took the street name as a good omen. For a couple of months she was free and growing as an independent woman further blossoming in his arms.

Soon after, though, she would find herself becoming jealous when he was at the bar talking to other women as she tried to work. That happens when a connection based on sex stays in that arena. He was her opportunity to try another relationship and she had it in her heart to make it work because she had left Christian and his familiar love which she'd known since she was a child. She did what she shouldn't have: she got pregnant, on purpose.

What she thought would have, should have, brought them closer together had the opposite effect. He pretended for a little while to take it seriously. He came to the bar but the look on his face changed. He was no longer carefree. He was now in a relationship of burden. They talked of the future and he made necessary promises that Kia tried to believe. But then he came around less and less. He told her he was just getting busier at the tattoo shop and people were booking appointments later into the evening. As her belly grew his presence dwindled.

Christian noticed her condition and was hurt and upset with her. And for himself, too, she was sure. He asked who she was with, and if she was just stupid? She couldn't get mad at him. She too was ashamed of her immaturity.

And then Zac was gone. After a week of his not being around, answering his home phone or being there at the tattoo shop, she went to his house on Santa Cruz to find a "For Rent" sign. Just like that she'd traded herself in, hoping another man would love her like Christian did.

CHAPTER 29

Jake is 7 now and lives with Christian on Silver Strand Beach. Sometimes all three of them surf together. It's so good that she has stayed friends with Christian, and that they excel at co-parenting—even after he remarried. His wife is supercool and loves Jake as her own. They have an 18-month-old baby girl and Kia loves her, too.

Then there is her other son, Joey, who is 6 going on 20. He's a little troublemaker just like his dad, who she lost her damn mind over. He's never even met Joey and she never heard from him again. Jake is a replica of Christian: blonde, blue-eyed and classically good looking. Joey, on the other hand, has naturally tanned skin, dark eyes and blonde ringlets that fall about two inches below his shoulders. He glows when he smiles which gives the false impression of innocence while his devilish little mind is working. Zac may have been Lucifer because Joey comes from the Devil.

Oh, Kia groans, she needs another drink.

The door to The Beachcomber opens, bringing temporary light into the dark bar.

Zane turns and sees Eddie walk in. He squints, adjusting to the dimness. He doesn't look happy. Eddie recognizes him and rushes over like he has been looking for him.

"Dude," he chokes, looking like he's been crying. "Henry . . . Henry . . ." he hangs his head in despair. "He's dead, man."

"What? What? What the fuck are you saying?" What do you mean Henry's dead? When? What happened?" Zane falls back against the pinball machine.

"He O.D.d."

Zane just stares at him in disbelief. "He was found by his girlfriend this morning, dead in bed."

Zane stands there stunned, picturing Henry's dead body lying in bed. A feeling of darkness makes his stomach lurch. "Shit," he mutters, "I thought he was off that."

Eddie turns around and orders two shots. Handing a shot glass to Zane, Eddie raises his glass, "To Henry!"

Zane looks up briefly and half-heartedly raises his glass. "To Henry." He tips back the shot but doesn't know why he s cheering Henry for being dead. He grabs a stool at the bar, putting his head in his hands. Fuck. Henry. Probably the nicest guy he's ever met, always happy and childlike.

Eddie orders two beers. Zane hasn't seen Eddie around much the last couple of years. He'd gone to his wedding three years ago and Eddie now has two little kids. He's settled into domestic life marrying a Catholic girl from a large Mexican family. They all stopped playing music together in their mid 20s. Henry got picked up by a popular experimental new wave/punk band and Eddie went to work out on the oil rigs. Zane's been doing construction, drywall in fact, and drinking. He still skates up and down the beach, surfs and plays guitar when he's drunk in the garage. He gets hammered and turns up the amp, until Kristen (yup, that's the baby's momma) comes in and bitches at him. What a fucking whore sac. Still hot, but a royal bitch. Shit, how will she go off when she hears Henry's dead? She'll make it all about her.

How Zane ended up with a girl who he has such disdain for still riles him up. He knew she was a whacko, lying bitch but after he and Erica split up he felt the familiar hardening of his heart begin to form again. He tried, didn't he? He chose to forgive himself and open to love once more. He'll never forget how that steel door of his heart opened for the promise of faith and love. Maybe it was just the after-effect of all the drugs he'd done before that night in his bedroom contemplating suicide. Yeah, he'd consumed a lot of mushrooms and alcohol and maybe he was just fucking tripping. But he did feel happy with Erica, really honestly happy. She was a beautiful pure girl and he really tried to change for her. But maybe it was because she showed up caring for him after that night and it was so unexpected he

270

believed it was a sign. Maybe from that smiling, surfing Jesus; so he went for it. He did the good boyfriend stuff, he didn't even fuck that crazy bitch in the van when he had the chance.But then she started accusing him of all kinds of crimes he didn't commit. He knew Kristen and Melissa were feeding her lies. They seeped out their poison onto Erica and she became confused. He did have a long-standing reputation as an asshole to overcome, after all, and a girl could only fight off so much backlash.

But in some moments alone, when that kind of paranoia wasn't going on, they laughed together and kissed delicately, holding each other tight. He needed redemption so badly. He needed her to give it to him. He needed to love her as much as he loved Aliah, and he really needed a happy ending. But over time the questions and accusations became too much to bear for either of them. Erica wasn't equipped to be angry and suspicious. She deserved to be sweet and trusting and he couldn't give that to her. As the tears pushed heavily from her eyes she broke it off. So that was it. The only thing that pushed that pain down was alcohol. In the years that followed, he played music, drank heavily and fucked anything he could. He figured he was dealing with the pain correctly by fucking and forgetting.

One night as he was at his usual stool at The Beachcomber, Kristen was also there with some dudes from Ventura's Pierpont Beach. Zane treated them all with disdain. The guys from Pierpont he recognized were part of a hood rat gang that ran that beach and they knew not to surf Strand as he knew not to surf Pierpont. There was an unspoken respect and understanding that everyone was protecting their break from each other, but more importantly from the others; the Valleys, etc. So as Zane

271

nursed his drink, he kept his eye on Kristen entertaining these hoodlums from the neighboring beach and making sure they didn't get too comfortable. He didn't trust her, yet she was a local in his eyes and so was considered family.

She came up to the bar stool next to him, her hair in wisps around her regrettably beautiful face and ordered shots for herself and her "friends."

"What's up, Kristen?" he asked out of the side of his mouth not looking at her directly.

"Oh hey Zane, didn't notice you sulking over here."

"Fuck you."

"Fuck you too."

She grabbed the shots two at a time scurrying between the bar and the table. In Zane's mind she looked like she was trying too hard to impress those dillrods. She laughed too hard and too quickly at the conversation.

And wouldn't you fucking know it, Bob Marley came on the jukebox singing "Could You Be Loved?" What the fuck?! his mind screamed. He sat still, taking it all in. That was the song Aliah used to whisper to him. He felt the words and was refilled with emotion that transported him back to a time before the hurt.

"They say only, only, only the fittest of the fittest shall survive, stay alive!," filled the air but it was only he who heard the words. At that moment Kristen laughed but was cut off by the sound of her body falling off her stool. One of the Pierpont

272

guys reached down to help her up, laughing. Zane glanced over and immediately felt sorry for her. She was trying too hard. What the fuck was wrong with her? She was gorgeous and didn't need to cater to these dumbfucks. She was local beach royalty. He couldn't stand to watch her prostitute herself any longer. As much as he didn't respect her, a part of him wouldn't let her take herself down and his world of Strand loyalty with her.

He got up before he even realized what he was doing.

"What's up?" he nodded to the familiar Pierpont dudes and their unfamiliar chicks.

"S'up Zane?" one dude reached out for a handshake.

"Hey," he said nonchalantly, more concerned about Kristen.

Her eyes looked blurry as she tried to focus on Zane.

"Go away," she mumbled.

"You OK?" he whispered in her ear.

She pushed him back with that familiar look on a drunk's face when they're too far gone to know they're too far gone. He remembered that night at the Casa Tropical so many years ago when Aliah showed up with that guy in the other band, pushing him away.

"Dude! Dude! What's up?" the other fuckhead took an aggressive mode.

Zane looked at them all then back at Kristen. She smiled

at him. This is when he would normally shake hands and go back to his drink. But that fucking song made him do something different this time.

"Eh, just checking on my girl you know?" he replied hands up in the air, head cocked to the side.

The guy stood up, "She's fine bro, go back to the bar," he pointed to where Zane was sitting.

Zane looked at Kristen with her chin nodding on her chest. She was a goner. The guy sitting next to her put his hand on her thigh caressing it up and up. He looked Zane in the eyes and smirked.

Zane felt it coming, his rage came up his spine to the top of his head.

He put the hood from his sweatshirt on, letting it fall low over his eyes.

He took a few steps backward putting his hands in the front pockets of his black Dickies.

"Yeah, man, yeah," he turned around and walked back to the bar standing in front of his beer draining it to the last drop. He looked down at his hand strangling the neck of the beer bottle. Then he swung around and charged toward the group of degenerates and clanked that beer bottle over the head of the guy sitting across from Kristen. The two girls sitting next to him screamed and stood up. Glass pieces fell to the floor off his head like amber confetti. The guy went down. Zane turned and

274

lunged at the guy who still had his hand on Kristen's thigh. She fell to the floor as Zane knocked him across the jaw. He wasn't thinking, he was raging. He got the guy on the floor and just kept punching.

The bartender ran out from behind the bar and attempted to pull Zane off. He got elbowed a few times before he was able to hook Zane around the elbows and lift him up.

"Zane! Zane!" he yelled in his ear.

Zane was panting as he stood over the dude he just beat the shit out of.

"Get out! Get the fuck out!" The bartender pushed him toward the door.

Zane looked at him and nodded. He walked over to Kristen and pulled her up—she was light as a feather—and put her over his shoulder as he walked out the front door into the summer sunshine, leaving the darkness behind him. He had a hero complex. Through saving her he was going to save himself. Redemption. He was going to have redemption.

He piled her into the passenger seat of his work truck and slammed the door. She was a limp doll. He got in the driver's side, slamming the door and locking it before reaching over and locking the passenger door in an abundance of caution. As he started the truck and tore off a bottle came flying and crashed on the cab of the truck. In his rearview mirror he saw two angry dudes yelling and cursing but he was now tearing down Ocean Avenue spitting sand behind him.

He didn't go home in case they decided to cruise down every street looking for his truck. Instead he got on Highway 101 and headed up the coast to Oil Piers on the outskirts of Ventura County before Carpinteria.

He ended up pulling over after exiting at State Beaches and parking far from all the carloads of kooks who had nowhere else to surf and party.

He rolled down his window lit a cigarette and stared at the ocean. He glanced over at Kristen who was passed out, her legs curled up in a fetal position.

Man, she was fucked up. And not just drunk, she was a fucked up human being. She was more like him than he ever realized. He was going to . . . what? What was he going to do? She couldn't stand him. He sat smoking and staring at the waves for an hour wondering how to redeem himself with a crazy girl like Kristen.

It was hopeless. He flicked the butt of his seventh cigarette out the window and took her home.

276

CHAPTER 30

As he pulled up to her house he woke her and helped her to the door. She mumbled and stumbled the entire time. The door was unlocked so he brought her in. She hung heavily on him. After taking in the huge living room and noting that no one was home, he turned toward the stairs half-dragging and half-pushing her up. He found her room and helped her on to her bed where she promptly passed out with her skirt raised up to her waist. Zane stared at that perfect ass highlighted by a baby pink lace thong. Her legs slightly spread, her hands up by her head and her hair flowing down her back. He couldn't stop staring. He bent down and gave a kiss to each cheek before covering her with a blanket. Then he looked around her room, took off his Converse sneakers and got on the bed, leaning against her headboard.

It was a long night in his head to say the least. So much pain came at him as he hid in the unfamiliar comfort of her sissy room. As she slept off the day's drunken comforts he tortured himself with bad thoughts and regrets. Why was he so fucked up? Why was he so angry? He got up and walked over to her bedroom window staring at the ocean in the distance roaring to shore. The room was dark, the house was silent. It was just them. It was just him, really. He turned and left her room walking downstairs. Everything was silent except for the sound of the ocean. He unlocked the back door to the deck and sat in one of the comfy cushioned chairs, then pulled out a smoke and lit it. For whatever reason he thought of Kia, she just came to mind. He actually gasped and shook his head. Then he thought of Henry and Eddie and growing up with them and laughing and playing music. They were all gone now. Kia was with Christian and having babies or whatever. Henry and Eddie had their lives wrapped up in other pursuits. He was alone. How in the hell did he end up alone? Shit. He looked up to Kristen's bedroom window and once again resolved to bring her to him. Maybe together they could redo the old times. Maybe they could bring it back. Life on the beach was infiltrated by the grommets now. Fuck them. They didn't know up from down. His mind was going crazy. He flung his cigarette and hopped over the railing toward the ocean. Without slowing his step, he dropped his pants, pulled his shirt off and ran toward the sea. Diving in head-first he dunked under the waves and came up laughing. Fuck 'em all, he thought. "I am the King of Silver Strand and I will have my Queen!"

After his proclamation and impromptu baptism , he ran back upstairs to shower. He ran the water hot and the room steamed up quickly. He stepped in and shut the curtain. He fumbled around with all of her bath products looking for a simple soap. She didn't own one. He lathered up with some coconutty

278

chocolatey body wash. Smelled pretty good. Smelled like her. As he was in the thralls of the exotic smells he heard the door open.

"Who's in here?" He heard Kristen mumble.

He stuck his head out of her curtain and smiled wildly. "It is I, your savior." Then he closed the curtain again.

"Zane, what are you doing here?" she mumbled again.

He popped his head out. "Come here beautiful. Let me take care of you. You had a rough day." Then he disappeared again. She walked over to the curtain pulling it back. She looked lost. She looked as she once had when she was an innocent child. "I feel like shit. What are you doing here?" she asked again.

He continued showering, and Kristen noted his tan and strong body making use of her expensive bathing products. The familiar smells made her feel a little better.

"Come here, sweetheart," he reached out his hand to her.

Slightly baffled, she wondered if she was in the middle of a very realistic dream.

He stood with his hand out and a sincere expression, not the usual asshole look he normally wore.

He smiled.

She stood there for a moment longer, then decided a shower was definitely looking good to her. She pulled off her clothes and stepped in.

He made room for her and they showered together as if it was perfectly normal.

He didn't try to touch her but he definitely took in her beauty as she washed her hair and soaped up that ridiculously gorgeous body.

He got out, dried off and put a towel around his waist before unfolding one for her to step into as he wrapped it around her.

She remained baffled.

He walked into her bedroom dropping his towel and slipping under the covers. She followed and did the same.

He pulled her into his arms and held her. He kissed the top of her head. She closed her eyes and snuggled next to him. They held each other for a few minutes.

"Zane," she whispered, " I don't understand what's happening."

He broke back from her so he could look into her eyes. "You are my Queen. You always have been. I'm so sorry that I've ever been mean to you, Kristen."

She searched his eyes for the cocky Zane she had always known. He wasn't there.

He kissed her and then he made love to her.

The next morning she woke up to find him in her bed. It was as though the night before was all a dream. She told him to leave. But within a few weeks she came to his house to let him know she was carrying his child.

She moved in and took over his home and his life. What he hoped he started in his head with a resurgence of the old-school hierarchy soon faded as their real identities took over. The fighting ensued, made up by the fucking that ensued. The bond that kept them together was called Madison.

And that was that.

CHAPTER 31

Kia decided to take her drink outside to one of the picnic tables on the beach and watch the sun set. Still hung up on being alone she mused on how unnatural it could feel sometimes. She had a good life, otherwise. She lived at the beach, she still looked good, and worked hard to support herself and her boys. Her parents were living at the mobile home park at Hollywood Beach and that's why she rented a condo there to keep their youngest grandson nearby. He didn't care much, he was more interested in getting into trouble with his friends. He was definitely like the boys she grew up with. He and his friends were like tiny versions Henry, Zane and Eddie. She remembered how crazy those boys were. Her son had already brought cops to her door twice for vandalism. She took a sip of her drink and looked at the ocean. She heard voices come out on her right and, no shit, it was Melissa and some chick she didn't recognize. Kia hoped she wasn't going to come over and start anything. They never really squashed what was between them. She purposefully looked to her left, toward the jetty, and figured she should drive over to Silver Strand.

As news of Henry's demise spread across the Strand, all the boys started to trickle into The Beachcomber to drink away the shock and sorrow. Within an hour the place was filling up with old faces—Ramsey, Mickey, Dave, all of them. Someone put some of Henry's band's songs on the jukebox and shots were going around. Zane sat on an end barstool next to the farthest wall, unhappy. He hadn't talked to Henry much over the last two years. Henry was busy touring and living in Hollywood, and Zane had his babygirl and was keeping busy with work and dealing with Kristen. He'd been depressed for a while. He stopped doing the hard drugs but the drinking had kept him from losing his mind.

The door opened and the light rushed in to reveal Kia. Fucking Kia. She walked in and he could see her trying to adjust her eyes to the dusky, filtered light. She self-consciously walked toward the bar and looked straight ahead at the bartender. Zane's heart skipped a beat. Wow, she looked great, still wholesome. This was crazy. How did she end up here, today? He sat back watching her. She ordered a cocktail and turned around, saying hello to some of the guys. She glanced in Zane's direction and caught him staring at her. He couldn't help it. She smiled shyly and walked toward him. He pulled out the empty barstool next to him and she sat.

"Hey, Zane," she smiled.

He couldn't respond. He lifted his shot glass, instead.

"What's going on?" she inquires looking around.

He clears his throat, " Henry died."

Her face said it all: shock, sorrow, surprise.

"What?" she leaned toward him.

"Henry's dead." He repeated.

"When? How?" she mustered.

"This morning," he whispered.

She took a few hard, deep breaths. "What happened?"

"OD."

She looked back down at her drink and sat quietly. He saw a tear slip down her cheek. Fuck . He looked back at his drink. He felt for her. His heart was in pieces, too. He couldn't help but reach out and grab her hand on the bar and give it a good squeeze. She looked over at him, her face was wet.

Zane looked her in the eyes. Out of everybody there telling stories about Henry he only wanted to talk to Kia. She squeezed his hand back.

"Zane, I'm so sorry."

They released hands and looked down at their drinks, the insight and connection between them fading.

It felt so weird to Kia to jet back in time so fast, sitting with Zane who she could never understand. And he was so vulnerable. She just wanted to hold him and touch his head, but he'd always been so hardened it broke her heart. She remembered when they were just kids and she got excited when he showed her attention . . . and then he made her feel like she wasn't good enough. Then Christian came in and changed all that. She loved Christian, she did, but Zane, he made her feel like she belonged for the first time. She thought he was sexy. After he and Erica didn't work out, he got with Kristen and had a baby. She figured that made sense, maybe he was always superficial, but somehow she knew he had more. There was passion in Zane, and darkness, and he had really loved someone before. She knew that because Brooke and Ami offhandedly told her about Aliah. She had hoped Erica could bring him back but that didn't last more than nine months before he cheated on her. Sad. Why was she sitting with him now, commiserating over Henry? Because he and Eddie were the two who were most devastated. She never really connected with Eddie much, though. Eddie was a one-note person. Zane had many levels and she remembered the day they did Ecstasy and she, Zane and Henry hugged. And the time she passed out with them on the beach, each with a hand on her boob flying on shrooms. It was simple, stupid and sweet, and she got it. We can only express ourselves as far as we've grown. But now we're grown, she decided, and it was time to connect for real with Zane. She straightened herself and asked for another whisky shot, plus one for Zane. Let's do this.

She grabbed the two shots and put one in front of Zane.

"I don't know," he hesitated.

"Come on, to Henry," she raised her glass in his direction.

He reluctantly put his hand around it. "Why are we cheering to Henry's death?" He had pain in his eyes.

She put her shot down and held his gaze. "We're not cheering to his death, we're cheering to his life," she explained. " Henry was different. He was special. He was funny. He was sweet. He was a big dork," she smiled.

Zane smiled to himself. "That he was. OK." He lifted his glass and she lifted hers. "To Henry, that big ol' dork!" They drank, then put their glasses back on the bar with a simultaneous thud.

She was starting to feel the effects of the alcohol. Turning around on her stool she looked at her old friends. She hadn't seen most of them for a few years. She moved back up to Santa Cruz for a while after having Joey. Jake stayed with Christian. Christian had a large family support system there at the beach and really did not want to be without his son. She wanted to go home again. She only moved back when her parents moved to the mobile home park. Up in Santa Cruz, she felt like her old self again. She looked up her childhood friends and rekindled those friendships with some of them. Some stuck, some didn't. She and Joey temporarily lived with her best friend Joanna from back then, in Boulder Creek until she got a job bartending at the Boulder Creek Brewery and could afford a little place of their own. She and Joey lived in a little one bedroom, next to a creek in Felton for a few years. She loved it up there. But honestly it reminded her of Ventura County. She lived 15 minutes from the Santa Cruz boardwalk and all the people she met up there reminded her of the locals from Silver Strand.

Her parents really wanted her to come back so they could be around Joey, so she moved back.

Now she was working as a bartender up in Ojai at the World Famous Deer Lodge. The drive at night sucked. It was a 45-minute commute and none of the locals she knew from the beach went up there so she hadn't really seen anyone. She had run into Morgan and Gerard at Mrs. Olsen's Coffee Hut when she and Joey were grabbing breakfast. She also bumped into Kristen's mom at the Rudder Room a few times while her mom was drunk off her ass as usual. That's how she knew Zane and Kristen had a baby together because that woman hung on her for hours one night divulging every detail along with her lack of approval.

She turned back to Zane and he was staring down at the bar looking forlorn.

What to do about him, she mused somewhat drunk.

"So tell me about your daughter."

"Oh, she's beautiful," a smile crept across his face. "She is really special. Nothing to do with Kristen though." The last sentence was said with disdain. "She's still a bitch." He looked back down.

Oh, Kia thought, baby good, Kristen bad.

"So, tell me about her. What's her name?"

287

"Madison. But her middle name is Lia." He looked at her.

"Lia? L.E.A.H.?"

"No, L. I. A."

"Wow, that's unusual. What a pretty name."

"Named after a pretty lady," he grinned.

Oh really, she thought. I wonder who?

"How old is she?"

"She's two. She's so cute. Calls me dad daw. Greatest smile! She's smart, too. And she can draw! I mean really draw, I think she is a little artist. I know all parents think their kids are special but I think she really may be."

"That's awesome, Zane," she smiled at him.

"So, I know Jake of course." He turned to her, more animated. "That boy can surf! I was out with him not long ago and he ripped it up. You have another kid, too, right?"

"Yeah, Joey. He's different than Jake, little more of a handful. In fact he and his two friends remind me a lot of how you, Eddie and Henry were back in the day. You little troublemakers!" she laughed.

"Where are you living?" he asked.

"I'm at a condo on Hollywood Beach. My parents are in the mobile home park down there and they wanted me to move back so they could be closer to Joey. But like I said, he's not like Jake. He doesn't really care about hanging out with his grandparents," she sipped her beer.

"Where did you move back from?"

"Santa Cruz. Remember I lived there before? You know, before my sister died.?" He nodded. "So I went back when Joey was little. I just wanted to see, you know, if I could change things back. I mean, Christian and I had a good thing, but I don't know, I had some healing to do I guess."

Zane let that sit for a bit. So, she wasn't completely happy with Christian?

"And how was it up there?"

She was touched that he was really showing some interest. Maybe a real bond would happen.

"It was good, Zane." She looked over, putting her chin on her right hand. " I loved being home. I would have stayed if I could. The mountains are full of redwoods and the beach is so fun. But you know, it still reminded me of being back here. So maybe this really is my home, after all." She looked away and finished off her beer.

Zane surmised that for a bartender she didn't look like a hard drinker. He could tell she was already buzzed. The old him would be scheming how to get down with her.

Ramsey came up to them throwing his arms around both their shoulders. "Hey you two, cozy like old times?" Before either could answer he went on, "So we are going to hit all of the beach bars in Henry's honor. Let's go! Mickey has his short bus. Let's go. Finish your drink, Zane."

With everyone jammed into the short bus, she found herself squished next to Zane. She could smell his scent and it made her heart skip. Weird how certain people's scents are instantly attractive.

They stopped by Christian's house and Ramsey went to get him. They got back on the bus and Christian's and Kia's eyes met. They smiled at each other and she gave him a little wave. He raised his eyebrows at who she was sitting next to and then gave a good natured laugh as he sat down. It was all guys and Kia on the bus rumbling down Victoria Avenue back to Hollywood Beach to go to the Rudder Room.

Zane sat with his hands in his lap and his left shoulder pressed up against Kia's right shoulder. Every time they hit a bump in the road, her right hand would grab his knee and then quickly go back into her lap. It was incredibly loud with Madness' "One Step Beyond" blaring from the radio and all the guys being boisterous and yelling back and forth.

Zane and Kia didn't attempt conversation the entire way there but he didn't think it was the noise level as much as it was the weird energy between them. It felt like old times, but better He was such a dick to her back in the day. He figured he would apologize to her at some point. Hopefully she would understand he was just a messed-up kid.

290

CHAPTER 32

Mickey found a spot to park and they all filed into the Rudder Room loud and unruly. The old guys sitting at the bar turned around to view the crowd pouring in. Everyone hovered around the bar getting drinks before taking them to the side patio. Kia ordered a Corona and walked outside to see Melissa and her friends still there. Not feeling entirely comfortable because she didn't know if she should sit with Christian or continue to talk to Zane, she just stood there. Come on, this isn't high school anymore, she told herself. Most of us have kids, we're adults now. But still, part of her shyness remained. Would she ever feel like she fit in? Hey, these were her people! These are her friends. Isn't that what she figured out in Santa Cruz? She strolled over to Zane and sat on the picnic bench next to him. She really did want to get to know him, now. OK, go with it, she decided. He smiled at her. She smiled back.

"Soooo," he said, "I wanted to say something to you, but not with everyone around."

"Huh? OK. Why not now?"

"I just don't."

She took a drink of her beer. She thought that was weird. She hated when people did that. Why say you want to tell me something and then don't? So now she'd have to wonder what was up. She looked around a little miffed. Why did he affect her that way? And then just because Melissa also pisses her off, Melissa strolled over.

"So Zane, how are you doing?" She ignored Kia completely.

"I'm good, Mel," he swigged his beer.

"How's Kristen?" She emphasized Kristen's name for Kia's ears.

"Still a bitch, Mel. You should call her sometime."

Kia laughed to herself.

Melissa looked over at Kia, ignoring Zane. "Hey."

"Hey."

Melissa then turned to her friends and walked away.

"God, she's such a bitch," Kia said.

"And a dyke," Zane added.

"Yeah, I thought so. I always thought she had a thing for

Erica."

"She did. Tried to break us up all the time. She was always telling Erica I was cheating on her. She would get Erica paranoid about it. The fucked thing was, I never did."

"Oh, I heard otherwise."

"That's what Erica ended up believing so she eventually broke it off. That sucked, she was a nice girl. . . like you." He glanced over at her and grinned. Kia's eyes grew wide and she took another sip of beer.

"That's weird. I thought you didn't like me."

"Well, ya, that's what I wanted to say to you earlier. I, umm, wanted to apologize for what a prick I was." He turned to her, "I was pretty fucked up back then."

"Yeah, you were," Kia smiled.

"Yeah well, I'm sorry. I didn't want to care about anyone after Aliah."

"What happened that made you try with Erica?" Kia was very interested.

Zane drank more of his beer gathering his thoughts.

"Well that one night I freaked out over at Mickey's on 'shrooms and threw the tequila bottle and shit, I was tripping on Aliah. I thought I saw her. I thought Kristen was her. I hadn't slept with a girl since Aliah died, except you know, what I did with you,

293

and then that night I was high, and I fucked Kristen thinking she was Aliah, I had kind of a breakdown or breakthrough I guess. He leaned closer lowering his voice, " Listen, I haven't told anyone about this but I was contemplating suicide. I was so fucking unhappy and I had this vision. I was going to drown myself surfing and I swear Jesus came to me as a surfer." He looked embarrassed.

"Yeah? Go on."

"And I don't know, I felt peace finally. Like I wasn't responsible for Aliah's death, and God loves me because, you know, I surf and maybe Jesus was a surfer too, you know since he walked on water. Maybe he was the first surfer, actually."

Kia tried to digest what he was saying. It sounded a little crazy, but if it helped him who was she to judge? She sort of liked the comparison.

"So what you're saying is you saw Jesus coming to you as a surfer, and you realized if Jesus was a surfer that God loves you and you are worthy of love?"

Zane nodded. Kia smiled and touched his hand.

"OK, Zane," she paused, "that means God loves Henry too and he's OK now, too, right?"

Zane looked her in the eyes and she could see his wheels turning.

"I hope so."

294

"Well, if it's the truth to you and you believe in it, then it goes for all surfers right?"

She could see tears forming behind Zane's eyes, he grabbed her hand, too.

"Fuck, Kia that's why I like you." He wiped away a tear that escaped down his cheek. He turned away from her staring at the wall across from him trying to collect himself.

She felt protective of him but released his hand and looked toward the crowd, casually sipping her beer so no one would notice he was losing it.

Looking around she realized one thing about being near these tanned, spirited men: The energy in the air was heavy with the feeling that everyone was sexy and blessed. They weren't mortals.

Damn, he thought staring at the wall. Henry, you are OK, man? You have to be. God forgave me, he'll forgive you, too. You're a better person than I am. Fucking drugs! They should have never started up again. Henry got deeper into the Hollywood punk scene and more and more lost. Last time Zane went to one of his shows Henry was distracted and so out of it. Now Zane had lost another person he loved to drugs. Suddenly he was pissed . . and sad.

He turned toward Kia, "Would you leave with me? Go for a walk or something?"

"Sure, let's go."

They got up and tried to slip past the crew. People kept stopping Zane and he would say he was going to the john. Kia just bee-lined to the front door behind him. Once out the front door they hurried down the street.

Kia laughed, "We need our skateboards."

She was referring to the night she, Henry, Eddie and Zane skated to the bonfire when, mistakenly, she thought she was Zane's girlfriend. Then the two of them skated back to her apartment. She thought she was going to lose her virginity that night. She ended up giving it to Christian.

Zane turned to her, "What?"

"We need skateboards!" she repeated wondering if he knew what she was referring to. Probably not. Her face flushed, "Anyway," she went on, "where do you wanna go?"

"I don't know," he paused looking around. "Do you live nearby?"

She felt a sense of déjà vu. Should she bring him to her house? Was it clean? She did a mental check. She didn't want to seem rude, he obviously wanted to talk.

"Sure, just a couple of blocks in those condos Morgan lived in."

He nodded and kept walking. The sun was setting and the sky was beginning to close up for the night with the first stars already out over the ocean. They walked in silence to her home.

CHAPTER 33

He followed her to her front door. He noticed wind chimes and hanging plants and a weathered wooden bench in front with seashells scattered across the seat like they were left there to dry. She also had one of those wooden signs of a big finger pointing to the shore. "SURF" was all it said. She took off her shoes and left them by the door in a pile of flip-flops and boy's Vans.

"Do you want me to take my shoes off?" he asked while she opened the door.

She looked back, "Yes please," and walked in.

He sat on the corner of the bench and removed his Cons. The front of her house felt more like a home than the entirety of the house he shared with Kristen. Her taste was all girly white wicker and pictures of flowers on the walls. Everything was white and pink like he didn't live there at all. The garage was the only place he was able to be himself with his music equipment, flyers from his punk rock days, surf posters, and his one lone Christy Brinkley poster that Kristen hated, which is why he refused to take it down.

He walked in, entering a hallway leading to her living room. She had wood floors and it smelled like a mixture of Nag Champa, ocean air and a hint of bacon that was probably cooked that morning. Her living room had a couple of indoor palm trees and he could see through her sliding glass door to the back patio and it was filled with plants. There were also a couple of chairs, a barbecue and a chiminea. The furniture in her living room was obviously used, but the couches were oversized and looked really comfortable. She had a couple of worn and torn Surfer magazines on the coffee table and a Nintendo hooked up to a pretty old TV. He sat on the couch closest to the coffee table and picked up one of the magazines.

"You wanna beer or something?" she asked walking into her kitchenette.

He could hear her open the refrigerator as he flipped the pages.

"Uh, yeah, whatever," he replied sitting back.

Kia peered into her fridge. Why did she feel so nervous? Relax! It felt so weird and inappropriately intimate to be alone with Zane in her home.

She grabbed two Heinekens and handed him one. He took it barely glancing up from the magazine and set it on the coffee table. She walked over to her CD player and turned on Sublime

298

and sat on the other couch.

They sat in silence, him looking through the magazine, her staring at him and then at the coffee table in a bit of a drunken haze. "What Happened?" played in the background. She got up and lit an incense (Nag Champa, just as he thought) and walked back by the coffee table to pick up her beer. She opened the sliding glass door, went out and sat in a chair in the patio. She took a pack of Marlboro Lights off the table by one of the chairs and lit one up, resting her feet on the base of the chiminea. She leaned her head back and took a sip of her beer. She looked up at the moon. Zane finished the magazine, grabbed his beer and stood in the sliding glass doorway looking around, looking at her.

"When did you start smoking?"

"When I started bartending. It was a good excuse to get away from the back of the bar and take a break," she looked at him and shrugged.

"Let me have one." He sat in the chair across from her. She handed him one and a lighter. He lit up and leaned back. Sublime's "Get Ready" started up. He smiled. He liked that song.

"Got any herb?"

She looked at him sideways, smirking, "You still owe me a baggie."

"Huh?"

"You had me give you my parent's pot and you sold it right in front of me. I was so pissed!"

"Oh, yeah," he laughed remembering.

"What a prick," they said in unison. Then they both burst out laughing.

Zane was enjoying himself. He felt comfortable with her. He quieted down and found himself looking at her feet leaning on the chiminea. She had tan legs leading down to pretty feet and toes. She had a silver ring on her toe next to her pinky toe on her right foot. She also had a red, yellow, and black Rasta type woven bracelet wrapped around her ankle. Little hippie chick. She always was. Cute. Man, he wished he was single right now. He would love to show her how he could make love to her now. All she knows of him is the stupid thing he did to her in her room years ago. Now he would fuck the shit out of her.

Kia felt a tingle go up her neck. Her heart began to beat a little faster. She let out a quick breath. Maybe it's the cigarette giving her a head rush. She put it out in the chiminea. She shook her head.

"What's wrong," he asked.

"Uh, I don't know just got a headrush I guess," she got up and felt fine. "How about a fire? I have some wood in the corner there. Let me get some newspaper." She disappeared into the condo.

Zane got up to retrieve the wood. He felt himself getting hard from the images of he and Kia naked together. Damn. He pushed it down with the palm of his hand. She came back with newspaper and crouched down balling up paper and placing it in the chiminea. He grabbed some wood and placed it next to her. She grabbed pieces setting them inside before getting her lighter to set it on fire. It was just enough time for Zane to sit down and cross his legs to hide his desire.

With the fire started Kia sat back down in her chair and noticed her cat Bob come to the doorway.

"Oh, shit Bob I forgot to feed you," she jumped up and went inside with Bob mewing behind her. She grabbed a can she'd bought earlier and put wet food in his bowl, petting him for a minute while he ate. Inspired by Bob's appearance, she changed the music from Sublime to his namesake Bob Marley's Legend. A little more mellow and relaxing, she decided.

She walked back out and sat down. Zane was smoking another of her cigarettes.

"So you wanna talk more about Henry?" she asked.

Zane just smoked staring at the fire.

" I haven't seen Henry for years. I didn't realize he was that bad into drugs," she said.

He continued to stare at the fire.

"Umm . . . we don't have to talk about him if you don't want to. I just thought we left 'cause you wanted to. And, you know, not to be around everyone . . ." she trailed off.

301

"Did you name your cat after Bob Marley?' he asked not removing his eyes from the fire. She was surprised at his question but went with it.

"Yeah, I love Bob. Both Bob's," she smiled.

"Cat person and a hippie, huh?"

"So? You got a problem with cats and hippies?" she teased trying to lighten the conversation.

"Just that both are pussies," he retorted.

She could tell he meant that and was a little offended.

"Well Bob's a great cat and I see nothing wrong with some hippie love," she said a little too seriously.

They sat in silence so she reached for another cigarette, lighting up.

"You got some hippie love for me, Kia?"

She didn't quite know how to respond to that. What did he mean? Was he joking?

"Umm, what?" she replied looking over at him, confused.

He put out his cigarette and turned toward her.

"You gonna show me some hippie love?"

Right away she recognized that side of him coming out. There was the old Zane laying a line on her, being sexual. Damn.

302

"What do you mean, Zane?" she was going to make him say it. She wasn't going to play this game with him like she was some dumb girl looking for the 'Great Zane's' attention. But goddamn if a part of her wasn't turned on by his charms. She had been feeling lonely lately and she always thought he was sexy. Even now with his bare feet and his blue Dickies that showed off his perfect ass, which she had noticed when she walked behind him. His lean and toned arms that she could see through his black T-shirt and his chest under it showing no hint of a beer belly. And his smell, that masculine aroma that was his essence. Stop it! Stop it, she told herself. He was with Kristen. She got her head right and steeled her brain against tempting thoughts.

"Aren't you hippies all free love and shit?" he smiled.

"Number one Zane, I think you are thinking of the '60s. Number two, and most importantly, I'm not going to fuck someone who is in a relationship, you turd." She sat back and ceremoniously took a drag off her cigarette.

"Too bad," he replied, " I would rock your world." Figuring he got the last word he finished his beer.

Her face flushed in a combination of desire and anger. She started pulling herself together before replying. Should she say what came to mind? Why not? He was pursuing her, this was her opportunity to show him she is not who he remembers her to be.

"You know, Zane," she started off, somewhat miffed, "I would love to fuck you," she wanted to get his full attention, "but I'm not that little girl back in the day who would lay down for you hoping that I could be your girlfriend. Which I did," she added.

303

" You say you changed, and now, I realize maybe you haven't. I thought at this point we could be friends. I thought you wanted to talk. This is my home where I live with my son. I'm not some slut you picked up on the beach so you could cheat on Kristen and escape your miserable life! I thought I was your friend." And with that she took another hit off her cigarette and scowled at the fire.

Zane listened to her surprised at her reaction, realizing he was being a dick. Half of him wanted to get up and leave and half of him wanted to stay and . . . no, he wanted to leave. He was miserable, it was true. He was hoping to escape back into the past with her and feel like he was special again. He knew how she felt about him back then. He knew she liked him and wanted to be with him and he played on that. He did that with many girls back when he was "someone." That was a long time ago. Now he was just some drywaller in a terrible relationship who played music by himself in his garage. His glory days were behind him. And with Henry dying he wanted some comfort. He wasn't good at talking or feeling emotion, but he could fuck and that's what he wanted at the moment. He made her mad and he didn't know now how to get what he wanted.

"Maybe I should leave," he said getting up.

She sat there with a miserable look on her face, not speaking.

"OK then," he said going to the door. He walked into the living room and toward the kitchen. He glanced over and saw her cat giving himself a bath, contented. He reached down to pet him. "Sorry Bob, I pissed off your mama. I'm a dick."

304

And then he was out the door grabbing his shoes, sitting on the bench putting them on, hoping Kia would stop him. As he stood up she appeared in the doorway. She looked at him and glanced down at his shoes on his feet.

"OK Zane, see you later I guess," and she shut the door.

He stood there for a minute looking at her closed door. A huge part of him wanted to knock on it and when she answered throw up his hands and ask her if he could start over. But he didn't have the guts. Fuck it. He turned and walked back down the beach to the Rudder Room to party with his boys.

CHAPTER 34

A few days later Zane stood on the shore by the jetty at Silver Strand for Henry's Memorial paddle out. He held Madison in his arms as he talked with various friends who showed up to pay their respects. There were over 100 people there from the beach community and the city of Hollywood. Though it was a beautiful sunny day, the overall feeling in the air was gray. Zane looked around and watched the tanned surfers in boardshorts mingling with the other side of Henry's life—the pale and tattooed freaks dressed in black. It was a scene from some movie where Beach Blanket Bingo gets invaded by Sigue Sigue Sputnik members sun-kissed blonde hair and purple and red mohawks everywhere Zane grinned at the absurd picture.

Madison squirmed to be let down. He gently put her down and held her hand. Kristen had dressed her up in ribbons and a pink frilly dress. Madison already had her hair ribbon out of her hair and had thrown it on the sand. Zane got the feeling Madison hated Kristen's taste as much as he did. She was happiest when she was running around in shorts getting dirty. He looked up and spotted Kristen surrounded by Melissa and Erica and some other chicks, and she was crying and carrying on like she was the widow or something. What an attention whore. He looked away from her and saw Kia getting out of a car with a young boy, and he guessed that was her other son Joey. The kid had a skateboard and took off from her skating around the parking lot. He watched her yell something at him and stand there for a minute staring off in the direction he skated to. Then she turned around and walked toward the group. She had on a little black sundress and flip-flops, her hair loose and wavy. He thought she looked beautiful. He looked back at Kristen who was sitting in the sand now smoking a cigarette and drinking straight from a tequila bottle laughing at something one of her girls said. Then he watched the group look back at Kia and huddle together whispering to each other. Just like fucking high school, he thought.

Erica walked away to stand by her husband. She had married some guy from Camarillo a few years ago and moved there to start a family. They had two little boys and he had not seen her for a few years. She looked good. She looked happy.

Kia walked over to Erica and gave her a hug. Zane watched Erica introduce her to her husband, and Christian walked over and joined them.

Zane looked away and walked Madison to the water's edge. He allowed her to get wet and listened to her squeal when the water lapped over her little feet. He had the sudden realization

307

that if he didn't become a happier person Madison might take after Kristen more. He wanted her to be an Erica or a Kia. What a sense of humor God had giving him a daughter. Karma. He decided to make some changes right then. He wanted to change! He wanted to do it for his daughter. But he had to do it for himself first. Even he was smart enough to know that much. He could see everyone starting to gather to get the memorial started. He scooped up Madison and dropped her off with the girls. Melissa reached for her and he reluctantly gave her his daughter. He went to get his board and stand in the circle to listen to Henry's girlfriend give a tearful speech about what a great guy Henry was, lots of nods of agreement, about how much she and everyone will always miss him, lots of nods of agreement, and different friends speaking up and telling stories. Zane just listened, too choked up to speak. He caught Kia looking at him, her face sad. He looked back down at the sand not wanting to feel what she was feeling or perhaps be encouraged to speak. Eventually, half the group grabbed their boards and paddled out. Someone had brought flowers that they gave to each surfer to place in the ocean for Henry. Zane put the stem in his teeth and paddled out with the group.

They formed a circle just past the break line. Zane closed his eyes in deep sorrow for his friend. In his mind he pictured Henry riding the waves in on his board next to Jesus, like the image he saw so many years ago. Henry was laughing and holding hands with Jesus as they floated down the shore. Zane said a prayer asking for Henry's protection and for help saving his own battered soul.

Kia watched the guys and a couple of girls paddle out. She

308

wanted to bring her board but thought she wouldn't want to leave Joey by himself. Of course Joey skated off once they got there. Jake and Christian were out there, along with Zane, Mickey, Ramsey and all the rest of the crew. Even Eddie paddled out and Kia could tell he borrowed a board because his belly was swelled by married life and work. He had a serious farmer's tan and hadn't been out for years. She longed to be out there paying her respects to Henry and to their history. She again felt like an outsider. Damn, she sighed. She felt the past creep up on her as Melissa and Kristen threw her dirty looks. Brooke, Vienna and Ami didn't even show up. She'd lost touch with them years ago, anyway. At least Erica had not changed and was nice enough to welcome her to sit with their family. She sat next to them on the sand watching the surfers throw flowers into the ocean for Henry.

Though it was a very sad occasion, it was a beautiful day. Kia closed her eyes and said a prayer for Henry. As she was doing this an image of a surfing Jesus filled her head. That's what Zane had told her about a couple of days ago. She smiled to herself and opened her eyes looking out on the water searching for that image of a surfing Jesus right now. That would be awesome.

Later that day after searching for and finding Joey hanging out in front of the Corner Store, they went home. She sat on the couch with Bob in her lap and Joey played games on the Nintendo. She drank a beer, glad she had called in sick. They would never give her a Saturday off otherwise. The manager was pissed but she felt only a small twinge of guilt. Fuck it. Some things are more important than work. She needed the money but she knew if she needed it her dad would float her

309

a couple hundred. Her dad was actually doing pretty well at the sanitation department. Her parents now lived below their means so they could enjoy their life more. Even her mom cut back on her hours at the hospital. Her mom had really changed in recent years and she was happier. Her dad got his confidence back and even lost some weight. They really turned their lives around and seemed closer than ever. Kia petted Bob and smiled. She thought briefly of her sister Bennie and wondered what she would be like in her life now. Who knows? She was just a baby when she died. But if she's in heaven she hoped she would be at peace that her parents were happy again. That's all Kia could wish for.

If Henry's in heaven what would he wish for? Kia sensed that he would want Zane to be happy. She remembered Henry pulling her aside when they were all on Ecstasy at the beach and telling her how happy it made him to see Zane happy again because of Erica. Henry just was never a normal, typical guy. He was almost a human puppy dog, always big-eyed and smiling. Kia lifted her beer in the air and said to herself, "Here's to you Henry. Love ya brother. Hope you are in peace."

CHAPTER 35

Joey put the Nintendo controller down at that moment and exclaimed, "I'm bored."

Kia shook her head, returning to the present moment. She looked at her youngest. He was so restless, always wanting to be on the go. He never relaxed.

"What do you want to do?" she asked.

"I dunno."

"OK, want to have a friend spend the night?"

He shook his head, "Nah, everyone is busy."

"OK want to see if you could go over to Nana and Papa's?"

He made a face.

"They would love to see you. Maybe they will take you to Red Lobster and a movie. Want me to call?"

He shrugged. Red Lobster was the ticket, his favorite place. She got up and made the call and they were delighted. They picked him up within 20 minutes. She hugged them both as they came in. It was decided they would keep him the next day, too, and take him and Jake to Magic Mountain. Joey lit up. He was so spoiled. Kia smiled. She really wanted him to get to know his grandparents. They adored him and maybe it would soften his angry little heart being surrounded by their love. God, he reminded her of Zane. She decided to once again try with him. If her parents can work their magic on Joey, she would try again for Henry to reach Zane. Maybe she needed to get laid first. The thought of him made her horny against her intentions.

Zane ended up at The Beachcomber again with the crew. Kristen left Madison with her mom and was already hammered. She was at the jukebox playing Henry's band's songs. She was swaying back and forth with a drink in her hand with Melissa and some other chicks. She was barefoot and had on a miniskirt showing off her tan long legs, a tank top barely containing her breasts that had grown after pregnancy. She was still gorgeous physically, but she was still ugly on the inside and that's all Zane saw now. His resolve to change strengthened and he knew it was over between them. He just had to figure out how to get out.

Kia closed the door after saying goodbye to her parents and attempting to give Joey a hug but he pulled away and jumped into the car. She sighed. Damn, he broke her heart. She jus couldn't reach him, never could. It was like he was born a badass. Even as a baby he was restless. There were moments when he loved being held by his momma, but they were fewer than she would have liked. Maybe because he never had a dad. Though Christian did try to kind of be a dad to him, and his brother Jake tried to hang out with him, they both also told her Joey was different. Christian and Jake were so laid back that Joey would complain they were boring. He didn't want to surf, only skate and listen to fast music. He had been talking lately about wanting a guitar so he and his friends could start a band, who does that so young?. It was déjà vu to Kia reminding her that it was a reemergence of Henry, Zane and Eddie '90s-style. She suddenly had a realization of how maybe she could help Zane and Joey at the same time. Maybe she could convince Zane to give Joey guitar lessons. This would either be a good idea or a very bad idea. But being the eternal optimist she figured it was too much of a coincidence to not be what should happen. Maybe Zane could be a mentor, he was more like Joey than Christian and Jake were. Maybe. The only very big problem was Kristen. She definitely wouldn't like the idea.

Kristen walked to the bar and ordered another shot. Zane glared at her sideways when she told the bartender he would pay for it. He shook his head at the bartender.

Kristen turned toward him, "Fuck you, Zane. Yes, he will," she said again to the bartender.

"No, I won't. Get one of your bitches to pay for it."

She stumbled back a foot and turned toward him pointing

313

a finger in his face slurring her words. "It's all you're good for, Zane. Now buy me a fucking shot!"

"Fuck you, Kristen."

She made a big show of looking amazed he would say that to her. "What did you say to me?" she said getting in his face.

He stepped back, "Fuck off! We're done."

She stood there slack jawed and speechless for a minute. She looked around trying to find her friends who were oblivious and still dancing. She looked back at him pissed. "No fuck you! You think we're done? You think you can do better than me!"she laughed. "You're a fucking loser!"

That was it, something snapped in Zane and the entire bar was now looking at them. He leaned into her and said inches from her face, "You are an ugly whore."

She slapped him and started to punch him, missing his face but landing a couple of blows on his chest. He wanted to punch her so bad for all the years he put up with her shit, but someone grabbed him from behind holding him back. Someone pulled her back, also.

"You're a fucking loser Zane! You're a fucking loser!" she screamed as he was being pulled back.

Eddie appeared in front of him. "Hey, let's go outside."

Zane was only seeing red. He wanted to punch something. He stormed out with Eddie on his heels. He walked to the street and

314

didn't know where to go. Eddie had his keys in his hand, "Let's go. My car is right there."

Zane followed him getting in the car and slamming the door. Kristen ran out yelling at him and kicking the car as they drove off yelling, "Fuck you! Fuck you!"

They drove down Ocean Avenue in silence. Zane was breathing hard. Eddie pulled up at the Corner Store and got out. Zane sat in the passenger seat seething and staring out the window. What a fucking bitch, he thought. Fuck her! Then he thought about Madison. How is he going to do this? His pictured Kristen keeping Madison from him and then he pictured her breaking all his shit.

Eddie got back in the car with lots and lots of beer. "Where do you want to go?"

"Take me home."

They drove to Zane's house and went inside. Zane ran to the bedroom and into the closet and started grabbing Kristen's clothes and throwing them on the floor. Then he tore past Eddie, who was standing behind him casually drinking a beer, and went to the kitchen grabbing trash bags and filling them with her clothes. He filled two bags and roared past Eddie again and out the front door throwing the bags onto the driveway. He came back in slamming the front door and turned to Eddie who was sitting on the couch looking amused.

"Dude, I'm barricading the front door. That bitch isn't coming back in. Are you staying or leaving?"

Eddie slowly got up from the couch. "Where's your phone? I'll call my wife and tell her I'm staying. It's about fucking time you dumped that bitch."

Kia grabbed a beer, put it in a bag and walked to the beach. The sun was just setting and she thought she would go sit in the sand and think about her plan. She sat there for 15 minutes feeling uninspired. She was lonely. It sucked. She wanted to call a friend to hang out but all of her current girlfriends—the few that she had since moving back—were working at the Deer Lodge. She took a pull off her beer and watched the sun set. Who could she call? It was rare to have a Saturday night off and also be kid-free. Her mind flew to a fantasy of being in bed with Zane and she wished he never put the thought in her head. Damn it! She got up and brushed the sand off her ass and walked home. Her house was too empty. Maybe hanging out with her other son would be good for her. She called Christian's house and Christian's wife answered and told her Christian and Jake were at The Beachcomber, a continuance of Henry's memorial. Did she want to come over? Kia did and thanked her. Christian's wife, Missy, was so nice. She should have thought of her in the first place. She needed some normalcy. She grabbed her keys and cruised over.

Zane sat on the couch drinking beers with Eddie watching a Lakers game. Before long the front door tried to open but they had blocked it with some heavy equipment from the garage. Then the pounding on the door started. And then the yelling. "Fuck you, Zane! Let me in you asshole!" Kristen screamed.

Zane turned to Eddie, they cheered their beers and turned

up the basketball game. She kept pounding and screaming. Then she went for the kitchen window and started pounding on it. The glass vibrated. He walked over and closed the blinds. The pounding and screaming grew louder. He heard Melissa screaming from behind the front door, "Zane you asshole!"

Eddie and Zane looked at each other smiling.

"She brought her dyke," Eddie said.

Then the glass broke. Zane jumped up to find shards of glass had filled the kitchen sink.

"You bitch!" he screamed. "Get the fuck out of here before I call the cops!" he said to the broken blinds.

"I live here, too!" she screamed back.

"Not anymore! I pay the fucking rent!" he yelled looking at all the broken glass.

"Fuck you Zane! Fuck you!" she started to cry.

"Get your shit and get out of here! LEAVE!"

"My hand's fucked. I'm bleeding," she whimpered.

"Serves you right! Fuck off!"

"Fuck you Zane! You'll never see Madison again!"

He closed his eyes afraid of that threat but he wouldn't do this anymore.

"See you in court, bitch." He walked back to the couch and sa
next to Eddie.